The
LIBYAN
BOMB

D1519936

A NOVEL BY

Alan Melton

2011 © Alan Melton. All rights reserved.

ISBN: 1463561571
ISBN-13: 9781463561574

Dedicated to all the FBI Special Agents who worked FCI before 9/11 made it career-enhancing to do so. Thank you.

OTHER NOVELS BY ALAN MELTON

THE CHAMPA FLOWERS

Author's Note

Students of nuclear physics will doubtless derive a good deal of amusement from my rudimentary description of neutron flux. That's okay. The object of the book is entertainment, not instruction.

This is a work of fiction. None of the characters (other than Moammar al-Gaddhafi, whose villainy and desire to get hold of nuclear weapons are both well documented) is modeled after any living person, nor are any of the characters intended to portray any current or past holder of any position at LASL, the FBI, the CIA or elsewhere.

Having said that, there is a TA-18 at Los Alamos. Skua is kept inside it, and Skua is pretty much as described, except a lot heavier. The protective measures at TA-18 are, however, far, far tougher than described herein, for which we may all be thankful.

CHAPTER ONE

April 15, 1986
Tripoli, Libya

"I want the Bomb! Libya must have a nuclear weapon! This must never happen again!"

Gaddhafi's voice was filled with rage. It was also shrill and shaky, and his face twitched in a manner his brother-in-law Abdallah had never seen before. That was hardly surprising, however, since the American bombers had flown away only ten hours ago. Had not the Italian politician Benito Craxi phoned to warn Gaddhafi of the imminent air raid, Gaddhafi would likely be dead. It had been a very close call.

Chairman Gaddhafi's office in the Bab-al-Aziziya Barracks reeked of the explosives dropped there the night before, although the office itself had not been touched by bombs. Electrical service had yet to be restored, and both men were sweating from the heat of the noon hour.

"Some years ago I directed you to create a cell of agents in the United States," snapped Gaddhafi. "Did you do so?"

Abdallah attempted to inject just the right amount of righteous indignation in his answer. "Of course I did it, Chairman. They are in place and well-established." Despite the family connection, Abdallah always addressed Gaddhafi by his official title, Chairman of the Peoples' Congress, during encounters involving state business.

Abdallah al-Sanussi was not only Gaddhafi's brother-in-law, he was also Deputy Director of the JSO-the Jamahiriya Security Organization-Libya's intelligence service. As such, he directed all of Libya's foreign intelligence operations, including both espionage and assassination. The action cell in question had been ordered by Gaddhafi in 1982 in response to his anger at American pressure on Libya following the Libyan incursion into neighboring Chad.

Over the ensuing years, Gaddhafi had not referred more than a couple of times to the American cell, and Abdallah sometimes wondered if he had forgotten about it. Obviously he had not, and now there had been nothing to do but answer the question.

"They have been there for a long time, then, doing nothing," Gaddhafi replied. "Perhaps they have been corrupted by soft living in that Godless place."

Abdallah shook his head. "No, Chairman. I have remained in contact with them through our intelligence chief in Mexico City. They are living in three different places in and around Houston, Texas, where there is a sizeable Libyan émigré presence. They are loyal, and not in the least corrupted. After last night's air raid, the problem will be not to prod them into action, but to restrain them until they receive your orders."

Gaddhafi's hand came down violently on top of the ornately inlaid desk top in front of him. "I do not want them restrained," he snarled. "You have my orders now: activate the cell. They are to take action immediately to find and steal enough nuclear material to make an atomic weapon for Libya. The accursed Americans must never again dare to attack me."

Abdallah inclined his head. "Bismillah, it will be done."

While being driven back to his office at JSO headquarters, Abdallah did some serious thinking about the interview he had just had with Gaddhafi. He hoped that he had not stuck his neck out too far with his assertion that the American sleeper cell was loyal and itching for action against their host country. He was not concerned about two of the four team members: the leader, Da'ud al-Musa, was rock-solid. Although a native-born Libyan, he had lived in the United States in his youth, spoke fluent English, and loathed the U.S. for the treatment he had received there.

The big man, Ibrahim, could be relied upon, as well. He was ultra-religious; so much so that it made Abdallah (whose name meant "slave of God) nervous to be around him, lest Ibrahim find him lacking in some aspect of religious obligation. Ibrahim no doubt found ten motives for killing Americans every day, just by walking down the street. He was not overly endowed with brains, but was hugely powerful, and willing to kill on command.

It was the other two team members that Abdallah was less sure of: Aziz was clever; sometimes too clever for his own good, as his past history had proved. In fact, one reason Abdallah had sent him to Texas was to keep him away from Gaddhafi's attention. Aziz undoubtedly loved it there; he was extremely westernized. Unlike Ibrahim, Aziz' religious fervor was zero, but his English was excellent, as well as his French and Italian, and he was possessed of a singular gift: he was a charmer. He could learn the life history of a total stranger in thirty minutes from a standing start, and that was a great and useful trait, which the team would need.

Finally, there was the woman: Sabana al-Murtada. Abdallah was grateful that Gadhaffi had not wanted to talk about the makeup of the team. He might have balked at the woman, especially when he learned her background, and that could have been awkward for Abdallah, who had insisted on including her, over the objections of Da'ud, the team leader.

She certainly had her shortcomings: she wasn't by any means a staunch Libyan patriot; she had been coerced into joining the operation. She was scarcely a moral paragon: she was not exactly a whore, but she had been the mistress of a succession of foreign businessmen. Her motivations were physical survival and money, in that order.

On the plus side, however, her English was excellent and she was gloriously beautiful. Only a saint could resist her, and Abdallah had been in the intelligence business long enough to know that the two primary reasons men committed treason were money and sex. To succeed at the mission he was about to give them, the team was very likely to need Sabana. It would be up to Da'ud to keep her in line.

And what were their chances of success? The team were the best people he had been able to find, and by now their covers were solid. He had only used them once; well, twice, counting the silencing of a potential witness, but it was over two years ago now, and there had never been any fallout from that episode, so he felt safe on that score.

The assigned target, however, was daunting. American nuclear material was extremely well-guarded, and the prospect of the Americans' reaction to the operation, if it succeeded, or even failed but was discovered, made him shudder. However, given Gaddhafi's current state of mind, Abdallah could not have talked him out of it. Indeed, had he tried, he would most likely have brought the Chairman's wrath upon himself.

He mentally shrugged his shoulders. Insh'Allah. He would provide the team with the best briefing he could give them, and after that it was in the hands of God.

As they neared JSO headquarters, Abdallah was startled by the amount of destruction he saw, in what he knew to be purely residential areas. The French Embassy appeared to have had a very near miss from an American bomb.

He had spent the morning, prior to his summons from Gaddhafi, in the bunker he had under his home, just in case the American bombers came back. From the bunker he was linked to JSO, the Defense Ministry and the Foreign Ministry, so he was aware that France, Spain and Italy had all refused to let the American bombers overfly their countries. Too bad the Americans hadn't killed the French Ambassador, he thought. That would have created a real problem for the bastards.

He was relieved to see that JSO was intact, but on arrival in his office, he was surprised by how few of his employees were present. His long-time personal assistant, Achmed al-Sanussi, a fellow tribesman, was nowhere to be seen. Indeed, the only person in his outer office was a relatively new employee whose name he had to ask for while inquiring for Achmed.

"My name is Samir, Deputy Director," was the reply, "and I am sorry to tell you that we fear for the lives of many of our fellow employees. Last night an American bomb fell on the Organization's apartment block for its employees, and many appear to have been killed, including perhaps Achmed. Only three of us reported to work this morning, and I took the liberty of dispatching the other two to help with the search for survivors at the apartment block."

The news was a shock to Abdallah, particularly the possibility of having lost Achmed, who was a trusted and reliable aide. He made a mental note to find out why he hadn't been advised of this disaster at his home.

"You did well, Samir," he said. "You don't have the combination to the vault, do you?"

"Oh, no, Sir", came the predictable answer. "I am too new to the office."

"All right," grunted Abdallah. "I have it with me. Let me open the safe while you get me a cup of tea, and then we will get to work."

After considerable difficulty (he hadn't personally opened the vault in years), he got the vault open and located the file he was looking for: Operation Sleeping Lion. He liked the name, which he had coined himself. He thought it fit the operation well.

He retired to his office and studied the file's contents for better than half an hour behind closed doors. When he had fully digested its contents he pushed the buzzer for his private secretary. Samir answered.

"Wa, ya Samir, are you still alone in the office?"

"Yes, Deputy Director. No one else has returned."

"Can you take dictation?"

"Yes, Deputy Director."

"Then bring a pad and come on in here. I need you to take down a message for our group at the Embassy in Mexico City."

CHAPTER TWO

May 8
Los Alamos,
New Mexico

It was noon in Los Alamos, and Willis Wilson drove home to eat, as he had almost every day for the past fifteen years. There was no one there to eat with these days, but habit was strong, and in any case, the idea of eating his lunch from a brown paper bag in his office wasn't attractive.

The Los Alamos Scientific Laboratory cafeteria was also out of the question, now that Tim Long had been named Facility Director at Technical Area-18, instead of Willis. Willis could do very well without the commiseration of his colleagues, whether sincere or (much more likely) otherwise, thank you.

Sarah used to prepare lunch for them at the house, but these days she was too engrossed in her business downtown for such domestic chores. That wasn't all bad. At least he didn't have to endure her chatter about her latest enthusiasm.

But her business really was booming. Willis hadn't approved of Sarah's taking Fred Herrman into business with her, when she first brought the idea up, a year ago. The man was crude and uneducated, and besides, Willis had suspected that he might be after her money. It was well known around town that she had inherited a fortune from her mother.

Sarah had gone ahead with it, however, in spite of his objections, and Willis had to admit that the combination of her designs---she really was quite artistic---and Herrman's metalworking skill had been a success. They had produced some very attractive jewelry, and the new business it had brought into Sarah's boutique kept her busy. She had been working late a good deal lately, sometimes well into the evening.

Willis drove out of the Los Alamos Scientific Laboratory area over the bridge that spanned Los Alamos Canyon. As he reached the town side, he noticed Deputy Sheriff Jess Lopez parked a few yards back up the first side street, poised to pounce on any speeder who came by.

Resentment rose in Willis at the sight, as it always did. Jess had pulled Willis over from that same location a few months earlier. The injustice of having to pay a twenty dollar fine for a three-mile an hour infraction, his first in a decade and a half of living in Los Alamos, still rankled Willis. He would have made an issue of it, if the vastly greater issue of the Facility Director position hadn't driven it from his mind.

He drove on into the residential area of the town, turning south on the largest of the lava plateaus on which the city had been built. He could have made the drive blindfolded. He had done it thousands of times. He might not be making it for much longer, however. He had been quietly making inquiries among the physics departments of the Ivy League. The slight of Tim's promotion was one he didn't propose to accept.

The LASL administrators had never liked him. His intellectual honesty offended the Washington politicians on whom they depended for funding. Tim Long, with his easy charm and glad-handing, was understandably more to their taste.

Willis parked in the driveway of his home on Camino Cereza and walked to the front door. He was a thin, slightly stooped man of forty, with receding sandy hair and freckles which appeared as if by magic anytime he was outdoors. He took the mail out of the box and examined it through bifocal glasses set in gold wire frames.

The mail was junk. He'd never understood why the postal authorities allowed the privacy of millions of Americans to be invaded this way by hucksters of trash.

He opened the door, bracing himself for the usual adoring assault by Heather's cocker spaniel.

Willis hated the dog. Its inane jubilation irritated him, and its jumping got his clothes dirty. But Heather doted on it, so that was that.

Curiously, the dog didn't greet him. Maybe Sarah had left it in the yard. He went through the house, opened the door from the kitchen to the yard and called. It wasn't in the yard, either. Had Sarah taken it to the vet? He frowned. She should have told him. He had better things to do with his time than hunt for the God-damned creature.

He closed the door and went to the refrigerator. There was an envelope taped to its door with his name on it in Sarah's handwriting. The mystery of the missing cocker was doubtless about to be revealed to him in prose.

He got a bottle of milk from the refrigerator, poured a glass, then put the bottle back and took the envelope and the glass of milk over to the breakfast room table. He took a sip of milk, slit the envelope open with the butter knife and began to read the letter.

He couldn't understand it. He understood the words, of course, but they made no sense. He read it again.

Sarah was gone. She had left him and gone to California to start a new life with Fred. She had taken Heather and the dog, leaving him both cars, the house and their savings. She didn't need his money.

She apologized for breaking the news to him this way, but she had not wanted a scene and this seemed the best way to avoid one. She had sold her business to some local investors, lady friends of hers.

As Willis read on, his initial disbelief and shock gave way to raging anger. The bitch! How dare she do this to him? How dare she just walk away without a word, as if he weren't worth the trouble to explain the problem to?

And for Fred? My God, she must have lost her mind! How could she even think of giving up her position as his wife and the intellectual stimulation of living in the most highly-educated community in America, to marry a foul-mouthed blacksmith? He, Willis, was nationally recognized in his field. Fred was a nobody, a nothing!

But Heather! The pain of losing his daughter was almost physical. She was his darling; so bright, so clever. What could Fred do for Heather? How could Sarah have done that to their child, as well as to him?

The LIBYAN BOMB

The letter closed with the statement that she would be in contact with him through her attorney and make arrangements for visitation privileges. She wanted them to be limited, at least at first, so as not to upset Heather. She hoped he would respect her wishes in that regard.

Willis' anger turned to fury. Respect her wishes, hell! He'd fight her for custody all the way to the Supreme Court. The bitch must have been lying to him for months. This was why she'd been working late! She'd been screwing Fred on the couch in the office of the boutique after the store closed.

In this one-horse town, where everyone knew everyone else's business, he was probably the only one who didn't know. It was humiliating. One of America's most brilliant nuclear physicists, cuckolded for weeks, maybe months, by a high school dropout hippy. Sarah had made him the laughing stock of the whole community.

He slammed the letter down on the table. The glass of milk tipped over and crashed to the floor. Broken glass and milk flew in all directions. Oh, shit!

He jumped up to get a towel and caught his ankle on the table leg. He tripped and fell to his hands and knees on the floor, slicing open the heel of his hand on a shard of glass.

The pain brought tears to his eyes. He sucked at the wound the mixture of blood and milk was nauseating.

It wasn't fair! First Tim's promotion over him. Now Sarah's betrayal. He hadn't done anything to deserve this, and especially not to lose Heather. He didn't have anything left, not even the God-damned dog.

Willis began to cry.

CHAPTER THREE

June 23
Washington, D.C.

The 9 millimeter Browning Hi-Power cocked in his two hands, Link stood poised on the balls of his feet, staring down the dark alley in front of him, waiting.

He could feel the tension in his back and shoulders, but the gun felt right: solid, balanced, ready, reassuring.

The silhouette of a man suddenly sprang into view twenty yards down the alley. Link reacted, without any conscious thought at all. His extended arms dropped, the barrel aligned itself before his eyes, and he fired, three times. He felt the gun bucking in his hands, but knew he was controlling the recoil as he should, knew that the shots were deadly, hitting the chest.

The LIBYAN BOMB

The silhouette dropped out of sight. Three tiny green lights came on above his head. "Nice shooting, Mr. Rowe," the voice of the range officer said over the loudspeaker above him in the firing booth.

Link cleared the weapon and backed out of the booth. He was sort of surprised to be shooting so well, considering how the weekend had gone. (Your Monday morning score on the range was an excellent indicator of how much alcohol you'd put away on Friday and Saturday night, and Link's Saturday night had gone on for a long time).

Link fired every workday morning, religiously. He hadn't shot at a human being for fifteen years, since Vietnam, but he'd come close a couple of times, and he'd learned in 'Nam that when the shooting starts, the man who reacts first and shoots straightest is the one with the best chance of survival.

He had to admit that hadn't kept him from getting his ass shot off in 'Nam, but he couldn't very well have reacted then, since he never saw the bastard who shot him. Anyway, in his business he was required to carry a weapon, and he damn well intended to be the one still standing after the fight, if he ever had to use it.

Of course, in this cruddy Headquarters job he had, it wasn't very realistic to imagine himself getting involved in a gunfight—unless maybe he went berserk and shot JJ—but the ritual of firing every day to preserve his reflexes and eyes made him feel less like a Headquarters weenie and more like a real, honest to God, FBI Special Agent.

Besides, if the truth were known, Link liked guns. He liked their sinister beauty, their single-minded functionality and the feeling they gave him of being able to deal with the world around him, no matter how nasty it got. There were a lot of guys like him in the Bureau. Guys who just didn't feel comfortable on the street unarmed. He suspected they got like that the same way he had: by being in a place where people were actively trying to kill you.

He moved off the firing line and leaned against the wall in the rear of the range area, waiting for Leo to finish firing. Link was a big man, six feet two inches tall and two hundred fifteen pounds, with unusually broad shoulders even for someone his size. His hair was anthracite black, and his eyes grey-blue under thick brows. His red cheeks and smooth brow made him look younger than his thirty-eight years.

The phone on the wall near Link rang. He flinched a little at the unexpected sound, then smiled a wry smile at his own jumpiness. The Agent on the other side of the instrument answered it. "FBI Range." He listened a moment, then held out the phone to Link. "For you, Mr. Rowe." Link took it from him. "Link Rowe speaking." He listened a second, then made a face at the mouthpiece. "Hi, JJ." (He made it rhyme with Mayday.) "How did you know I was here?"

"Where else would you be at this time of day, Wyatt Earp?" said the voice in his ear. "Certainly not at your desk."

Good old JJ, Link thought. One of these days . . . "Okay, you've found me," he said. "What do you want?"

The answer, which went on for a little while, replaced his irritation with interest. "Hey, that's something new," he said at the end of it. "When? . . .Just now? . . .Okay, I'll be right up."

He hung up, and turned to find Leo standing in front of him. "Got to get upstairs, Leo," he said. "The Mossad liaison guy over at the Israeli embassy wants to talk to me."

Leo's eyebrows went up. "What's that about?"

"Beats me," said Link. "It's the first time he's ever called a non-scheduled meeting, which probably means bad news."

Among Link's primary duties was maintaining liaison with the Washington representatives of security services of friendly countries, among them the Israelis. Since arriving at Headquarters, Link had meet them only four times, always on a pre-arranged schedule, and all of those meetings had been essentially social in nature, just keeping the lines of communication open.

Link and Leo left the basement range and took the elevator up to the offices of the Anti-terrorist Section, which overlooked the Justice Department building across Pennsylvania Avenue. They separated at the front office door, Leo going left down the hall to his desk, and Link opening the door marked "Chief/Anti-terrorist Section."

Link walked through the reception room which separated his office from JJ's. He didn't see Barbara. She must not be in yet. He wanted to talk to her.

The plastic plaque on his office door said, "Lincoln A. Rowe, Deputy Chief, Anti-terrorist Section."

Eleven moths ago, when Link got this Headquarters assignment, everyone in the New York Field Office told him what a great job it was.

The damn liars. He would give anything to be back in New York again.

In New York, he'd had a real job to do, a job that you could get some satisfaction from doing: putting bad asses in jail. Sitting on his butt in Washington reading about what other guys were doing wasn't Link's idea of a job. It was just barely a job description.

He opened the door and went in. He had a nice office. His position as Deputy Chief of Section entitled him to carpet, a big wooden desk and a leather swivel chair, plus exterior windows with a view of the roof of the Justice Department building.

When John Joseph Maloney, C/ATS, showed Link the office for the first time, he had made much of the view and the fact that it had not one, but two, windows.

Link had never thought of determining the importance of a job that way, and said so. It had gotten him off on the wrong foot with Maloney, and it had been all downhill ever since.

On his first day in the unit, Link shortened Maloney's names to JJ ("it rhymes with payday.") The nickname spread through the unit like prairie fire. Maloney didn't like it, and said so, more than once, to everyone in the unit, but the name stuck. Link expected JJ to take his revenge when he wrote Link's Efficiency Report. No problem. He could handle a bad E.R., especially if it helped get him back into the field office.

He went into his office, unlocked the safe and got out his classified in box. He took it to his desk and had just sat down at the desk when there was a soft knock at the door.

Barbara entered with the morning traffic. At thirty-four, she was four years younger than he, with a mass of light brown hair framing an oval face. Her eyes were the blue of Delft china, and her teeth were very white and even. She had a beautiful smile. Link noticed that she wasn't smiling now.

"Good morning," she answered, putting the sheaf of papers in his in-basket. She didn't meet his eyes. She didn't say she was glad to see him, either. He'd suspected she might not.

Their Saturday date had ended with her telling him she didn't want to see him again outside the office. It was now Monday morning. She didn't seem to have changed her mind.

She walked back across the office and shut the door behind herself without saying another word. He felt his temper rise.

They had been dating since last fall, had been lovers since early spring, and now she had come down with an attack of acute matrimonyitis, which she clearly felt it was his duty to cure.

Well, she'd had minor attacks before, and he'd been able to bring her around. It wasn't as if he'd misled her. He had told her, right up front, when they began dating, that his disastrous marriage had left him permanently soured on that institution. If she didn't want to play it that way, there were plenty of other women who would, and anyway, right now he had some official business to worry about.

He pulled a Rolodex out of the box he had taken from the safe, looked up a number, and dialed it.

An hour later, he knocked softly on the door of a suite in the Marriott Hotel in Rosslyn, just across the Potomac in suburban

Virginia. The door opened a crack, and a dark brown eye appraised him for a second before it swung open and he was waved inside with a smile by a short, stout man in his forties.

"Hello, Link. I'm glad you could come. Sorry about the short notice."

The man spoke one hundred percent American English, and why not? He'd been born, raised, and gone through grade school in Chicago, but his parents had then emigrated to Israel, and he was now an Israeli, and the Washington representative of the Mossad, his adopted country's intelligence service.

He was declared as such to both the FBI and CIA, since it was his job to be in contact with those agencies on matters of mutual interest. Most of the Mossad's business was with the CIA. The fact of the short-notice, non-scheduled meeting had definitely piqued Link's interest, but he wanted to seem cool about it, as if it were all in a day's work.

"No problem about the short notice, David. It's a work day."

First names were the rule in liaison relationships. It prevented awkwardness when one side or the other was goosey about revealing a true last name. The two men shook hands. David introduced him to the other man in the suite.

"Link, this is Sol. He is one of our senior officers. He just arrived this morning from Israel on a matter of great urgency. I learned that he was coming only last night."

Link was surprised at the man's age, perhaps in his upper sixties. He was thin to the point of looking frail, but there was nothing frail about his handshake or the piercing look he gave Link. His eyes were a very bright shade of green, almost chartreuse. They reminded Link of a cat his mom had once owned.

David waved Link to a chair. He poured a Coke for Link, and bottled water for himself and Sol.

"Well, Link," the visitor began, "I must also thank you for being so prompt in responding to our call, and apologize to you for the lack of warning and the mystery of all of this." His English was fluent and precise, but heavily accented.

Link dismissed the problems with a wave of his hand. "No sweat, sir. What brings you to Washington?"

The question wasn't just courteous. In the anti-terrorism business, a flying visit by a high-powered foreign intelligence officer almost certainly meant trouble.

"We have acquired some information which we wanted to get to your government as rapidly and as confidentially as possible," said the Israeli. "You may judge its importance by the fact that I am here on the personal orders of the Prime Minister of Israel."

"Whoa," Link thought to himself. Out loud he said, "Excuse me, Sol," Link said, "but if you're operating at that level, I think I ought to make an appointment for you to meet with my Director, instead of me."

The Israeli shook his head decisively. "No. Because of the need for absolute secrecy, I was ordered to deliver the information directly to the Counter Terrorist Section. I don't want to show up on any high-level appointment calendars, from which my presence might leak to the press."

No question about it, Link concluded. This is Bad News. He decided to dispense with any further protocol. "Okay," he said. "We'll hold it very close. What's happening?"

Sol nodded to David, who turned up the volume of the TV in the room. The older man hitched his chair toward Link and spoke almost in Link's ear. "We have been advised by a very sensitive agent in Tripoli that Gaddhafi has a team of agents in your country. They have apparently been here for some time. He has now ordered them to avenge the recent American air raid, and to deter the United States from any future attacks on Libya, by stealing enough weapons grade nuclear material to make a Libyan atomic bomb."

Chapter Four

June 23
Washington, D.C.

"Jesus! They took their sweet time in letting us know about it!" JJ's voice was half an octave higher than usual. "The air raid happened over two months ago. Did you ask them about the delay?" He and Link were in JJ's office, half an hour after the close of Link's meeting with the Israelis.

Link bit down on his irritation. "Of course I asked them, JJ. They explained that the agent is super sensitive—I could believe that—and isn't met in person. He reports via impersonal means, what ever that might be, and his reporting has to pass through a cut-out in a third country before it gets to the Mossad. Then, when they finally got it, there was an argument over its validity. Obviously, if they passed it, the doo-doo was going to hit the fan on our side, so did they want to put their credibility with us on the line? Finally, they figured out that was a political decision that needed to be made at the top, so they passed the buck to the Prime Minister, blah, blah, blah. Result, over two months went by."

"Okay," said JJ. "What about the credibility? How much faith do they have in this agent?"

"That was the first thing I asked them," replied Link, "and they waffled on it. The problem is, the guy is a new source. They've only heard from him twice before, and that reporting was on much more mundane subjects, to which they knew his job gave him access, so that gave him some credibility. By the way, I also asked where he worked and what his access was, and they weren't about to tell me."

"This report", Link went on, "is sourced to, quote, a senior officer of the Libyan intelligence service, unquote. That's a level to which their agent would normally not have access, so they wonder about that. On the other hand, the agent's explanation of how he happened to come by the information——and again, they didn't tell me any details——seemed reasonable. So, short answer, they weren't going to bet the family kibbutz on it. But at least, the Prime Minister did understand the downside if it turned out to be true and they hadn't passed it, so they finally kicked the ball to us, and we need to run with it, fast and starting now."

"Hold on, hotshot," said JJ. "The Izzies are right about one thing; this is political, one million percent. The minute after we tell the Director, it's going to be at the White House, and I'm not going to tell the President a cock and bull story that'll come back to haunt me. You just hold your horses for a couple of hours. I'm going to go talk to the Libya guys at the Agency, and see what they think." JJ reached for the secure phone on his desk.

Just as Link handled liaison with foreign security service representatives in Washington, JJ, as chief of ATS, maintained official contact with other government agencies, including the CIA, and Link, although the news he'd gotten from the Israelis had fueled a huge sense of urgency in him, had to admit that JJ was right. Before they sprang this news on the Director, and the President, they needed to check it with all the U.S. government agencies who might be able to shed some light on it. A couple of those agencies occurred to him now. He headed back to his own desk and secure telephone.

It turned out to be more like three and a half hours before JJ returned from his visit to Langley and called Link into his office.

"The Agency doesn't buy it", he told Link without preamble.

Link was taken aback. "What don't they believe? That the Izzies have an agent in Libya, or the story itself? I've always thought they had a lot of respect for the Mossad over at Langley."

"It's not the Mossad they doubt, it's the agent's story. They've apparently got some guy of their own, with more or less the same access—and boy, did they tap dance around that tidbit of information–, and they haven't heard anything like the Mossad's story from him. I went around and around with them over it. I saw the Division Chief, and the deputy Director for Operations, and we all wound up in the Director's office—that's why I took so long getting back here. I got them to agree to direct their sources, world wide, to look into it, but for the moment, they're not prepared to join us in scaring the White House out of its mind, and if that's good enough for them, it's good enough for me."

Link couldn't believe his ears. "Whoa, JJ," he sputtered. "We can't sit on something like this. This is dynamite. We've got to send it upstairs."

"Oh, hell, Rowe, I'm not going to sit on it. I'm taking it to the Criminal Division chief right now, but I'm going to make sure he hears all the caveats and doubts that both the Mossad and the CIA have expressed. If I go up there all hot and bothered, and get the Division chief and maybe even the Director excited, all hell will break loose, with our office right in the middle of it. We've got plenty to do here without leading the whole US government off on a wild goose chase after a bunch of people who probably don't exist in the first place, and couldn't carry out their mission if they did. The nuclear material in this country is guarded tighter than the gold in Fort Knox."

Ah! Link got it. It wasn't an undue flap JJ was trying to avoid. It was the workload that a full court press would cause for him, the lazy bastard.

He made a Herculean effort to get his tongue under control before he answered. "Actually, JJ, it's not all that well guarded, at least not some of it. While you were gone, I spent the whole time on the secure phone with the Nuclear Regulatory Commission and the Immigration and Naturalization Service."

Seeing JJ's frown, Link held up a placatory hand. "Not poaching on your territory, JJ," he said soothingly, "just getting some information." JJ continued to look unhappy, but didn't say anything, and motioned for Link to continue.

"The guy at NRC scared the crap out of me," Link told him. There is highly enriched Uranium-235 all over this country: at the weapons manufacturing and storage facilities, of course, but also at the national laboratories, Lawrence Livermore in California and Los Alamos in New Mexico, and, what I hadn't even thought about, at the research reactors at universities and medical centers; there are well over twenty of them, and they all have to be refueled periodically."

JJ looked pained. Link pressed his point. "We just can't ignore this, JJ. Even if we keep our cool in reporting the Mossad information, we, our office, ATS, have to be busting our asses to check it out, with or without the support of the Agency."

Link found himself surprised by the force of his need to convince JJ, and by the fluency of his presentation. He hadn't said that much to his boss at one time since joining the office. He was also pleasantly surprised by JJ's apparent consideration of Link's statement.

'Okay, Rowe,' JJ finally said, "you've obviously got a bug up your ass about this. What do you think this office ought to do about this story? And how many damn' Libyans can there be in the United States anyway?"

Link was delighted. JJ was actually thinking about it! "Last question first," he answered. "There are a lot more Libyans here than

I realized, which is bad news, but there's some good news in that: most of them are in Houston, Texas, which the INS tells me is the third largest Libyan city, population-wise, on earth. So it seems like the ones we're looking for might have settled there, figuring to disappear in the crowd. At least, that's where I think we ought to start looking. And, of course, we need to alert all the storage facilities under government control or contract, and send people out to talk to the folks who run the research reactors at the universities; see if they've hired any Middle Eastern- looking folks lately or seen any lurking around."

JJ shook his head. "Oh, my God, Rowe," he said. "You have no idea what you are getting us into."

Link played his trump. "I'll do it all myself, JJ," he said. "You manage the day to day business of the office and I'll take on this Libyan thing. That way, we don't lose any of our usual coverage, but if something does come out of this story, we're covered. No one can say we weren't working it."

JJ stared off into space for a bit, apparently lost in thought.

"Okay," he finally said. "Notifying everyone who has anything to do with enriched U-235 or plutonium is something we have to do, I agree. And yeah, we'll notify Houston to start looking at the Libyans down there, but with a big population like that, it'll take forever, and INS isn't going to be any help. Houston's going to pitch a fit."

It was an article of faith in the Bureau that getting paperwork out of INS was impossible. INS was willing, all right, but their records were a disaster. The favorite Bureau theory was that the INS filing system consisted of one little old lady wearing a green eye shade, sitting all alone in the middle of a gigantic warehouse piled to the ceiling with stacks of immigration paperwork in random order.

"Okay," JJ repeated. "You're on, but remember, it's all your baby."

That was all Link wanted to hear.

Chapter Five

June 24
San Diego, California

Sprawled naked on his bed, Da'ud watched the video cassette of the man and woman making love on the TV screen across the room. The light level was a little low, but the faces were easily recognizable, and that was the main thing.

Naked or clothed, Da-ud was a handsome man. He had often been told that he looked like the Egyptian movie star, Omar Sharif. The first time he heard that, he had shaved off his mustache to lessen the resemblance. Sharif was a traitor to the Arabs, a defector to the American-Zionist side.

People had also told him that he looked like the Mexican singer, Jorge Negrete, and that was the resemblance he wanted to enhance now. It made for excellent cover here in San Diego, so he was growing the mustache back.

It amused him, now that he wanted to pass for a Mexican, to remember how he had fought the American boys for calling him one, back during his boarding school days in Texas,

The man on the TV screen was approaching orgasm. He humped the woman under him furiously, then collapsed on her, kissing her face and neck.

Watching, Da'ud felt himself getting hard. He reached over beside himself on the bed and put his hand on the tangle of curly black hair between Sabana's legs.

At his touch, she rolled up on her knees and began kissing him, open-mouthed, caressing him expertly at the same time. He became fully erect almost immediately. "Sit on me," he grunted in Arabic.

She swung one leg over his body and guided him into her. She moved slowly and rhythmically forward and back, up and down, smiling down at him and pinching his nipples with her fingertips.

Then her movements became faster, her face contorted. She leaned forward, bracing herself against his shoulders with fully-extended arms, moving herself on him as hard and fast as she could. He lay still, trying to retain control.

"Aii," she cried suddenly, twisting and writhing on him. "Aii, oh, God, oh!"

Da'ud rolled her over on her back. She locked her legs around his waist. After no more than a dozen strokes, he drove himself to the hilt inside her, and emptied himself with slow, languorous movements. Sweat poured from his face onto hers, despite the air-conditioning.

"You are my life, you are my soul," she panted. "No man in the world but you can make me come like that. You are a stallion, a he-camel."

Now that his lust was stated, the practiced words repulsed and angered him. "Is that what you were saying to your skinny engineer?" He motioned with his head toward the now-dark television screen. "It's what you say to every man who gets inside you."

She stiffened at the insult, and tried to get out from under him. "You bastard," she snarled. "Let me go."

He pinned her to the bed with powerful arms, enjoying her futile struggles. Only when she subsided, gasping for breath, did he pull out of her and roll off to let her up.

She scrambled off the bed and faced him. "You just can't be nice to me, can you? You have to treat me like a whore. Well, if I disgust you so much, why can't you keep your pecker out of me?"

He watched her march to the bathroom, her stiff back radiating indignation. Her full buttocks jiggled beneath the mane of midnight black hair. Her skin was the color of honey, its lightness an inheritance from the English soldier who had uncaringly planted her mother in her grandmother's belly.

Sabana had to be the greatest whore alive, Da'ud reflected. She was a beautiful woman, a marvelous piece of ass, a wonderful actress, and didn't have an honest bone in her body.

She had made a good living with those talents, too—using her job as a bilingual secretary with an American oil company in Tripoli as a springboard to the bedrooms of its senior officers, and once there, finding ways to rob their dollar accounts.

Unfortunately for her, one of her lovers had complained to the police, and she had thus been brought to the attention of Abdallah al-Sanussi. He had recruited her by giving her the choice between serving her nation or going to jail.

And she had beguiled even Abdallah. He had assigned her to Da'ud, over Da'ud's strong objections, with the assurance that Sabana's terror of the male guards in the women's prison in Tripoli, plus Da'ud's own sexual dominance, would assure her loyalty.

After four years, Da'ud knew better. Her only loyalty was to herself. He wished for the hundredth time that he didn't have to use her. Their mission was too important to entrust to a half-breed slut and thief, but like it or not, he did have to use her. In fact, she had now become the key to their operation.

As team leader, it was therefore his duty to control his distaste for her, stop insulting her as he had just now, and play on her vanity, even make her think that he really cared for her.

In all probability they would not have to use the video tape he had taken surreptitiously of Sabana and the engineer making love last night in her apartment, next door to his in their apartment complex. Blackmail could easily backfire, and once Sabana got her hooks in a man, she could usually convince him to do anything.

Da'ud had not been happy with his choice of General Atomics as the target, but it was the only one which combined some hope for success with cover for their foreign appearance, and it now looked as if his fears had been groundless.

He had left Aziz in Santa Fe as a fall-back position, but now that Allah, via Sabana, had delivered the engineer into their hands, perhaps he ought to have the little man join them. They would need all the manpower possible when the time came to make the final move. Ibrahim was already here, in another apartment block a mile or so away.

Sabana came back out of the bathroom, her heavy breasts bobbing as she walked toward the chair where she had thrown her clothes. Still angry, she wouldn't look at him.

"I am sorry, my dove," he said. "I spoke out of jealousy. It made me angry to see you with another man. I apologize."

She sulked. He held out his arms to her. "Come to me," he coaxed.

She made him wait a moment more before choosing to forgive him, then ran to the bed and knelt on the floor between his legs.

She threw her arms around him and pressed her face against the mat of hair on his chest. "Please don't say things like that to me again, Da'ud. You hurt me so much. After all, it was you who told me to go to bed with him."

She looked up at him with huge eyes, wide set and long lashed. "How could you be jealous? How could I feel anything for a skinny runt like that? Your prick is bigger around than his arm." One of her hands slid down between his legs and began to squeeze him, ever so gently.

"I hate your being with him," he told her earnestly, "but I must tolerate it, just as you must, for the sake of our cause. I promise, I won't be unkind to you again, and you must do everything in your power to turn this clever Yankee engineer into a whimpering puppy."

33

She smiled. "It will be easy. He thinks I'm a poor, sweet Latina refugee, practically a virgin. "He is a child, a fool." She giggled.

Her squeezing had aroused him again. He pushed her gently on her haunches and pulled her head into his groin. "Show me that you forgive my unkindness," he said.

✧ ✧ ✧

Nine hundred miles to the east, in Los Alamos, Linda Long pulled her nightgown back down over her hips. Beside her, Tim was already beginning to breathe deeply. She nudged him. "Tim?"

He grunted. She nudged him again. "Tim, don't go to sleep yet. What about Willis? Did you talk to him?"

"No, honey," he mumbled sleepily, I didn't have a chance."

She propped herself up on one elbow. "Tim, you promised!"

"I know honey, but we got busy."

"Tim Long," she said accusingly, "You're lying to me and we both know it. You just don't want to do it."

"Linda," he groaned, "I can hardly keep my eyes open. Can't we talk about this tomorrow? I won't see Willis again until Monday."

"We've already talked until I'm blue in the face from it," she retorted. "You're the one who has to talk, and not to me, but to your precious Willis. I know it's hard for you, Tim. I know how much you respect him, but you owe it both to him and to yourself to do it. You're responsible to all the other men up there, too. Suppose he makes some awful mistake when he's hung over some Monday morning?"

"Linda, let's get some sleep." There was an edge to his voice.

She lay back down beside him silently for a moment, then felt for his hand and gave it a squeeze. "All right. I'll get off your back. I'm just worried for you. I don't want you to get in trouble because of Willis. Go to sleep, sweetheart. Good night."

She kissed his stubbly cheek. His breathing became deep again almost immediately. Poor thing. He'd worked hard in the yard today.

He was so loyal to his former professor, who later got him the job at Los Alamos Scientific Laboratories, that he couldn't bring himself to talk to Willis about his obvious increasing use of alcohol since his abandonment by his wife six weeks ago.

Tim would do it though. She would see to it. Willis Wilson may have gotten Tim his job, but it was because he knew Tim was a brilliant physicist, not out of the kindness of his heart.

She had never been able to like Willis, although for Tim's sake she had always been cordial to the man. He was so arrogant, such a monumental egotist, and his friendship for Tim had disappeared damn fast, too, when Tim got the top job at TA-18 instead of him.

She was sorry that Wilson was taking Sarah's desertion so badly, although she suspected that he was mourning more over his wounded ego than for the loss of his rich, artsy-fartsy bitch of a wife.

"That was an unworthy thought," she scolded herself. He was probably truly mourning the loss of his daughter, and Linda could feel for him in that loss. The little girl, Heather, had been adorable.

Nonetheless, sorry for Willis Wilson or not, she was going to stay on Tim's case until he did something about the situation. Gossip was beginning to spread through the little community, and working with enriched uranium, everyone in the facility had to be on his toes all the time. She hoped Tim could help Wilson get back on his feet, but whatever the outcome for Willis, she was determined that his problems were not going to ruin Tim's career.

✻ ✻ ✻

Thirty miles southwest of their bedroom, in Santa Fe, Aziz gently ushered his last customer out of the bar and locked the door. It was a quarter past one a.m., closing time. The customer had been drinking since shortly after eight, and was visibly the worse for the experience. He weaved slightly as he stood in the corridor beside Aziz.

The man had become a regular on weekends over the past month or so. Aziz had talked to him on a number of occasions, and had found him not inclined to chit-chat. Still, Aziz had learned some things about him, notably that his wife had left him, "kidnapping" their daughter.

"That's what you get for being a Christian," Aziz had thought when he heard about the wife's desertion, more for his own amusement than because he had anything against Christians. "If you were a Moslem, you'd have three more wives at home to keep you happy."

"Are you all right, Sir?" Aziz asked now.

"Hmmm? Oh, sure, I'm fine. Jus' tryin' to find the key." Aziz observed with amusement that what the man was actually trying to find was his pocket.

"Are you a guest at the hotel?" Aziz hoped so. To turn the man loose in a car would be murder or suicide, or both.

"Yeah, sure, spending the weeken'." The man had finally located his coat pocket and now retrieved a hotel key. He smiled triumphantly at Aziz. "I 'preciate your concern," he said. "I'll go to the room now. Little house — out in the garden. Good night." He turned and started down the hall toward the door out to the street.

Aziz hurried after him. "Let me accompany you, Sir. The grounds can be quite confusing in the dark." Aziz didn't want to have to explain to the manager why he'd let an obviously intoxicated hotel guest wander off into the night.

The Posada de Santa Fe Hotel, of which the Staab House bar was a part, had large grounds, on which were a number of guest houses. Aziz took the man's key and noted the number of the guest's "casita" before they stepped out into the darkness of the garden.

The sky was very clear, and even the lights of downtown Santa Fe couldn't obscure the brilliance of the stars. Although it was late June, there was a touch of crispness in the air, and the fresh smell of pine and pinon came to Aziz on the night wind.

The little man breathed deeply. "What a lovely place this is," he thought. "Maybe I can come back here some day and retire." The idea amused him.

Many of Aziz's ideas amused him, and much of everything else that he saw or heard, as well. For some reason, the All-Bestowing had seen fit to lavish the gift of laughter on him. Aziz was very grateful, even if he didn't believe in the All-Bestowing for a minute.

Living under the orders of a fanatic like Da'ud al-Musa, however, did not amuse him, although Aziz had been able to retain his sense of humor here in Santa Fe, far from Da'ud and the others.

He could face Da'ud with a clear conscience if he had to. He had carefully followed his instructions about trying to meet employees from Los Alamos Scientific Laboratories. That nothing had come of his efforts suited Aziz very well, but it was not his fault.

His presence here in the United States, on the other hand, was his fault. In his previous life in Libya, he had been the commercial agent for a number of Italian enterprises, and his fondness for the good life had lead him to begin fudging on his accountings with them. Unhappily, that had led him into the clutches of Abdallah al-Sanussi, and from him, ultimately, to Da'ud.

Up to now, however, that had been a blessing in disguise. The previous four years in Houston had been infinitely better than Aziz had feared when they departed Libya on this mission. He had loved his job in Texas, as a travelling salesman for a bar and restaurant supply company. He had four different American girl friends at the same time, all of them blonds, carefully located in widely dispersed parts of the state. It was also through that job that he had acquired the skill of bartending, which he had come to enjoy, mostly for the opportunity it provided for meeting women. Best of all, he had been under strict orders to have no contact with Da'ud, whom he both feared and despised.

What he emphatically did not enjoy, indeed what horrified him, even here in Santa Fe, was the mission on which he was now embarked with Da'ud and the others. He regarded it as sheer madness.

The dangerous part, however, seemed to be presently taking place far away from him, and he devoutly hoped that it stayed that way.

The man shambling along beside him stumbled and almost fell, bringing Aziz back to the present with a jerk. "Come on, Sir," he said. "Up we go. We're almost there."

Aziz got the man moving again with some difficulty. The alcohol he had consumed was about to overpower him.

They reached the door of the casita and Aziz wedged the guest upright against the door frame while he worked the key in the lock. He got the door open, turned on the room light and pulled the weaving man into the room after him.

The guest started down again. All Aziz had time to do was push him toward the living room couch. He fell face down across it, knees on the floor, and immediately began to snore.

The bulge of the wallet in the man's hip pocket arrested Aziz's attention. He stepped to the door and looked outside. No one was around.

Aziz closed and locked the door, walked back over to the snoring form and pulled out the billfold.

"Let me see who this drunken ass might be," he said to himself, "and how much money he is carrying. It might be that he wouldn't miss a twenty or two."

Chapter Six

July 9
Washington, D.C.

Link called JJ on the intercom. "Are you free? We've got something you need to see."

"Okay, come on over".

Link walked across the reception room into JJ's office. Barbara didn't look up as he went by. He handed the sheet of paper in his hand to JJ. "Take a look at this telex. I think we're finally onto something."

JJ looked like hell. His normally pink jowls were putty-colored, his white hair had acquired a suspicious yellow tinge, and there were dark rings under his eyes.

Link didn't feel so hot, himself. He'd been averaging 4 or 5 hours of sleep a night for the past three weeks.

JJ's plan to play down the significance of the Israeli report had not been too well received by the Chief of the Criminal Division, and it died stone cold dead on the desk of the Director, when they took it up to him.

"I don't give a damn what the CIA thinks about this story," The Director had said. "I'm responsible for counter-espionage inside the United States, not the CIA, and no one is going to be able to say that I dropped the ball on this," and with that, he had gotten on the phone to request an appointment with the President, who, on hearing the story, had immediately agreed with the Director's attitude.

Ever since, the NRC, the CIA, the INS, all the nuclear-related agencies, plus selected elements of the armed forces, and, of course, the FBI, had been working non-stop to increase the protection surrounding the country's nuclear material and find the as-yet unknown terrorists. ATS had become the center of a maelstrom. Unfortunately, until this very minute, the total result of all the activity had been exactly zero.

The pressure from the White House to find and neutralize the Libyans before the story leaked was tremendous and growing daily, given the potential for national panic. The President had sworn everyone who knew the story to secrecy, but considering how many people were in on it by now, it was a miracle that the story hadn't hit the papers already.

JJ took the telex – it was from the Houston Field Office – and scanned it, then read it again, slowly. "Huh", he grunted. "Well, it's not the pot of gold, but it does look like a lead, and at this point, I'd be grateful for a lot less."

He looked over the desk at Link, and waved the telex at him. "Get down to Houston and find these people."

Link could hardly believe his ears. JJ was ordering him back to the field! "Me?" he asked inanely.

"Yeah, you. You're our expert on these bastards. What does Houston know about terrorism? Take Leo with you, and anyone else you think you need. Take Barbara, too. She can handle your admin and communications with me. We've got to get this thing off our backs. I'd go myself," he said, "but the Director won't let me out of here." Link repressed a smile. JJ hadn't been in the field in almost twenty years.

Back to the field! And having Barbara to himself in Houston was frosting on the cake. He stood up, popped a mock salute and left before JJ could reconsider.

He used his credentials to bump some hardworking taxpayer off the first flight for Houston from Washington National that afternoon.

He was met at the airport by the Special Agent in Charge, whose warm greeting proved he was A Good Soldier. Link knew the SAC must be royally pissed to have some Headquarters weenie come down and take what could be the biggest case of his career out of his hands.

The SAC briefed him on the background of the case during the interminable drive into town from Houston Intercontinental.

"Houston has a huge Libyan population because of the oil industry connection," the SAC told him. "It took a long time to check out the community for new arrivals in the past three to four year time frame, even with every man in the office on the street, and INS working around the clock, and it was all for nothing—I mean, zip. That's when we decided to review the files of the Libyan permanent residents in whom we'd had some previous interest, just in case, and we came up with this guy, or rather, these guys."

"Thank God this man is smarter than I am," Link thought. "If he hadn't had that idea, I'd still be sitting in Washington, without a clue." He didn't think that saying it out loud would do anything for his credentials as the Bureau's master anti-terrorist expert, however, so he just nodded encouragingly.

"The trouble is," said the SAC, "we missed them by six weeks. They quit their jobs and told everyone that they were leaving for better positions in Saudi Arabia. They paid all their bills, closed all their accounts, sold their cars and left no forwarding addresses anywhere. If it hadn't been for the alert we got from your office, they could have had forever to do whatever they're planning to do."

The SAC turned right off West Memorial Drive just past the bridge over Buffalo Bayou, and they drove into the compound of Memorial Creole, a condo-apartment complex in which the buildings were built in imitation of the Louisiana style, the upstairs units supported by pillars and reached by wrought-iron staircases. Link liked it.

"Nice neighborhood," he observed.

"Yeah, it's pretty, isn't it? Well, this Da'ud al-Musa guy was a geologist for Esso Exploration, so he made good money."

The LIBYAN BOMB

They parked in front of one of the units at the far end of the complex, where the bayou made a bend. The apartment for which the SAC had secured a search warrant prior to Link's arrival was upstairs.

A number of agents were already inside the empty apartment, dusting it for fingerprints.

"Let's wait out on the balcony," suggested Link. "No use getting in their way in there. Tell me some more about this guy, al-whatshisname."

"Da'ud al-Musa. Calls himself Dave Muse for American consumption. If these guys are involved in some terrorist plot, he'll be the brains of the bunch. He's an interesting guy. He was an orphan, adopted in Libya by an American oil man, raised and educated in Texas. He's a naturalized U.S. citizen. When he was still in college at A & M, his adopted parents were killed in a plane crash. Their natural-born children got together and froze Da'ud out of their folks' will. It was a really ugly story, and got into the papers. They really shafted the kid."

"He got enough money to finish his degree, but as soon as he did, he went back to Libya, and according to his job application at Esso Exploration, worked for the Libyan National Oil Company. About four years ago, he came back here. He brought a Libyan wife with him. She's a knockout, they say. All the men in the neighborhood had the hots for her, but their wives all thought she was nice."

"On the surface, they were a model couple. He paid his bills on time, got along with the neighbors, even took their kids to baseball games."

"The reason we got interested in him was, a couple of years ago, one of our informants in the Libyan expatriate community told us that one of the other guys who's missing, Ibrahim something or other—he's got a hell of a long last name—had killed one of the anti-Gaddhafi activists in the Libyan community on al-Musa's orders."

"Unfortunately, before we could even get started with an investigation, our informant was fished out of the ship canal with his skull smashed in. We've never gotten anything to confirm the informant's story, or even to confirm that Ibrahim and Da'ud were acquainted. We interviewed both of them. They denied knowing each other, or the deceased, and that was that."

"This Ibrahim guy is as different from Da'ud as night from day: Da'ud is pretty big, my guy who met him says, maybe 6'1", 190 pounds, but Ibrahim is huge: 6'4" or more, 250 pounds and pretty much all muscle. He worked at a local mosque—he's a super devout Moslem, gave the impression of being a little slow upstairs, and of speaking very little English."

"What about the third guy you mention in the telex," asked Link.

"He's the wild card. His name is Aziz abu-Rizq. He was a restaurant supply salesman. He has a clean record and no known connection with either al-Musa or Ibrahim, except that he left the area at the same time they did, and in the same way, with the same story."

"Do we have anything besides the story from this dead informant of yours that ties any of these people to Libyan intelligence?" Link asked him. "I agree that it's funny, their all disappearing together after the Tripoli raid, but I've got to have more than an unsubstantiated accusation and a coincidental disappearance before we start turning the country upside down looking for them."

"Not a damn thing that's really evidence," said the SAC, "but aside from the disappearance, here's the reason I sent you that telex: the only pictures of any of these people that we can find are on their Texas drivers licenses, which, by the way, were all acquired within 6 weeks of each other, back in 1982."

"We showed those pictures to everyone who knew them, and not one single person could positively ID any of them. They apparently had their pictures taken in disguise. Doesn't that sound like an intelligence operation to you?"

"Well. yeah, it does," said Link, "but no pictures? How can that be? I mean, after four years in Houston?"

"Link, we turned Houston inside out looking for pictures of these people, and we didn't get shit."

"What about visa applications, naturalization certificates, stuff like that? There are pictures on them. Thumbprints, too."

"We've asked State Department and INS for them," the SAC answered, "but have you ever tried to get records from INS?"

Link nodded glumly. "Maybe we'll have some luck with State." He added, "I'm sure you've got folks working on composite drawings with people here who knew them?" It was a dumb question, practically an insult, coming from one professional to another.

The SAC silently nodded assent. Link admired his restraint.

He could feel excitement rising inside him. Ever since he heard the story from the Israelis, he'd been viscerally certain that the story, and the threat, were both real. In his mind, what he'd just learned confirmed it. In the espionage business, there was no such thing as coincidence. No useable photos? These were the people they were looking for! To the SAC he said, "They did a real number on us, didn't they?"

The SAC nodded. "Yeah, they did, but maybe we can find something here in the apartment. Prints might be very useful, down the line."

As if on cue, the agent in charge of the finger printers came out on the balcony with them.

"What have you found," Link asked him.

"Nothing," came the response. "There's not a print in the place."

Link stared at him. "They lived in that apartment for four years and there aren't any prints? Since when did Arabs get to be such good housekeepers?"

"They painted every inch of it before they left, and what they didn't paint, they washed in paint thinner. That apartment isn't just clean, buddy. It's as sterile as an operating room."

Chapter Seven

July 9
Houston, Texas

Barbara's eyes widened. "Really? They painted and washed down the apartment? Then don't they almost have to be the ones we want? I mean, innocent citizens don't do that."

Hot damn, she was talking to him again!

"Yeah, I think they're the ones we want," Link said, "and it's not just the apartments either. These people had been here for almost four years, but they didn't own anything—no cars, no furniture, no nothing. They rented everything, and turned it back in as clean as the apartments."

Barbara and Leo had arrived late in the afternoon. Link was briefing them on the events of the day in a Vietnamese restaurant out on West Memorial Drive that one of the Houston agents had recommended to him.

Link liked Vietnamese food. The subtlety of the tastes and the smell of charcoal smoke and garlic coming from the kitchen evoked for him the good part of the time in Vietnam: the tropical weather, the bright flowers and beautiful girls in their bright-colored ao dais.

He thought he'd set the evening up pretty well. Barbara couldn't refuse to come along, since it was official business, and Link had arranged with Leo to get lost after the briefing.

Leo and Link went back a long way. They had gone through training at Quantico together and then pulled their first tour, in Newark, at the same time. Separated for a tour after that, Leo had come to New York at Link's request, and then followed him to Headquarters, a decision he now probably regretted. Link was afraid to ask him about it.

Anyway, Leo didn't need any persuading to leave him alone with Barbara. He was always telling Link that he ought to marry her.

"So what are we going to do?" he asked Link now, speaking around his last mouthful of sticky rice and mangos.

"We're going to find them, buddy," Link answered. "Somewhere, somehow, one of these people has to have forgotten his cover story, left a forwarding address, or dropped a hint that will point us in the right direction. We'll start first thing in the morning, interviewing everyone we can find who knew them. The whole field office will be involved. We've asked INS to check flight manifests leaving Houston for overseas destinations just after they left the area, just in case they're legit, but if you'd like to make a bet, I've got a hundred bucks that says we won't find anything. They're still in this country, and we're going to get 'em."

"I hope you're right," said Leo, "but if they are still in the U.S., here's a bet I will take. Ten to one says they're not going to still be using the names they went by here."

Link nodded glumly. "Yeah, that had occurred to me, too. They didn't go to all that trouble to clean up behind them just to keep on using their true names. We've got nothing but the composites to go with. But hey, that's a hell of a lot more than we had this time yesterday." He nodded emphatically. "We'll find 'em."

That was Leo's cue, and he fielded it with aplomb. "Well, if I'm going to spend tomorrow on the street, I'd better get to bed early. Us old married men need our sleep." Barbara was only half way through her dinner.

"Okay, Leo," said Link. "I'll take Barbara back to the hotel. See you at seven in the coffee shop.

Leo left his share of the bill and departed. Barbara devoted her attention to her sautéed shrimp. When she finally looked up, Link was delighted to see the hint of a smile at the corners of her mouth.

She struggled to contain it, but couldn't. She finally burst out laughing. "Honestly, Link, you and Leo! You're both as transparent as glass."

He tried to look innocent, but gave it up in the face of her laughter. "It's your fault," he said. "You haven't spoken to me in over two weeks. I have to get sneaky."

The merriment left her face. "I'm sorry about the silent treatment, Link, but working together in the same office every day, the only way I could get by was just to pretend you weren't there."

Oh, oh. That didn't sound good. "Well, for crying out loud, at least tell me what it is that I've done to deserve all this non-attention."

"We've been over all that before, Link. It isn't what you did. It's what you didn't do, and won't do. I really don't think there's anything left to say about it."

"Look, Barbara, we've been going together for months. We like each other a lot, and all of a sudden, without any argument or anything, one night you suddenly decide you won't see me anymore. It seems to me that you owed me some warning that I was in trouble."

Her clear blue eyes were somber. "Liking each other doesn't have anything to do with it, Link. I went from liking you to loving you a long time ago. Otherwise, we wouldn't have become lovers. And you got plenty of warnings of what was on my mind. You just didn't want to hear them."

She put down the chop sticks she had been toying with and looked squarely at him. "At my age, Link, loving a man who isn't going to marry me is not only too painful to endure; it's also a waste of time that I haven't go to spare."

There was a hint of moisture in the blue eyes now. "I don't want to grow old by myself, Link. I want to share my life with someone. If you're not interested in being that person, I have to try to meet someone else."

She dropped her eyes and frowned at her plate. "I don't know why I'm baring my soul to you this way," she said bitterly. "Please take me back to the hotel. I'm not hungry anymore."

Her rock-solid honesty was something he had liked in her from the start, but sometimes it had an edge. She had just driven it into him up to the hilt. He couldn't think of any rebuttal that wouldn't sound trite by comparison. He tried to get the attention of the waitress.

Link had married three months after getting out of the Navy hospital, and two months after meeting the girl. He was twenty-three years old. The marriage ended thirteen months later, when he came home early one afternoon to the trailer park where they lived outside Camp Lejeune, and found her in bed with the next-door neighbor.

He hadn't seen it coming. He hadn't had much experience with women at all before his marriage, and he'd fallen head over heels in love with Susan. Maybe his close encounter with death in Vietnam contributed to that. He realized that he didn't know much about her. She never talked about her family or her life before they met, but he was so crazy about her that it didn't seem to make any difference.

Her betrayal had devastated him. The divorce hadn't hurt him financially-the neighbors knew what was going on and testified on his behalf-but he became so depressed that he couldn't focus on anything, including his job. That ultimately resulted in a medical discharge from the Corps. His combat record in 'Nam earned him the sympathy of the evaluation board.

He'd bummed around until his money was gone. His dad had persuaded him to go to college on the Vietnam G.I. bill, and he did, just for something to do, earning mediocre grades until he happened to enroll in a class in Criminal Justice, which caught his interest.

He changed his major, made good grades from then on, and on graduation got a job with the Cincinnati Police Department. He worked there for four years before applying to the Bureau. His combat record once again helped him get preference in the selection process, along with a glowing reference from the C.P.D.

In all that time, he'd scarcely dated. After he joined the Bureau he immersed himself in his work, and even when he was in town, he might not get home for days at a time. There had always been women available to him for casual sex, attracted by his size and looks, but he'd never formed an emotional attachment to any of them. He'd never wanted to take the chance of being knifed in the back again. It was a lot safer emotionally to be the one waving goodbye than the one being waved to.

He didn't feel very emotionally secure right now, however. Barbara had succeeded in making him feel guilty, and dammit, he wasn't guilty of anything.

"Barbara, it's not like I lied to you. I told you when we started dating . . . ."

She held up a hand to silence him. "I know, Link. You were very frank about your intentions, or lack of them, I guess I should say. I was so glad you wanted me that I just fooled myself into thinking that you'd change your mind someday. Not your fault at all. You were completely honorable and honest. I just fooled myself."

The blue eyes were definitely wet now, and her voice was beginning to quaver. "Can we please get the damned check?"

Her discomfort with him made him suddenly angry, whether with himself or with her he couldn't decide. He waved imperiously at the waitress, who came running. He paid, left a minimum tip and started around the table to hold Barbara's chair. She was already standing when he got there.

They walked out to the car. He opened the door, let her in, then said, "Wait a second," and went back into the restaurant and doubled the tip. It would be pretty crappy of him to take his frustration out on the poor little waitress.

Not a word was exchanged on the way to her hotel. She was out of the car and on the sidewalk before he could get his door open.

"Goodbye, Link," she said through the open window.

He was really unhappy. If she was trying to pressure him into proposing, it wasn't going to work, but the idea of not even seeing her again didn't sit very well, either. He needed time to think about this one. "Dammit, Barbara, can't we even talk about this?"

Her face crumpled and tears began to flow. "No, Link, we can't. It's going to be hard enough, working together in the same office, without having you trying to jolly me back into bed again. It you care for me at all, I hope you'll show it by leaving me alone."

He felt his cheeks getting hot. Was that all she thought he cared about?

She was crying openly now. "And tell that damned JJ that we've broken up," she sobbed. I'm sick to death of his leering at me every morning." She turned and marched into the hotel.

He drove back to the Best Western next to the Loop where his room was. It was near Pat O'Brien's restaurant. He'd hoped to have eggs Benedict there with Barbara tomorrow morning.

A stop light turned red on him. He swore viciously at it, and ran it. A screech of tires and blare of horn sounded behind him. He didn't even look in the mirror. Screw 'em. A miss was as good as a mile.

The way he felt took him by surprise. Barbara had his number, all right. He HAD thought he could "jolly her back into bed," as she'd put it. Maybe too many easy lays over the years had made him complacent. Woman-killer Rowe. But dammit, she wasn't just a piece of ass to him. And she knew it.

Was it just a ploy, a pressure play? The memory of her tear-streaked, distorted face made him dismiss that theory. Barbara wasn't an actress. What she felt, she said, and what she said, she meant. A real straight arrow.

She'd said she loved him. She'd never said it before, not that way, just straight out, "I love you." That made him feel good, but a fat lot of good it did now.

Did he love her? He thought about that as he parked the car and took the elevator up to his floor. He really couldn't say. He didn't feel the same way about her as he had about his wife. He'd been out of his mind about her, and look what he'd gotten for it. Of course, he wasn't twenty-three years old anymore, either.

He certainly thought about Barbara more than he had about any woman since his marriage, and not just sexually, but in other ways, all kinds of ways. It suddenly occurred to him that he knew her a lot better than he'd known Susan.

He'd jokingly told Leo that he guessed it was a sign of middle age, having a steady girl. Leo just smiled and said, "Maybe you're finally getting lucky."

Maybe he ought to talk to Leo and see what he thought.

He lay awake in his bed for a long time, thinking about her, and what she'd said. The idea of not seeing her anymore really bothered him. Maybe he was in love with her.

Jesus, what a day. His head ached worse now than it had this morning, he'd been dumped by Barbara and he didn't have the faintest fucking clue where the Libyans had gone to. Leo's observation about them changing their names was probably right on the money, and was going to make Link's job a thousand percent harder. JJ wasn't going to like that.

Speaking of JJ, Barbara said he'd been leering at her. He knew they were lovers, of course. That asshole. He wondered why she'd never mentioned the leering to him before. Probably afraid he'd punch JJ out. He might, yet. It was about the only satisfaction he was likely to get out of the deal.

He had to turn off his mind and get some sleep. Tomorrow was going to be a bear. "One thing about it," he thought. "It's got to be better than today. It can't get any worse."

Chapter Eight

July 17
Los Alamos,
New Mexico

Ed Adams looked out the window of his office on the top floor of the Los Alamos Scientific Laboratories Administration Building. He had a magnificent view of Santa Fe and the Sangre de Cristo Mountains behind that city across thirty miles of intervening valley.

The mountain air was so clear that he could distinguish the birch trees on the mountains from the darker green of the pines. It was a view that normally lifted his spirits and soothed his soul.

It wasn't doing a damn thing for him this morning.

The LIBYAN BOMB

The reason was the classified telegram from the Nuclear Regulatory Commission, which he held in his hands. It was the third one he had received in the past two weeks.

They had all said about the same thing. "Don't tell a soul, but there's a bunch of crazy camel herders out there somewhere trying to steal nuclear material. And it might be yours that they're after, so watch your ass."

"Jesus, Mary and Joseph," he thought. "With a little over six months to go to retirement, I don't need this."

Ed was the Chief of Security of LASL, and in addition to the general dislike that anyone in that job might have to being targeted by someone bent on nuclear theft, he had some very specific worries: worries that had kept him from sleeping much lately.

First of all, he had a hell of a lot of weapons-grade material to worry about. Los Alamos was the nation's primary plutonium re-processing center, and there was a very large (classified) amount of plute stored on-site. Besides that, there was weapons-grade U-235 in Technical Area-18 and in two or three other areas under his jurisdiction.

Second, he didn't even come close to having enough people to protect the stuff, even under normal circumstances, let alone with a threat of this magnitude hanging over his head.

In a period of declining budgets, security naturally had a very low funding priority, and LASL had been balancing its budget on Ed's back for years. In an establishment populated almost universally with PhD's, Ed reflected bitterly, a cop with an Associate's Degree didn't cut much ice. The tiny Los Alamos Police Department and the Sheriff with his handful of deputies, weren't equipped to be of any help against a terrorist attack.

Finally, and the reason why he was looking with such a jaundiced eye at the magnificent scenery in front of him, was that the goddam scenery was made to order for terrorists.

LASL and the two bedroom cities that supported it were built on the tongues of a massive lava flow, which began at the foot of the Big Meadow, the huge ancient volcanic crater a couple of miles north of where he stood, and spread south to the Rio Grande.

The lava had solidified into a series of mesas, which stood a hundred feet or more above the surrounding land. Between the mesas were canyons, some of which came to within a few feet of the perimeter fences of his most sensitive areas. Overgrown with pinon and other scrub trees, they provided ideal cover for an approach to LASL by anyone bent on mischief.

And if a band of terrorists DID take aim at LASL, the country-side around the perimeter was so vast and so thinly populated that the chances of their being discovered before they made their move was very small indeed.

"Jesus, Mary and Joseph," Ed thought again, rubbing a hand wearily over his florid face. "I really don't need this shit. I'm going to talk to Pearl about retiring early."

July 17

Washington, D.C.

"Wrong again, Rowe," Link thought, staring morosely at the roof of the Justice Department. He'd never made a lousier prediction in his life, that night in Houston, over a week ago, now, when he'd told himself that things couldn't get worse. They had – a lot.

Interviews of everyone who had known or might even have conceivably known the Libyans had produced exactly diddly-squat in the way of new information, and not one photograph had come to light.

With the help of the Libyans' former neighbors and employers in Houston, they had put together what they said were pretty good composite pictures of the suspects, but that was it. If the bad guys had missed a trick, Link hadn't been able to discover it.

Increasingly frustrated by both the lack of results and non-stop telephone harassment by JJ, Link left the Houston SAC (who was visibly glad to be rid of him) in charge of the investigation there and returned to Washington.

That had been another bad judgment call.

The heat on the Bureau from the White House had gone up about a thousand degrees during Link's absence, and JJ was driving everyone in the unit absolutely batshit. If he told Link just one more time about White House interest in the case, Link swore that he would deck him.

Nonetheless, JJ was right. It was an election year and the White House was VERY interested in the case, and for that matter, interested in how the Bureau was handling it.

For example, Link had wanted to flood the country with the composite pictures of the Libyans. It would greatly increase the chances of finding them, and the charge on which they were allegedly wanted could be fudged to keep the real situation a secret. And, if the Libyans themselves saw the posters, maybe it would scare them off. It looked like a no-lose idea to Link.

The President nixed it, saying it might lead to public panic. The White House was hoping the Israeli agent in Tripoli could identify the Libyans' target, so the Bureau could lie in wait and trap them without the necessity of going public. In the meantime, the State Department was sending "signals" to Libya, what the hell ever that meant.

Barbara was back from Texas, too, of course. Every day she said exactly four words to Link: "Good morning," and "Good night."

All in all, he couldn't remember a less satisfactory time since the day he got shot, in Vietnam.

The ringing of his phone saved him from losing his staring match with the Justice Department roof. "Rowe here."

"Okay, Bryan," he told the caller. "I'll come down and get you. JJ's waiting for us."

As soon as he got back from Houston, Link had called Bryan James, a friend of his in the Nuclear Regulatory Commission, who knew a lot about the security systems used by NRC. He also knew about the Libyans, of course. NRC was as much under the White House gun as the Bureau.

The LIBYAN BOMB

Bryan and Link had spent the last two days looking at the potential targets from what they hoped was the Libyans' point of view, and had come up with a working theory. If JJ bought it, Link hoped he would be able to get out of Washington again.

✵ ✵ ✵

"I'm glad to meet you, Mr. Maloney," said Bryan to JJ after the introductions. "I hope what Link and I have come up with is useful to you."

"I hope it is, too," grunted JJ. He sounded doubtful.

"Well," began Bryan, "I know you've all got a huge problem trying to find these guys, but they've got some big problems, too, even without knowing that we're on to them."

"First, there are only four of them, as far as we're aware, and they're said to be all pretty much typical Arab types, so there are certain parts of the country where they'll be quite noticeable."

"For that reason, the weapons depots are almost certainly not what they've targeted. Those are very heavily guarded, and no one who looks like a foreigner is going to get close to one of them unchallenged. Anyway, a nuclear bomb weighs a hell of a lot. You don't just stick one in your pocket and walk off with it."

He warmed to his subject. "Of course, if what Gaddhafi wants is to blackmail the US into laying off Libya, he doesn't need plutonium, which would be the hardest for him to get. He could make a gun-type device out of Uranium-235 an awful lot easier. It worked on Hiroshima. It could work on Manhattan."

JJ looked as if he had developed a stomach cramp.

"It seems much more likely to me," Bryan continued, "that they will go for one of the secondary sources, like the scientific laboratories, commercial manufacturers or experimental reactors. Those aren't nearly as heavily guarded as the weapons are, but some of them have weapons-grade material."

"I know, I know," moaned JJ. "And there are lots of them."

"There are quite a few, Mr. Maloney." Bryan agreed cheerfully, and began ticking off points on his fingers. "The Babcock-Wilcox plant in Lynchburg, Virginia, manufactures fuel for the navy's nuclear subs, although I don't think they'd go for that, either. It's highly guarded, and Lynchburg would be very tough for them. Everyone in town is either black or Anglo-Saxon. Four Arabs would stick out like sore thumbs. There are highly enriched U-235 experimental devices at Los Alamos," Bryan went on, "and every nuclear physicist in the world knows it. They're locked up damn' tight, but there's not much firepower protecting them. Furthermore, the Libyans would look more or less like the local Hispanics. On the other hand, Los Alamos is a very small place, everyone knows everyone else, plus, it's in the middle of the country. How could they get the thing back to Libya after they stole it?"

"Lawrence Livermore Laboratory —L cubed, to insiders – is the national weapons design center. Whether there's weapons-grade material there is so classified that even I don't know the answer, but you guys can find out. The Libyans sure might think there is, and it's an easier target for them than Los Alamos. There is a big local population for them to hide in nearby, including Hispanics, and it's only thirty miles from San Francisco Bay, which could facilitate their getting it out of the country."

"Long story short, if I were in their shoes, I'd go for California. There are just so many viable targets there. Rockwell International makes enriched fuel for the Department of Energy at Canoga Park, and General Atomics in San Diego makes fuel for its own experimental reactor, the TRIGA, plus there are five TRIGAS in California that use high-grade fuel."

"Jesus," JJ sighed again.

The end of the sigh was cut off by the buzz of the intercom. JJ picked up the receiver.

"I thought I said we weren't to be interrupted," he snapped. Link recognized Barbara's voice on the phone, explaining something. "Okay, okay," JJ said ungraciously, "I guess you were right to break in."

He passed the phone to Link. "It's your Mossad buddy, who got us into all this shit in the first place."

Link took the receiver. "Hello, David . . . No problem. What've you got?"

The Israeli spoke for less than thirty seconds, but it seemed much, much longer to Link. "Well," he said, when the caller fell silent, "thanks for letting us know. I'm sorry about your man . . . Yeah . . . OK . . . So long."

He handed the receiver back across the desk to JJ. "The Israelis have monitored a Libyan internal broadcast announcing the execution of what they called, 'an Israeli-American imperialist spy'."

"Well? What of it?"

"David said the guy they executed was the Mossad agent who tipped us off to this shit, as you put it. You can tell the White House to forget about any breakthroughs in Tripoli."

Chapter Nine

July 17
San Diego

Sabana cradled Dave's head against her breast and played with his blonde curls. A fine sheen of perspiration covered her body and the air conditioning made her feel chilly, but she didn't want to break the mood by pulling up the sheets.

"Daveed?"

"Hmmm?"

"What is your job? I know you are ingeniero, but kind of work you do?"

"I'm a nuclear engineer, baby. I work at General Atomics."

She jerked her head away to look at him in feigned shock. "Atomico General? You work with bombas atomicas? Que horror!"

He laughed and pulled her back close to him. "No, baby, I don't work with atom bombs. We produce an experimental nuclear reactor. We sell it to universities, mostly. It's to teach people about nuclear energy."

"But even if is not a bomb, it mus' be very dangerous. Does it not have la radioactividad?

"Yes, it does involve radioactivity, but we are very careful with it. I'm in no danger at all."

"How can be no danger, if you work with reactor? She hugged him tight. "Daveed, if something happen to you, what will I do? I love you so much."

He returned her hug. "I love you too, baby. Don't worry. We've got dozens of TRIGAs running, all over the world, and we've never even come close to an accident."

She wouldn't be appeased. "Maybe no, but what is inside el reactor is very dangerous, no? If you in charge, don' you have to take out an' change sometimes? I read that if the radioactividad hit your – you know, down there – you no can make love anymore. What will I do then?"

He grinned at her. "We use a special, lead-lined truck to move the rods, and when we change the fuel, believe me, baby, we are very, very careful."

He kissed a breast. "Now that I know what it's like to make love to you, I'll be careful. Where did you learn so much about atomic energy, anyway?"

Careful, Sabana, she warned herself. Too much, too soon. "Oh, I learn in the school," she answered. She took his face in her hands and looked at him with pleading eyes. "Please, Daveed, promise me, you tell me when you do this dangerous thing next time, so I can go to church the whole day and pray to the Virgin for you."

His eyes softened. "All right, baby, we've got a re-load to UC-Berkeley in September. I'll tell you when it happens and you can pray for me." He smiled at her and kissed her gently on the tip of her nose. "I love you, Maria."

"I love you, too, Daveed."

Two months! She had to drain this idiot's balls and send him home, so she could go tell Da'ud.

July 18

San Diego

The rising sun shone straight in Da'ud's eyes. He wished he'd thought to bring his sun glasses.

He drove slowly east down Genesee Road from its junction with North Torrey Pines Highway, heading toward Interstate 5. At six a.m., there was no other traffic.

He passed Tower Road. The entrance to the General Atomics plant was just beyond view to his north. It wasn't far enough to the Interstate to give them many choices: only about three-quarters of a mile.

He already knew every inch of the area. During the team's first weeks in San Diego, he and Ibrahim had spent every afternoon up here, hiding in the thick brush and Torrey pines on the slopes of the canyon he was now beginning to drive down.

They had studied vehicles coming out of Tower Road at quitting time through binoculars, noting the make, color and license tags of cars with General Atomics parking stickers.

After three weeks, when their list seemed to be complete, they'd begun loitering in their own cars on North Torrey Pines and further down Genesee at quitting time, waiting for cars on their list to come past.

What they were looking for were the GA employees who habitually stopped somewhere for a drink on the way home. Their system was to follow the same car for a week, using a different team member and vehicle every day.

Da'ud had allowed a minimum of eight weeks for that portion of the operation, but luck, or Allah, he didn't care which, had given them the engineer in less than a month. The guy stopped for a beer two or three evenings a week at a cocktail lounge in the La Jolla Village Square shopping center.

With Sabana's looks, it had been easy for her to get a waitress job there and child's play after that to get the engineer in her bed.

The road Da'ud was driving on suited his purpose well. It was four lanes wide, divided by a median thickly planted with palms, oleanders and other shrubbery. Cars coming up-hill wouldn't have a clear view of what was going on in the east-bound lane.

Traffic coming downhill behind the truck with fuel rods would have to be stopped somehow – just a few minutes were all that was needed. Aziz could devise some diversion – perhaps a stalled car or minor accident. Da'ud made a mental note to have Aziz come join them. No need to worry about a fall-back position now.

The LIBYAN BOMB

The road dropped downhill quite steeply from its crest. He was now perhaps a hundred feet below the level of the land above the canyon. There were no residences or business anywhere around. The slopes were thickly covered with a variety of bushes and thick brush, which came all the way down to the edge of the road. He and Ibrahim could hide with no difficulty next to Sabana's car.

Her's would be the critical job of stopping the truck. She should be able to manage that, however, with the hood open and a small smoke charge giving the appearance of an engine fire. As soon as the driver was looking into the engine compartment, Ibrahim and Da'ud would take him.

The biggest problem was going to be getting the fuel rods out of the county, either by truck into México or on a ship docked at San Diego or San Pedro. Since the alarm was sure to be sounded soon after they snatched the rods, it would be necessary to off-load them immediately into some pre-rented storage facility until the search died down. The GA truck was completely unmarked, so it would not attract attention, but handling the weight of the rods with only three men: could they do that? He needed to make contact with Tripoli to discuss that part of the operation. He would have to go to Mexico City and use the code machines at the Embassy there. Happily, they had time to make these arrangements: almost two months.

All at once, the ideal ambush site appeared in front of him. Genesee Road made a slight turn southward, blocking the view from the rear, and the Interstate was still not visible ahead. The plantings on the median were quite thick, and so was the brush alongside the road.

Da'ud made a careful note of his odometer reading, and drove back to the apartment for breakfast.

Chapter Ten

July 18
Livermore, California

"Look JJ," Link snapped into the phone, "just because we haven't found 'em yet doesn't mean we won't. We've still got plenty of places to look out here, and even if we learn they're not in California, at least we'll know that, which is more than we know now, and in the third place, when the Director asks you what we're doing about these guys, you can tell him something besides, 'sitting on our asses in Washington'." Link hung up.

After Bryan's briefing and the bad news from the Israelis, JJ had agreed to Link's plan for a massive investigation in California. Given the pressure from on high, they had to do SOMETHING, and in the absence of hard information, the number and variety of nuclear facilities in that state made it the most likely target for the Libyans.

The top brass had agreed, put the San Francisco Field Office at Links disposition, and pulled in other agents from all over California for more manpower.

For the past three days, Link had had two dozen special agents, each with composite drawings of the Libyans, interview all of the employees, contractors and sub-contractors of Lawrence Livermore Laboratory. A hundred more had covered Livermore and the towns around it, door to door. An equal number of special agents under Leo's direction had done the same around Canoga Park.

The total results to date had been nil.

This morning, Link's task force was starting in on the experimental reactors, and Leo and his team were in San Diego, interviewing the staff at General Atomics.

In spite of what he'd just said to JJ on the phone, the lack of results tarnished Link's delight at being back in the field again. He had really thought the Libyans might be going after L-cubed. Bryan had made it seem so logical.

The lack of progress wasn't made any easier to swallow by JJ, who was on the phone two or three times a day, shriller with each call.

July 18

San Diego

In the office that the General Atomics official had made available to him, Leo handed the composite likenesses to the man across the table. "Take a look at these pictures, Mr. Lewis, and tell me if you've seen any of these people around the area in the last few months."

Composite likenesses are made with an Identikit, a set of transparent acetates, each containing a single facial feature. People who have seen the face being re-created are asked to compare different face shapes, nose, ear, eye, chin and eyebrow types as they are laid on top of previous acetates. With good witnesses and a little luck, a remarkable resemblance can be obtained.

The General Atomics engineer across from Leo barely glanced at the drawing of the male suspects, but the likeness of Sabana al-Murtada held his attention. He frowned at it for a good while without comment, then looked up at Leo. "Could I ask what this woman is suspected of?"

Excitement flickered in Leo. "I'm not free to provide all the details, Mr. Lewis, but basically she is suspected of conspiring to steal nuclear material. Have you seen her?"

Lewis's frown deepened. "What's her nationality?"

"She's an Arab."

The frown disappeared. He handed the composite back to Leo. "You had me worried for a minute," he said. "I know a girl who looks a lot like this, but she's no Arab."

"Oh? Where's she from?"

"El Salvador."

Leo's excitement faded. "How long have you known her," he asked.

"Oh, not long. Five, six weeks."

The timing was right. Leo got interested again. "How do you know she's from El Salvador? I mean, besides her saying so."

Lewis' frown came back. "Well, I've never seen her passport, but she speaks Spanish and is a Catholic."

That sounded pretty convincing to Leo too, but what the hell, it was the only lead he had. "Does she live around here, Mr. Lewis?"

The frown became a furrow. "Look," the engineer said, "suppose she turns out to be an illegal alien? Are you going to throw her out of the country, or put her in jail? I'm not going to be a party to something like that."

The guy's tone of voice got Leo a little hot. "Mr. Lewis," he said, "I don't care if she machine-gunned her way over the border with twenty kilos of coke on her back. If she's a Latin American, she's home free. Do you know where we might find her at this time of day?"

The engineer obviously didn't like that idea. "Well," he said finally, "she works during the afternoons at a cocktail lounge down in La Jolla."

"How about running down there with me? We won't take more than five minutes of her time."

"I think I ought to call her first and tell her what's up. I don't want you people to scare her to death."

"Look, Mr. Lewis, you apparently suspect that she's an illegal alien. Now, if she is, and you tell her that the FBI wants to see her, it may not scare her to death, but it could sure scare her out of town. This is a very serious case we're working on here. If she runs, I won't have any option but to put her on a nation-wide wanted list. Do you want to do that to her?"

The frown almost turned to a snarl. "You can't threaten me, mister. This girl hasn't' done anything but try to get away from the CIA killers in El Salvador."

"Oh, shit," thought Leo. "That's all this investigation needs." He made a quick decision to be a nice guy. "Okay," he said. "Tell you what. How about letting Special Agent Hidalgo here listen on the extension while you talk to her? If he says her accent is legit, maybe we won't have to see her at all."

Lewis reluctantly agreed. He fished a card with the woman's phone number on it out of his billfold, and dialed. Hidalgo got on the extension in the next office. Lewis asked whoever answered to let him talk to Maria Gomez. She came on the line a few seconds later.

"Maria? Hi, baby, it's Dave. I'm sorry to bother you at work. We have some people here at the plant doing an investigation. They want to make certain that any foreigners our employees know well are from friendly countries . . . No, they're from the FBI. They want to meet you and . . ."

From the look on Lewis' face, Leo gathered that her reaction to the idea wasn't enthusiastic agreement. He looked inquiringly at Hidalgo through the glass partition. The agent mouthed the words, "scared shitless." Illegal alien, sure as hell.

Lewis started talking again. "Okay, baby, I understand. Now listen. Don't panic and run out on me. They don't care if you're not in the country legally. They just want to be sure you're from El Salvador. If you don't have a passport, just talk Spanish to them."

He listened some more, nodding. "Okay, baby, we'll see you there. Don't worry. I'll be right there with you. I won't let them do anything to you."

He hung up. "She's afraid her boss will fire her if any police come into the lounge asking questions about her. She gets off at seven-thirty, and she'll see us at her apartment about eight."

Leo tossed a quick glance at Hidalgo, who shrugged noncommittally. "All right, Mr. Lewis," Leo said. "Thank you for your cooperation. Tell us where her place is and we'll meet you there this evening."

The furrow on the engineers brow as he left the office was deep enough to plant beans in. "He's afraid she isn't going to show either," thought Leo. "Shit. I should have leaned on him for an unannounced interview."

Hidalgo returned from the other office. "You know, Leo," he said, "the way that woman talked didn't really sound like any Spanish accent I ever heard before. Do you think she could be the Libyan gal we're looking for after all? I mean, this place is a target, and the timing's right."

Leo pondered for a second. "I don't know. Link says that GA isn't really a likely target, because the fuel for their reactor isn't metal, and it would be real hard for the Libyans to move enough to make a bomb out of. And another thing is, where would the Libyans have learned Spanish?"

His own question gave him an idea. "Tell you what. Just for the hell of it, let's send a telex to Houston and have them do a quick run-through of the local language schools with the composites. We ought to have the answer back before we go see her."

Hidalgo went off to the communications office. "God, I screwed that up," thought Leo. 'Even if she isn't the Libyan babe, if she runs out on me, what am I gonna do? If I wind up putting a goddam' illegal on the most-wanted list, I'm gonna be laughed out of the Bureau. I'd better call Link."

Chapter Eleven

July 18
San Diego

Leo and Hidalgo met Lewis in the parking lot in front of the apartment building at a quarter after eight. Since they were on daylight time, there was still plenty of light.

Houston hadn't responded to the telex yet, but Leo understood why. With the two-hour time differential between California and Texas, most of the language schools had probably closed for the day before the inquiry got under way.

He didn't think it was essential, anyway. Lewis swore up and down the woman was from El Salvador, and when Leo checked it out over the phone with Link, he'd agreed that she was probably an illegal.

He'd chewed Leo's ass for not forcing the interview, because he was afraid she wouldn't show either, but as Link's ass-chewings went, it was pretty mild. Leo had had a lot worse.

Link was coming down on an evening flight, but mostly just for something to do. He told Leo to go ahead and check it out before he got there. Leo didn't' think he needed any more backup than Hidalgo.

Like Hidalgo said, even if he couldn't place the woman's accent, the story Lewis had told them about her wanting to light candles so he didn't get his balls fried off by the TRIGA sure sounded like a Latina.

The apartment was typical San Diego modern: white stucco over cinder block, lots of glass, semi-tropical plantings everywhere, and a pool in the interior patio with a bunch of young women splashing around in mini-kinis.

Leo sighed for his lost youth as they followed the engineer up the stairs to the third-floor apartment. According to Lewis, his girl didn't have a car, but got a ride home with another waitress. The engineer was still mumbling under his breath about Gestapo tactics. Leo couldn't figure out why he was so hostile. He was too young to be a flower child. Maybe his mother had been frightened by a runaway police car.

Lewis knocked repeatedly on the apartment door, but there was no answer. "She's probably not home yet," he told Leo. "Her relief at the lounge may have come in late." He sounded worried. Leo and Hidalgo looked at each other.

Fifteen minutes later, she still hadn't showed up. Lewis sounded mad now. "Goddamit," he said. "You scared her. She's probably gone back to El Salvador, and I don't even have an address for her down there. Is that all you guys have to do, go around hassling illegals?"

The guy was beginning to get Leo's goat. "Listen, buddy," he said, "I've told you already. What we're doing here is investigating a conspiracy to steal nuclear material. That's not like a traffic violation. In the second place, if she's really Salvadorian, the whole fucking Marine Corps couldn't scare her into going back home. She's probably staying with some friend of hers for a couple of days. Why don't you call the cocktail lounge, and see when she left there?"

Lewis and Hidalgo went downstairs to use the pay phone by the pool. They were back in three minutes. Lewis was boiling. "You can't get away with strong arming me," he fumed.

Leo was getting sick of Lewis. "What's he mad about now?" he asked Hidalgo.

"She wasn't still at the bar," answered the agent. "I asked Mr. Lewis here to let me talk to the folks there, but he wouldn't. When he started to hang up, I took the phone away from him."

"So?"

"I talked to the manager. He said the Gomez woman took off like a scalded cat about thirty seconds after Lewis called her this afternoon. He said he told her she was fired if she left like that, and she told him to go fuck himself." Hidalgo grinned at Leo. "The manager said that was the clearest English he'd ever heard her speak."

"Well, shit," said Leo. "There goes Monday night baseball. Okay, let's call for a search warrant and fingerprint team."

He turned to the engineer, who was still sputtering. "Mr. Lewis, simmer down. You've got no one but yourself to blame for this. I warned you she might run if you told her we were coming."

Lewis didn't say anything. Leo went back into his reasonable cop routine. "I'm betting that she didn't go far," he said, "and that she'll be contacting you, so I'm going to delay putting her on the wanted list for a few days.However, if I don't hear from you by, say, next Tuesday, I won't have any choice but to list her, and then she's going to have every federal agent in this country looking for her. If you really like her, you'll be doing her a big favor to call me. Okay?"

Lewis scowled for a moment, then nodded. "Okay. If I hear from her, I'll call you."

"That's fine," Leo said heartily. "I really am sorry to have caused you all this trouble." The engineer grunted and clomped off toward the stairs.

When he'd rounded the corner, Leo turned to Hidalgo. "We'll have to stake this place out, starting tonight," he said. "I don't trust that asshole to call me. Let's go see what the apartment manager knows about this babe. Maybe we can talk him into letting us into her place without a warrant, just to look around."

As they started toward the stairs, he had an idea. "You go on down and see the manager. I'll talk to the neighbors. Maybe somebody can I.D. her as Salvadorian, and save us a ton of trouble."

Hidalgo nodded and went on down the stairs. Leo walked back to the apartment next to the one where they'd been waiting, and knocked on the door.

No one answered. Leo was just about to knock again when the door opened. A big, good looking guy in his underwear opened the door and stood blinking at Leo in the sunlight. "What do you want?" he asked.

Leo showed his badge. "I'm sorry to disturb you, sir. "I'm a special agent of the FBI. I'd like to ask you some……"

The man's eyes flew open at the words "FBI." Leo broke off the question in mid-phrase. Jesus, the guy was a dead ringer for the composite of Da'ud whats-his-name!

Before he could react to the thought, the man stabbed his right fist into Leo's solar plexus. Leo grunted and fell to his knees, paralyzed. The man grabbed his hair and pulled him forward, then brought a vicious chop down on the back of Leo's neck. Darkness fell on him like a tree.

✡ ✡ ✡

Leo dragged himself agonizingly back toward consciousness. He was dimly aware of movement near him, of sounds that he couldn't identify, of the man's voice, muttering to himself in a foreign language.

Leo still had his gun. He could feel its bulk on his belt. He tried to reach for it, but he couldn't make his arm move.

The man was standing near him. Leo could see his feet through half-closed eyes. He had his shoes on. He must have dressed. Shit, he was going to run for it!

Leo grunted with the effort of trying to move. A violent kick landed on his shoulder near the base of his neck. Leo lay still. He had to fake unconsciousness until the man left, then follow and take him from behind. God, if he could only breathe better!

Through slitted eyes, Leo saw the man step over him and open the door. Leo saw one foot draw back for another kick. He made an enormous effort and rolled away. The man grunted his surprise and anger, then slammed the door.

Leo tried to get to his feet. His legs were made of putty. He could hear the clatter of the man's shoes on the concrete walkway. He somehow reached the doorknob and heaved himself erect. The blinding pain in his neck almost made him black out again.

He pulled the door open and staggered out onto the open walkway. He tried to call Hidalgo, but his voice was a pathetic croak.

Holding himself up on the metal rail of the walkway, he began dragging himself toward the stairwell. In some vague corner of his consciousness, he was aware of the girls by the pool gaping at him.

The sound of footsteps on the stairs stopped abruptly. Leo heard a loud exclamation, then another, the second one in a voice that sounded like Hidalgo's. Then there was a single, thunderous gunshot. The girl's in the pool started screaming.

Ignoring them and the screams coming from his own body, Leo started down the stairs. His legs gave out twice, and only the banister rail kept him from falling on his face. He could hear footsteps running across the asphalt of the parking lot in front, then the sound of a car door opening and slamming shut.

The LIBYAN BOMB

At the bottom of the stairway, Leo stumbled over the body of Hidalgo. He was stretched out on his face in a spreading pool of blood. Leo recovered his balance somehow and lurched through the entryway. If he could just move a little faster! In the parking lot, a car engine roared to life.

Leo hobbled around the large oleander bush at the edge of the sidewalk, and past the van in the first parking space. The sound of the car's engine was getting louder.

He stepped beyond the van and looked left. A Toyota Camry was heading straight for him. The driver's left hand was outside the window, an automatic pistol clenched in it. Leo's mind identified it as a Walther PPK.

The Camry was right on top of him. Leo tried to throw himself backward, behind the body of the van, but his forward momentum was too great. He couldn't stop.

The right fender of the Camry took Leo above the knees at thirty miles an hour. He felt both legs break, and he slid helplessly up the hood toward the windshield. He had somehow pulled his own gun and was trying to aim it, but his arm wouldn't work right.

The hand holding the Walther moved toward him. Leo could see the Arab's grimace of hatred and triumph as the barrel lined upon Leo's face. "I'm dead," he thought.

An instant later, he was.

Chapter Twelve

July 19
Mexico City

The cab dropped off Da'ud and Ibrahim at ten-thirty in the morning. They walked the remaining two blocks down a narrow cobble-stoned side street to the house Abdul had rented in the Pedregal de San Angel district of the city.

All the seats to Mexico City from Tijuana had already been booked when Da'ud and Ibrahim crossed over the border on their forged Mexican passports. They had caught a flight to Torreon, spent the night there, and taken the first Mexicana de Aviacion flight today to Mexico City.

They reached the entrance to the Spanish colonial style home leased by Abdul, the JSO officer in the Libyan embassy, as a safe site and staging area for Sleeping Lion.

They had called Abdul from Torreon last night to announce their presence in Mexico, telling him only that they had to communicate with Tripoli, and agreed that they would call him at the embassy as soon as they arrived at the safe house.

Like the other houses nearby, the house presented a blank wall to the street, broken only by the massive wooden driveway gate. Set in the gate was a smaller door, large enough to admit just one person at a time.

Da'ud fitted a key into the newly-installed Abloy lock in the small door, and pushed it open. He waved Ibrahim in ahead of him and took a last look up and down the street. It was empty. They had been very alert for surveillance both before and after crossing the border, but they had seen nothing.

They walked down the long drive to the door of the house itself. The same key fit it. They let themselves in.

Ibrahim suddenly held up a hand in warning. Da'ud felt instinctively for his gun, but he had dropped it in a trash can in San Isidro before crossing the border.

"Quien es?" called a timorous female voice from the living room.

Da'ud's lips tensed into a hard line. "Don't be afraid, Sabana," he called in Arabic. "It's Ibrahim and I. Praise Allah you are well. We have been worried about you."

Sabana ran through the entrance to the living room and threw herself in his arms, kissing him feverishly. "Oh, thank God," she panted. "I was sure you had been captured."

Da'ud pulled her down on the sofa beside him. "I almost was," he told her. "I had to shoot my way out of it. Tell me, what happened to you?"

"Well, I had to work late because my relief didn't come. I didn't call because I knew you were sleeping. David came into the lounge a little before eight with some men I didn't know." She hesitated and licked her lips. Da'ud nodded encouragement.

"When David told me they were from the FBI, I was terrified. He said they just wanted to make sure I was from El Salvador because he works with atomic material, but I could see it was a lie, so I told them sure, and said I would go back to the employee's room and get my passport." "It was a genuine Salvadorian passport," Da'ud said gently. "You had nothing to worry about."

"But I was so afraid, my darling. I could see that they were lying to me. I – I panicked. I took my purse and ran out the back door. I caught a cab to San Isidro. I called from there to warn you two. First I called Ibrahim, but no one was there. Then I called you, but a strange voice answered."

"I thought they had captured you. I was so afraid." She looked from one man to the other piteously. "I crossed the border and tried to get a flight last night, but they were all booked. I checked into a hotel and took the first flight this morning. I got here just a few minutes ago. I am so glad to see you." She threw herself at Da'ud and kissed him passionately.

He pushed her slowly away to full arms length with his left hand, then slapped her on the mouth with his right as hard as he could hit her.

Blood spurted from her split lip. He backhanded her, and she fell off the couch onto the floor.

"Not in the face," she screamed. "don't hit my face again."

"Da'ud dragged her upright, then slammed a right and left into her breasts. The breath whistled out of her lungs, she grunted in pain and fell heavily back to the terrazzo floor. He stood over her.

"Cunt," he raged, panting in fury. "Filthy, treasonous whore. I'll kill you." He kicked her hard in the ribs. He heard them crack. Sabana screamed, and he kicked her again.

"It is a lie, you pig, a lie," he screamed at her. "They came to the apartment and caught me unawares, but I killed them and got away. I drove to the lounge to get you, but you were gone. The manager told me when and why you left." He kicked her again. "You had all afternoon to warn us, but all you could think of was yourself. You left us to be taken by the Americans, you half-breed slut."

She sobbed. He stalked the room, went to the kitchen and found a butcher knife in a drawer. He returned to the living room, knelt beside Sabana, and yanked her head back by the hair, exposing her throat.

She grunted in agony as her broken ribs were compressed. When she saw the knife, she gibbered in horror, foam flecking her lips.

"Scream all you like," he told her. "There is no one to hear you."

He put the point of the knife against her belly. "For your betrayal," he told her, "there can be only one reward, "I am going to gut you like the pig you are. You will be able to watch yourself die." He clapped a hand over her torn lips. His arms tensed for the thrust.

The bell on the driveway gate rang. Ibrahim spoke for the first time since entering the room. "Better wait. Suppose it is the police? We don't want a body on the floor."

Da'ud didn't want to wait. The urge to kill her was overpowering. "The police can't enter here. This is a diplomatic residence."

Ibrahim's expression of disapproval brought a measure of sanity. "All right," he told the big man. "Answer the door."

He brought the knife up to Sabana's throat. "Silence, whore," he hissed at her, "or you drown in your own blood." She nodded understanding, gurgling with fright.

Da'ud heard the sound of the metal bar on the front door sliding back, followed by the creaking of the massive hinges and the sound of indistinct voices. He strained to make out the language. Perhaps it was Abdul, although they had not yet notified him of their arrival here in the capital city.

The bolt slammed shut again and the sound of returning footsteps came to his ears. Da'ud could make out the odd word of Arabic. It must be Abdul. Ibrahim came into the room.

Behind him was Aziz.

The little man looked silently for a moment at the tableau before him, his face solemn. "Ibrahim has told me what happened," he said. He walked over and looked dispassionately down at Sabana. Then, unaccountably, he smiled.

"I am glad I arrived in time," he said to Da'ud. "You would never have forgiven yourself, had you killed her."

The little man's smile infuriated Da'ud. "What the fuck are you talking about," he snarled.

Aziz's smile broadened as he answered. "I want to introduce her to a new friend of mine."

Chapter Thirteen

July 21
Washington, D.C.

"It was the Libyans, no doubt about it. We showed the composites to the neighbors in the apartment house. The 'Salvadorian' refugee woman was Sabana, and the so-called Mexican who lived next door to her was her husband, Da'ud al-Musa."

Link had just arrived from Washington National airport. He, JJ and Barbara were in JJ's office, waiting for the call to go up and brief the Director. Barbara thought Link looked awful. His face was drawn and there were deep, dark circles under his eyes. His suit looked as if he hadn't been out of it for days. He probably hadn't. Her heart went out to him. He and Leo had been close friends.

"We found the car he drove away in, parked in the lot of the lounge where Sabana worked," Link went on. "It was a rental in a phony name, wiped clean. We located the cabbie who took him from the bar to San Isidro."

"The Immigration people at the border couldn't give us a positive ID on him, but they remembered Sabana, all right. She crossed in the late afternoon, only about half an hour after the call to the lounge, using a Salvadorian passport with multiple entry visa. We've asked the US Consulate in San Salvador if it's legitimate. No answer yet."

"We hit pay dirt on the three of them with the local television showing of the composites," Link said, "including a bunch of positive IDs on this Ibrahim character, too. He lived in a rooming house about five miles south of Da'ud and Sabana, and worked as a sacker in a grocery store. He went through the border as a Mexican."

"We got plenty of fingerprints out of their rooms," he went on, "so if INS can ever find their residence and naturalization documentation, we'll be able to get an ID that will stand up in a courtroom."

"Christ, Link," said JJ. "We couldn't try these guys—except maybe Da'ud for murder—if we had them all in jail. You don't think the White House would go public with this now, do you, with midterm elections coming up in November? We had enough trouble getting their permission to show the composites on San Diego TV in connection with the shooting. Anyway, the nuke theft case is closed. The Libyans are gone and they didn't get away with any bomb material."

Link shook his head. "I don't know, JJ. If they don't know we were on to them, they might just think they were unlucky, and that we've bought the illegal immigrant yarn."

JJ leaned forward across his desk. "How in the hell could they not know? Remember the Israeli agent they caught? They tortured him. They know what he knew."

Link's face took on what Barbara called the bulldog look. She wondered how many days he'd gone without sleep. Poor thing.

"Yeah, JJ," Link said, "but suppose he didn't talk? I mean, if they knew we were on to them, why was Da'ud still in the apartment when his wife had been over the border for hours? That makes no sense."

JJ's face got red. He pointed a finger at Link. "Now listen to me, goddammit! If you even breathe that cockamamie idea at the Director, so help me, I'll crucify you! I've had the White House shoved up my ass for the last month, and I'm not anxious for any more of it. The fucking case is closed!"

Link looked even more stubborn. "So how come showing the composites on TV didn't give us a hit on this Aziz character? He disappeared from Houston the same time the others did, in the same way, but we don't have a sniff on him. That worries me."

"If you want to worry about something," snapped JJ, "worry about why you didn't have enough brains to order backup for Leo when he went out to check the only lead we had."

Link went rigid, and his face turned very pale. Barbara was horrified. What an awful thing for JJ to say! She was afraid Link was going to hit him. She was moving forward to get between the two men when the intercom buzzed.

JJ picked up the phone. He listened, then put the phone down again. "The Director's ready." He wouldn't look at Link. He knew he shouldn't have said that.

Link took a deep breath. He got up and started toward the door without a word. The look on his face was terrible. JJ followed him, well behind.

Forty-five minutes later they were back, JJ looking grimly satisfied, Link looking just plain grim. They went into their respective offices and closed their doors.

Barbara sat at her desk for a few minutes, undecided what to do. She finally dialed Link on the intercom. "Can I come in for a minute?"

"Sure." His voice sounded strange. She found him behind his desk, staring out the window. In front of him was a single sheet telex.

"What did the Director say?"

"He bought JJ's argument." His voice still had that strange sound. He didn't look at her.

"The case is closed. Everyone in town, from the President on down, wants this case to be over with. The White House will probably send a message to the Libyan government through some intermediary, letting them know that we were aware of the plot and warning them what will happen if there's a repeat."

He sounded completely defeated, not like himself at all. She tried to cheer him up. "Link, I know how you must feel about Leo. I'm sick about it, too, but there is a bright side. Just think what might have happened if they had gotten away with it, or even had a chance to try. Lots of people might have been killed and not just FBI agents, but innocent civilians, too."

He turned and looked at her. His eyes were wet.

Barbara was shocked. She'd never seen him cry. She couldn't even imagine him crying.

"I killed Leo, Barbara," he said. "He called me for instructions. I fucked up, and got him killed." His face was haggard.

"How could I have been so careless?" he berated himself. "I believed the Libyans were in California. I'd been briefed that they might go for General Atomics. That's why Leo was in San Diego, for Christ's sake!"

He was talking more to himself than to her. "The engineer Leo interviewed was a perfect target for them. So why didn't I have Leo take an army with him to meet that woman? Because I've got shit for brains, that's why."

It really frightened her to see him like this. "No, Link, you mustn't blame yourself for that," she said. "The engineer insisted that she was a Latin American; that she spoke Spanish, that she was a Catholic. Leo thought it was a false lead himself. You just took his word for it."

Link pushed the telex on the desk toward her. "I just found this thing in my jacket pocket. I've been carrying it around for three days."

Barbara moved to his side and took it from his hand. It was from the Houston Field Office. It read: "All suspects studied Spanish at language schools in Houston for periods ranging from 8 months to 4 years."

Link's voice was thick with self-directed anger. "That came into the San Diego office the morning after Leo was shot. I keep asking myself; why in the hell couldn't I have thought of that during all the time I was in Texas? If I'd just asked that one simple question, we'd have known what we were looking for and Leo would still be alive."

"Link, you have to stop blaming yourself. No one could have guessed that they'd studied Spanish." She put a hand on his shoulder.

"Leo was an experienced agent, Link," she continued, "He didn't smell trouble, and he was right there on the spot. How could you have foreseen it, talking to him on the phone from hundreds of miles away?"

He looked up at her. "I've got to go see Leo's wife this afternoon. I've known her forever — ever since Quantico days. They have three kids. Christ, I'm even the godfather of one of them. I don't know how I'm going to do that. I killed him, Barbara. How the hell am I going to tell Mary that I did that?" There was agony in his eyes.

Without even being aware of having moved, suddenly she was holding him in her arms, pressing his head to her breast, kissing his hair. "It's all right, Link, it's all right, honey. Just tell her you're sorry. Tell her you loved him too. She'll understand."

He pulled her tightly against him and buried his face in her blouse. She petted him and rocked him in her arms.

A voice in the back of her mind was shouting at her, "No, no, you ninny. You're making an awful mistake. You're going to start it all over again. Stop this!"

The LIBYAN BOMB

She knew the voice made sense, and she didn't want to go through the pain of the past weeks again either, but what could she do? He needed her love, and she needed to give it to him.

Chapter Fourteen

July 22
Tripoli

Gaddhafi's voice cracked with rage as he handed the sheet of paper across his desk to his brother-in-law. "Look at this. Look at the arrogance of these people!"

Abdallah was taken aback by the change in the Chairman's appearance since the air raid in April. They had met four times since April, and it had seemed to Abdallah that Gaddhafi was losing weight, but now the weight loss was very obvious, and there was a tic in his left eye which Abdallah had never seen before. He took the proffered document from Gaddhafi's trembling hand, and read it.

It was a diplomatic note from the United States Secretary of State. A note in the margin indicated that it had been transmitted through the Italian Embassy, which had often served as a conduit for

The LIBYAN BOMB

American communications to the government of Libya, with which the U.S. had no formal diplomatic relations.

The note was quite undiplomatic in style, and very much to the point. It stated that the United States was aware that the Libyan government had made an illegal attempt to steal highly enriched Uranium-235 on American soil in the recent past, in the course of which an American government official had been murdered in cold blood by a man identified as Da'ud al-Musa, a native of Libya, but an American citizen. Two other Libyans were implicated in the plot: Sabana al-Murtada, wife of the said Da'ud al-Musa, and Ibrahim Abd al-Din al-Masrata.

Abdallah noted with interest that there was no mention of Aziz Abu-Rizq. The note further stated that the government of Libya was requested and required to arrest these individuals and turn them over to American authorities (utter nonsense, of course, since there was no extradition treaty between the two nations). Should the Libyan government repeat such an outrage at any time in the future, the government of the United States would respond militarily

The language of the note made Abdallah blink. He doubted that any communication between two sovereign states had ever been couched in such blunt terms in the history of diplomacy.

He looked up at Gaddhafi. The tic in the left eye was very noticeable. Careful, Abdallah, he told himself. In his mind, the note required the immediate recall from Mexico of the team, whose long debriefing cable he had received the day before. His appointment to discuss that cable, which outlined the disaster in California, was scheduled for tomorrow, and he had been dreading the Chairman's probable response. Gaddhafi's summons this morning had pre-empted him.

The American note he had just read made that probable response a hundred times worse, since Gaddhafi now knew the bad news in unvarnished form, and it absolutely precluded Abdallah's even mentioning the team's proposal for a new operation aimed at the Los Alamos National Laboratory, which Abdallah had in any case decided not to approve, since it was, to his mind, virtually suicidal.

"Well," demanded Gaddhafi. "Is it true?"

Abdallah nodded. "Yes, Chairman. That is the sad news which I would have told you at our meeting set for tomorrow."

Gaddhafi's face turned red. He slapped the desk top. "Why was I not informed immediately?"

"I wished to have a full report for you, without the possibility of error, and it is contained in a very long and detailed cable from our embassy in Mexico City. I have it here." He made a move toward his briefcase, which Gaddhafi cut short with a violent gesture of his own.

"Is this true, about killing the American official?" The Chairman motioned with his head toward the paper before Abdallah.

"Yes, Chairman. Our principal agent was surprised in his apartment by an FBI officer. He knocked the American unconscious and attempted to escape, but the American followed him with a weapon in his hand, and our agent was forced to shoot him. It was that or be taken prisoner."

"Good!" Gaddhafi's response took Abdallah completely by surprise, and caused him to close his mouth on his next planned words. The Chairman's face was contorted with a blend of fury and triumph. "At least we have killed one of the enemy! And our people, are they all safe?"

"Yes, Chairman, they are all in an Embassy residence in Mexico City. They crossed into Mexico using documents with names other than these," he nodded toward the note, "so they should be safe from arrest by the Mexicans. In view of this note, however, I will order their immediate recall."

"But we were not able to obtain any nuclear material? None at all?"

Again, Abdallah was startled by the thrust of Gaddhafi's question. He had expected approval of his proposal to recall the team. "That is correct, Chairman. The operation had not yet reached that stage. I must add, in justice to our team, that they made no mistakes." (He thought it best to pass over the fact that the Americans had somehow connected the true names of his deep cover team in Houston with the Hispanic aliases they'd used in California).

"So we have no one left in the United States who can continue the mission?"

Abdallah was not just astonished by the question, he was horrified. He hoped with all his heart that his face didn't betray his emotions. Surely Gaddhafi was not thinking of continuing this quest for a nuclear bomb in America? Not in light of this brutal note from the Department of State!

Gaddhafi's jet-black eyes, focused on Abdallah's face, did not permit him, in spite of his fears, to speak anything but the truth. "One member of the team remains in America, Chairman," he replied reluctantly. "He was not with the others in California, and no mention is made of him in this American note. To the best of our knowledge, the Americans are not aware of his presence."

"Where is he, and what is he doing?"

Abdallah felt his guts shrink. If he told Gaddhafi the truth, he would inevitably be led into a revelation of the new target discovered in Los Alamos by Aziz, and he had a terrible premonition, fed by the Chairman's unexpected questions, that the American note had not induced prudence in Gaddhafi's attitude, but the contrary.

He took a deep breath and told the truth. "His name is Aziz Abu-Rizq, Chairman. He is working in Santa Fe, New Mexico, as a bartender in a large hotel."

Gaddhafi's face twitched in distaste at the idea of a Libyan bartender. "Is there any nuclear material near Santa Fe?"

For an instant, Abdallah contemplated lying, but the habit of obedience, coupled with physical fear, forced the true answer from his lips. "Santa Fe is very near the Los Alamos National Laboratory, where a great deal of weapons-grade uranium and plutonium is stored."

Gaddhafi's gaze had the focus of a cobra about to strike. "And has he made any useful contacts, there?" he asked softly.

Abdallah nodded. "He is in contact with a scientist who works on a daily basis with highly enriched uranium experimental devices."

Gaddhafi's expression gave Abdallah no option but to continue. "The team has proposed another operation, against this man, whose wife has recently left him, who is drinking heavily, and whom the team believes would be vulnerable to our female agent." *Allah preserve me, my family and clan, and Libya,* he thought, as he waited in dread for Gaddhafi's response to that news.

The Chairman's face was now completely composed, almost ethereal, as if he were in a state of religious exaltation. "God is great," he said to Abdallah. "Continue the operation. I will never submit to the threats of these arrogant infidels."

Chapter Fifteen

August 1
Technical Area 18,
Los Alamos

"You wanted to see me, Tim?" Willis stood in the door of the office of the Facility Director. The office that by rights should have been his, not his former student's.

"Yes, Willis. Come on in. Have a seat." Tim Long was four years younger than Willis, and looked even younger, despite a rapidly receding hairline. He was one of those people whose skin never wrinkles. He had been Willis' graduate assistant at MIT, and had later followed him to Los Alamos.

Willis slumped in the government issue brown leather chair. It was just before noon on Friday, and he felt as if the week had lasted a month. He hadn't been sleeping at all well lately. Tim was fidgeting behind his desk, seemingly having trouble organizing his thoughts. "Well, Tim? I'm listening."

"Willis, I had a visit this morning from Ed Adams."

Willis felt anger rising in him, at the mere mention of the man's name. "That Nazi? What did he want?"

Back in the days of the Vietnam War, which Willis and Sarah had vigorously and vocally opposed, Willis had made a public anti-war statement at a rally in Albuquerque. The rally sponsors had caused it to be played in the press under a headline of "Nuke Builder Hates War," or some such thing.

Adams, then a security underling, had called Willis into his office, and in a fit of patriotic zeal, had given him a tongue-lashing. Willis had made an issue with LASL management of the right of the staff to publicly speak out on any issue they cared to, and had demanded Adam's dismissal. It became a cause célèbre in Los Alamos.

Because most of Willis' professional colleagues felt the way he did about the war, Willis' position carried the day. Adams retained his job, but had to write an apology to Willis, who had it published in the local newspaper. It was a memory which Willis relished, even after sixteen years.

Tim seemed uncomfortable. "I don't like to say this, Willis, but he wanted to know if you appeared to have been drinking or hung over on the job. He said that you had been seen in Santa Fe in pretty bad shape."

Willis saw red. "That sneaky son of a bitch! This time, by God, I'll make sure he loses his job. He'll wish he'd never been born."

Tim looked unhappy. "It may not be that easy, Willis. He apparently has talked to some people who saw you in a condition Ed described as 'so drunk you couldn't walk or talk'."

"That's a God-damned lie, and even if it weren't, who gave him the right to send his spies snooping around after staff employees in their off-duty time? The bastard should have been born in Germany. He's a natural SS trooper."

Tim looked at him soberly. "Insulting Ed doesn't solve the problem, Willis. The function of Security at LASL goes well beyond watching out for theft and changing safe combinations. This time, Ed's on solid ground legally. It puts me in a real bind."

Willis couldn't believe his ears. "Jesus! Whose side are you on, anyway? I got you hired here, or have you forgotten that, now that you're Facility Director?"

Tim gave him a look such as he had never given Willis before. "No, Willis, I haven't forgotten that at all. And for the record, I'm on your side against Ed Adams until hell freezes over, but that doesn't change the situation. Now you calm down for a minute and listen to me."

Willis resented Tim's tone of voice, but he sat back in the chair. "Okay, boss," he said. "Fire away."

"I didn't say so to Ed, Willis, but it is a fact that on more than one Monday morning during the last couple of months, you've come to work obviously hung over. Now, no matter how much I owe you personally, my first duty is to the safety of this facility and the people who work here. Anyone who is not feeling up to par for whatever reason shouldn't be manipulating weapons-grade uranium."

Willis started to protest, but Tim cut him off. "Let me finish, Willis. I'm not the only person in the facility who has noticed your condition. In fact, it was first brought to my attention by one of your co-workers. That's probably how Adams got wind of it."

"These God-damned busybodies . . . ," sputtered Willis.

"Willis, be quiet and listen. It's not being a busybody to be worried about one's own safety. Furthermore, your colleagues here are your friends. They are just as sorry about what Sarah did to you, and as concerned about you now, as I am."

"Unfortunately, that is not the case with the Chief of Security. When you publicly humiliated Ed Adams, you made an enemy for life. He wants to pull your clearance, Willis. He recommended to me that you undergo a full-scale psychological evaluation."

That shocked Willis. My God, they couldn't pull his clearance! Okay, maybe he had been under the weather a couple of times after a Santa Fe weekend, but he wasn't a criminal or a security hazard. He was the innocent victim of a conniving, round-heeled bitch, and he was hurting. Couldn't LASL have a little compassion, for Christ's sake?

"What's the status of the next Skua experiment," Tim asked him. It took Willis a second to follow the abrupt change of subject.

"Uh, we're scheduled on the twenty-seventh. My part of the calculations is complete. Dr. Lundstrom will do his part when he gets back from leave."

"How much annual leave have you got left this year?"

Another non-sequitur! Tim must be losing his marbles. "All of it, or nearly all. I've taken a day or two. Why?"

"All right, Willis. I want you to go on annual leave, effective at noon today. Take three weeks. Get out of Los Alamos. If you stay here, Adams will have his people here watching you, ready to pounce."

Tim got up and came around to Willis' chair. "I know it takes time to get over what Sarah did to you, Willis, and I've done my best to give it to you, but Adams has forced my hand."

He patted Willis on the shoulder. "It's a bad break, Willis, but Ed's out to get you, and the only way you can beat him is to come to terms with your situation before you come back to work. Good luck."

✫ ✫ ✫

Willis checked into the Posada de Santa Fe around three-thirty, unpacked, put on his bathing suit and took a sunbath beside the swimming pool. What in the hell was he going to do with himself for three weeks? He wanted to see Heather, but he didn't even know where she was, and Sarah probably wouldn't let him visit her if he did.

Fury at Ed Adams festered inside him. Tim sure hadn't put up much of a fight for him, either. He'd become a "manager" the way a duck takes to water. "Good luck," he'd said. A fat lot of good that did.

Well, screw them all at Los Alamos. He didn't have to take this kind of treatment. There wasn't a physics department in the country that wouldn't jump at the chance to have Willis Wilson on the faculty. Maybe he ought to drive back east and visit some universities.

The more he thought about that idea, the better he liked it. Tonight after dinner, he'd make a few phone calls.

His skin began to feel unpleasantly warm. He went to his room to shower and dress for dinner. He'd drop by the Staab House bar for a drink before he ate, and shoot the breeze with Saafi. Talking with the amusing little Moroccan would cheer him up.

At six o'clock that evening, Ed Adams and Pearl were having dinner. Ed had just finished giving his wife a blow-by-blow account of his day; and a very satisfying day it had been, too.

It had started with the receipt of a telex from the NRC, declaring the Libyan terrorist threat to be at an end. That had been a huge relief.

Ed had been vacillating about retiring early ever since he first learned of the possibility of nuclear theft. He had actually written out the memo, but had never submitted it. He was thankful now that he hadn't. He would have felt like a dope tonight, if he had. Now, he could wait out the balance of the leave year and hang it up in January.

The frosting on the cake, though, had been running Willis Wilson out of town. He had heard from the Sheriff's office that Willis had driven out of town toward Santa Fe in the early afternoon. The Office of Personnel confirmed that he had taken annual leave.

It hadn't surprised Ed a bit that Wilson hit the bottle after that bitch wife of his ran off with the hired man down at her store.

He might be a whiz kid in physics, but he didn't know shit about the real world, and couldn't handle it when it jumped up and bit him.

For all the smarts Wilson was supposed to have, he was really a dumb shit. Ed had known for months that his wife and the gold-smith were screwing around, but Wilson hadn't had a clue.

Well, taking off on leave, wasn't going to solve his problems, and he couldn't stay on leave forever. He'd come back and when he did, Ed would be waiting. No one shit on Edward Dooley Adams and got away with it. Ed couldn't think of a more satisfactory way to wind up his career than torpedoing that over-educated asshole, Willis Wilson.

Chapter Sixteen

August 4
Santa Fe

"Look, over there, across the valley. That's where I work."

Willis and the woman were in the Sangre de Cristo Moutains, high above Santa Fe. There was no snow left, even in the shade, but the air was cool, and the view was magnificent.

In the gin-clear mountain air, Los Alamos was easy to see, even though it was almost forty miles away. "If I walked into that hick country club up there with this woman on my arm," Willis thought, "their eyes would fall out."

In the Staab House Bar on Friday night, Saafi had introduced Willis to his sister, Samira, whose impending visit Willis vaguely remembered hearing the bartender mention at some earlier date. She had divorced her husband, which was apparently a scandalous thing to do in Morocco, and had come to the United States for a visit to let the scandal die down.

She had been in a car accident shortly before leaving Casablanca, and its effects were very visible, but broken ribs, split lip and all, she was one of the loveliest women Willis had ever seen.

On Friday evening, Saafi had asked Willis, as a favor, to sit with his sister in the dining room, so that she would not be approached by other men. Willis had done so, and they had been together almost continuously ever since.

He was amazed at how easy it was for him to talk to this woman. He had been an only child, a studious boy who had never had a chance to talk much with girls. Even after years of marriage to Sarah, he still was not good at social chit-chat, but he was never at a loss for words with Samira.

Her educational level was far beneath his, of course,—she said she had graduated from the Lycee in Morocco— but she seemed very well informed about world events.

And, my God, she was beautiful. They had toured Santa Fe on Saturday, gone out to dinner on Saturday night, and spent Sunday in Albuquerque until late in the evening.

Samira had told him this morning, when they started out again, that Saafi was beginning to wish he hadn't introduced them. She laughed about it. Willis didn't think it was funny at all.

They talked and laughed all the way back to Santa Fe. As he parked the car near the Plaza, a thought struck Willis. "Two days ago," he told her, "If someone had told me that I would be laughing before the weekend was over, I would have called him a fool.

You're what has made the difference, Samira. I'm so glad Saafi introduced us."

She dropped her eyes. Her lashes were so long they looked false. "I'm glad I have been good for you, Willis. I have enjoyed myself very much also."

They had dinner together again that evening, and as always, they found a hundred things to talk about. Tonight, she told him about her childhood in a traditional Moroccan family; the marriage arranged for her by her tyrannical father to a friend of his, to which she had agreed, believing that the groom, a widely traveled man, would prove more sophisticated and modern in outlook than her traditional father, and of her ultimate disappointment, rebellion and divorce.

Her story both fascinated and repelled Willis. It was hard for him to believe that such medieval customs still existed in the last quarter of the twentieth century.

He told her about his career, his domestic disaster, and his terrible longing for his daughter. It seemed to him that their present situations had a great deal in common, despite their disparate backgrounds.

After dinner he raised the idea that had been simmering in his mind for the last twenty-four hours.

"Samira, do you remember telling me how Saafi wasn't going to be able to get off from work as much as he had hoped, and how disappointed you were not to be able to tour the Rockies with him?"

"Yes. I am truly desolated to be able to see them in the distance, and not be able to go there."

Willis took the plunge. "Let me take you."

Her magnificent eyes widened and darkened.

"I don't mean anything improper at all," he hastily assured her. "We would have separate accommodations, of course. I wouldn't dream of forcing my attentions on you."

She still looked doubtful.

He pleaded his case. "It just seems such a shame that you can't fulfill your dream trip the way you want to."

She looked at him in silence for a long time, as if to gauge his intentions, then gave him one of her dazzling smiles. "I think that would be a wonderful thing to do." She put her hand on his for an instant. "First, however, we will have to tell my brother. I don't think he will be as pleased as I am."

✲ ✲ ✲

They sprang the idea on Saafi in the lobby at midnight, after he closed the bar. The little man drew himself up to full height, his eyes bright with indignation. "It is absolutely out of the question."

"Saafi, you don't understand."

The bartender cut him off. "No, Professor Wilson, you are the one who does not understand. You are a decent man, but that is irrelevant. My father will simply not allow a woman of his family to travel with a man who is not a relative."

"Saafi, stop being silly," Samira snapped. "I am a divorcee, thirty-four years old. I live apart from my father's household and I have earned my own living. I have come all the way from Morocco to see this country. You cannot accompany me, and Dr. Wilson has offered me his protection. I have every confidence in him."

She smiled warmly at Willis. It made him feel like some modern-day Sir Galahad.

"You can tell me you're a grown woman all you want to," the bartender replied, "but that isn't going to mean a thing to father."

He turned to Willis. "Professor, I have to warn you. If anything happens to my sister, you are in deep trouble." He stalked out of the lobby.

"Don't worry about Saafi," she told him, as he walked her to her room. "An Arab man always has to have the last word. It doesn't mean anything."

She shook his hand firmly. "I'll meet you at breakfast. Good night."

The top of her head came up to his eyes. Willis had to exert real will power not to kiss her on the forehead. He went to his own room, packed, showered and went to bed. Images of their coming trip kept him awake for hours.

Sabana lay on her own bed, waiting for Aziz to knock on her door. Her mind was a jumble of emotions, all of them negative.

What was she doing here? They couldn't possibly get away with this insane business. Da'ud had killed an officer of the FBI. The whole American government must be looking for them, but Da'ud didn't care.

He didn't care that they had lost the vital element of surprise, any more than he cared about his, or her, safety. The only thing that mattered to him was his stupid mission. He was obsessed, a madman.

During the time they waited in Mexico City for her new identity documents, every word he'd said had been a litany of hatred: hatred for the Americans, and for her.

She shook her head in anguish, and her broken ribs lanced her with pain.Da'ud had done that, she thought viciously, the syphilitic son of a whore. She had been in pain ever since.

How in God's name could Da'ud expect her to get the American to commit treason, when every step she took made her want to cry out? And how in hell was she supposed to make love to him, when she couldn't even lie down on a bed without wincing? She whimpered.

She didn't want to be a spy. She wanted to be safe, to stay in America.

She loved America. The four years in Houston, even though she'd been blackmailed into coming here, and had to submit to Da'ud and his loathing for Texas and the Texans, had been the happiest years of her life.

She'd made friends with some of the non-working wives in the apartment complex, and they'd gone out together during the day, while Da'ud was at work: shopping, to the movies, to lunch. How she had loved that!

To Sabana, coming from the Muslim Arab society in which her mixed blood and single status made her the constant target of either contempt and lust, or both, America was paradise. She was accepted as a pretty, friendly woman, like any other. She wanted to stay here forever, to find an American husband whom she could bind to her with her face and body before she lost her looks. He didn't even have to be rich, just a decent man who loved her.

Instead, she was ensnared in this insane conspiracy of Gaddhafi's and Da'ud's.If she continued on with it, she would almost certainly be captured by the Americans and thrown in jail for the rest of her life, or perhaps even killed. Da'ud would not be taken alive. He would go down shooting.

She had thought a hundred times over the past few years, and especially now, after the failure of the mission in California, about going to the nearest FBI office, turning herself in and betraying the others. After all, she hadn't killed anyone, or stolen any nuclear material. As a cooperative witness, she probably wouldn't even be put it jail, and she had heard that the FBI even hid such people from retribution; created new lives and identities for them.

God, how she wished now she had done that in San Diego, instead of fleeing across the border to Mexico! She wouldn't be lying here hurting all over. Well, she could still do it! All she had to do was reach for the phone.

But she was so afraid! The horror of that morning in the safe house in Mexico City would remain etched in her mind for as long as she lived: the mad fury in Da'ud's eyes and the knife in his hand, its point already piercing her belly. She shuddered at the memory. It paralyzed her, destroyed her will. Da'ud had threatened her that if she betrayed the plot, Gaddhafi would never stop trying to find her.

The LIBYAN BOMB

Da'ud, or if he were dead, someone like him, would hunt her down and kill her.

She believed him. They would find her, and kill her, and they would enjoy doing it. They hated her, all of them.

Her courage failed her. She dared not betray him, not now. No matter how frightened she was, she had to go through with it, at least for now. She dared not give Da'ud an excuse to use the knife.

There was a soft tap at the door. She rolled painfully off the bed and went to answer it.

Aziz was all smiles. "Congratulations, sister," he whispered. "You have hooked him."

"Not yet, not yet," she replied to Aziz's compliment. "It is only a beginning." She hurt too much even to enjoy his flattery. She turned to business.

"Da'ud and Ibrahim must be here before we return from the trip", she told him—they were still in Mexico, waiting for their own new identity documents. "I don't know how long we will be gone, but Willis has to return to work in less than three weeks."

Aziz nodded agreement. "I will tell them. I have Wednesday off. I will fly to El Paso, cross to Juarez and call Mexico City from there."

"Good. Before you go, drive up the road to the ski basin and look at the cabin I saw when Willis drove me up there. If it looks

116

good to you, rent it for them. You can't miss it; there is a for rent sign in front with a number to call."

"All right. Shall we go ahead tomorrow as we have planned?"

"Yes." She looked at his narrow, intelligent face with the lively eyes. He was not a fanatic like Da'ud or Ibrahim. In spite of his eternal good humor, she knew, from a remark Da'ud had once made in Houston, that Aziz', too, had been coerced to assure his cooperation with them. She longed to confide her fears to him, but she didn't dare. He might tell Da'ud, and that was a chance she dared not take. The memory of the knife was too fresh.

Chapter Seventeen

August 5
Santa Fe

They left La Posada on Tuesday morning.

Willis was dismayed to find Saafi hanging around as they packed the car. He muttered in Arabic to Samira, who paid no attention to him.

After they had got in the car and were buckling their seat belts, Saafi came around to Willis' side and thrust his face in through the window.

"I don't care what my sister says about this, Professor," he snarled. "If something happens to her, you're dead."

Samira put her hand on his arm. "There is no point in trying to talk to him, Willis. Let's just leave."

He pulled out of the hotel lot. He could see Saafi in the rear view mirror, standing in the hotel driveway, glaring after them.

✡ ✡ ✡

Aziz watched them leave with a sense of mixed relief and apprehension. He was relieved to get Sabana out of Santa Fe. Her Moroccan passport was a work of art, but if she were ever challenged, she couldn't defend that cover for a minute. Unlike Aziz, she couldn't speak Maghrebi Arabic, and she didn't have a word of French to her name, which most Moroccans spoke, at least a little.

He'd argued with Da'ud about it when they were all together in Mexico. They should have covered Sabana as a Tex-Mex: the Texas drivers license was absurdly easy to reproduce; it would get her across the Mexican border, along with a tourist card, and Sabana spoke excellent English and passable Spanish.

Da'ud had over-ruled him. He wanted to take advantage of the solid relationship Aziz had built with Willis Wilson to introduce Sabana to him, and the story they had concocted for the later stages of the operation relied on an initial Moroccan cover.

Da'ud and Ibrahim also had Moroccan documentation, genuine passport blanks like Sabana's, into which JSO's master forger had added both Mexican and American visas, but in their cases there was no problem. Both spoke fluent Maghrebi dialect. Da'ud also had a Texas drivers license in a new name, which would be handy if he had to make a quick trip back to Mexico.

The principal cause of Aziz's apprehension was the prospect of having Da'ud and Ibrahim in the same city with him. This whole new plan was insanity. They should have thanked God for their safe escape from California, and admitted defeat.

That, of course, was an idle dream, considering the character of Moammar Gaddhafi, Da'ud and Ibrahim. They were all madmen. Aziz would have to be very lucky to escape from this new scheme a free man, or even alive.

And Sabana, newly named Samira? The memory of the scene he had walked in on in the safe house in Mexico flooded into his memory. His arrival had most certainly saved her life then, but in his heart, Aziz was sure that when her usefulness to Da'ud had ended here in New Mexico, he would kill Sabana. Da'ud would never forgive her failure to warn him in San Diego. Well, Allah hir hamha– God have mercy on her. Aziz needed to focus on saving his own skin, and, to that end, on another new friend he had recently made.

✠ ✠ ✠

Willis and Samira drove along in strained silence for several minutes. "I don't really understand what happened just now," he finally said. "Saafi wasn't this angry last night. I know he feels responsible for you, but surely he knows you're safe with me."

"I'm very sorry about this, Willis. "Saafi is still frightened of our father, even here in America. He was afraid he would be blamed for letting me go off with you. To get off the hook, he called father last night and told him about our trip."

"Oh, hell. What happened?"

"Father was furious, of course. He threatened all sorts of terrible things if Saafi didn't stop us. Saafi came to my room after you left me and told me about it. I refused to give in, and that made him even more angry and frightened. He was taking it all out on you just now, that's all. Don't worry about it."

"But I can't just ignore it, Samira. I don't want to be the cause of a row between you and your family."

Willis was beginning to wonder if he wasn't getting out of his depth. These foreigners were really unbelievably emotional in their behavior.

"It is not your fault, Willis. This is a rather common story in the Arab world today. My father was born in a tent in the desert. The end of colonialism made him a powerful politician, but in his heart he is still a Bedouin, a man of the seventh century. Anything which does not accord with his beliefs is wrong, a sin, evil."

"Most of my brothers and sisters have accepted his rule. Saafi rebelled and ran away, years ago. I, too have spent my whole life trying to free myself from him, and at last I have done so. He can't do anything about our trip, no matter how little he likes it." She put her hand on his for an instant. "Let's just think about all the beautiful things we are going to see and do together."

They reached Taos before lunch, and stayed there for three days, exploring every inch of the little old town and dutifully visiting all of the tourist attractions: the Kit Carson Museum, the Governor Bent house and the nearby Indian pueblos.

They ate good food, poked through art galleries, and talked. By tacit agreement, there was no more discussion of the threats made by her father and Saafi.

He was amazed at how quick she was to grasp ideas; even technical matters in which she had no background, and she was more than intelligent and beautiful. She was a tease, in spite of the pain her ribs caused her. She made him laugh. After the past months of bitterness, she was like a tonic. Willis couldn't get enough of her.

By Friday, when they drove on up to Red River, he couldn't keep his hands off her any longer. He took her arm at every curb as they wandered around the little resort town, and fabricated reasons to touch her as they walked together. She didn't seem offended. Sometimes he thought she responded.

On Saturday morning, he borrowed a fly rod from the manager of the Tall Pines Camp, where they had adjacent cabins, and they set out to try his luck with the trout in the noisy little stream that gave the town its name. Samira came along as his cheering section.

In an hour's time, he had caught three. Samira squealed with delight at every catch, and wanted to try it herself, but with her broken ribs, she couldn't raise her arms to cast.

"Let's see what we can do with some teamwork," Willis told her.

Below a small pool, he positioned himself close behind her. He reached around her with both arms, the rod in his right hand. Pulling off line with his left, he made a few experimental casts up the pool until the length of line suited him. The closeness of her body and the fragrance of her hair made him ache with desire.

He let the salmon egg-baited hook drop into the water a couple of yards above a boulder in the center of the stream. "We'll float it down past the rock," he whispered in her ear. "Be ready to take the rod from me if we get a strike."

As the bait swept around the side of the boulder in the current, a trout streaked out of the shadow at its base and sucked in the hook. The rod bowed and the line began to thrum in his fingers.

He passed her the rod and line. "Keep the rod tip high, and pull in line with your left hand to keep the leader taut," he told her.

"Oh, oh, I have one!" Samira shrieked. She turned with the trout as it ran back and forth across the pool. With every turn, Willis could feel her breasts under the thin blouse.

Working together, they gradually brought the trout into the shallows of the gravel bar on which they were standing. Willis reluctantly released his hold on her left arm. "Reach down and take the leader just in front of his head," he told her.

She picked up the fish by the leader and turned to show it to him, pulling his right arm behind her back. Her face was flushed with exertion and excitement and her laughing mouth was bare inches from his own.

Overwhelmed by her closeness, he pulled her to him and kissed her.

She grunted with pain and dropped both the rod and the fish. "Willis, stop. You're hurting me."

He felt as if he were drowning in a whirlpool of emotions. "Darling, forgive me. I'm sorry. I couldn't help it. I love you, Samira." Her breath on his face was like an angel's kiss.

Still panting with pain and surprise, she looked up at him with her enormous dark eyes. He could feel her body trembling. It took heroic will not to pull her tight against him. He covered her brow and bruised cheeks with tender kisses.

She took his hands in her own and very slowly raised them to her breasts. "You are the kindest man I have ever known," she whispered to him. I love you, too." He caressed her, shivering with happiness and desire.

Fishing forgotten, they walked back to Tall Pines hand in hand, as the daylight faded behind a growing wall of white cumulus clouds. When Willis came back from returning the rod to the manager, the rumble of thunder reached his ears from the south.

He cleaned the fish behind her cabin. She made a salad and French fries. While the trout cooked, they sipped iced tea, saying little. Looks and kisses replaced words.

The sky grew steadily darker and the sound of the thunder began to echo off the mountains surrounding the town. As the sun disappeared, the temperature dropped, and Willis laid a fire to ward off the chill. The seasoned pine caught easily, and by the time the meal was ready, the cabin was bright and warm.

The storm broke with full force while they ate. Rain roared on the tin roof and stroke after stroke of brilliant white lightning poured down onto the peaks from the clouds above them. The electricity failed almost at once, but they didn't care. They had their fire.

After lunch, Willis took her hand and gently led her into the bedroom. They undressed each other without a word. The lightning flashes revealed her beauty to him in micro-second images of white-hot light.

When they were both naked, he pulled her toward the bed.

"Willis," she whispered to him, "I want to please you, but you must be very gentle. I cannot stand your weight on top of me."

He was quivering with lust, as hard as a rock. "What can we do?" he heard his voice shaking."

"Stand there." She painfully crawled up on the high old-fashioned bed. The next lightning flash showed her presented to him like a cat: head low, buttocks raised and thighs spread.

He was so inflamed he couldn't think or speak. He entered her, possessed her, holding her thighs in his hands, slamming himself against her buttocks until he came in a heart-stopping convulsion, and all the time she cried, "Gently, Willis, you're hurting me. No! Stop! Oh, oh, oh!"

During the next week, time stood still for Willis. They left Red River after two more days and drove north into Colorado as far as Denver, then Southwest to Crested Butte and back south through the Rockies by slow stages.

Willis lost all track of time. He had no idea what day of the week or month it was. The only tiny contact he maintained with the world he had lived in before he met Samira was the "having a wonderful time" post card he sent Tim Downs from Gunnison, Colorado.

He laughed as he dropped the card in the mailbox, thinking about how little Tim would be able to imagine just how wonderful a time Willis was really having.

When he and Samira finally arrived back in Taos, he couldn't recall anything of the scenery, the towns, the pack trips into the high meadows or the fishing expeditions.

125

For him, those days and nights were nothing but Samira: her eyes, her mouth, her arms and her magnificent, yielding body, all his. His alone. He wished he knew how to reach Sarah, so he could tell her how glad he was that she had given him this chance to know what a real woman was like.

✡ ✡ ✡

When they got back to Taos, Sabana finally managed to get out of Willis' sight long enough to find a pay phone and make a call to the Staab House Bar. Saafi answered.

"Listen well, I don't have much time," she told him. "Where is Da'ud?"

"He and Ibrahim are here in Santa Fe, staying at the Ramada Inn on Cerrillos Road, the road to Albuquerque. They have rented the cabin you found, too. What has happened with you?"

"Tell Da'ud that he'll have no cause to be unhappy with me this time. His plan has a good chance to work."

"Allahu akbar," Aziz crowed. "God is great"

"I will call you again when we get back to Santa Fe," she told him. "Thank God this is almost over. If I don't get away from him before long, I'm going to lose my mind."

She hung up and leaned her forehead against the side of the phone booth. She had just told Aziz a lie, and she had never felt more frightened, and more ashamed of herself, in her life.

Chapter Eighteen

August 16
Santa Fe

"What do you say? Shall we stay at La Posada again?" They had almost reached the Santa Fe city limits.

"Oh, no. We can't!"

The urgency in her voice startled Willis "What do you mean, we can't? Why not?"

"I don't think my father's threats to Saafi went any further than talk, Willis," she told him, "but until I am sure, I don't want to take a chance. One of my brothers might be waiting in the lobby to take me back home by force."

"You can't be serious, Samira. This is the United States."

She started to say something, then apparently changed her mind and sat still, staring straight ahead. She had been in a strange mood all day, scarcely saying a word since they left Taos.

"Willis," she said abruptly, "I must confess something to you that I should have told you long ago. Saafi and I have lied to you."

"Huh?" This time he almost swerved into the on-coming lane.

"Stop the car, Willis, before we have an accident, and I will explain." He pulled into a way-side a hundred yards up the road, parked and turned to look at her.

"Willis, Saafi and I are not Moroccans at all. We are Libyans."

"Libyans?" He didn't know what to make of it.

"Yes. I am terribly sorry to have deceived you. You see, many Americans are hostile to Libya because of Gaddhafi's terrorist acts against America and Israel. After some unpleasant experiences, Saafi found it easier to say he was a Moroccan, especially since the air raid in April"

Willis still couldn't think of anything to say.

"Of course, I couldn't get a visa to the U.S. as a Libyan," she continued, "but because my husband was Moroccan, I was able to get a Moroccan passport, using his family name."

"I did it without his knowledge, of course. That is one reason he, and my father, are both so angry with me."

She looked pleadingly at him. "What else could I do, Willis? I had to get away. Father wouldn't accept the fact of my divorce. It dishonored him. He threatened to force me back to my husband." She sobbed, and winced as her still-tender ribs reacted.

He was instantly filled with sympathy for her. What a strange world she had grown up in! "I can't believe a father would treat his daughter like that. Of course you had to get away." He returned to the original question. "Well, where shall we stay, then?"

"How about one of the motels we passed on the day we went to Albuquerque?"

"Okay, fine. Let's see where there's a vacancy." He reached for the key, and she put a hand on his arm.

"There is one more thing, Willis. Please don't think I am being hysterical, but if anything happened to you, I couldn't bear it."

"What do you mean, happen to me?"

"Well, Saafi knows that we are due back in Santa Fe about now, and knows who you are. I think it would be safer to register in a different name, just in case."

He didn't like the sound of that. "Honey, don't you think you're getting a little carried away? Besides, I think it's illegal."

"How can it be illegal? It doesn't hurt anyone. And no, I am not carried away. Do you remember a few years ago, when a Saudi prince had his own granddaughter executed because she ran off with a commoner, against his wishes? My father is a man like that, Willis."

She leaned toward him and put a warm hand on his upper thigh. "It is your safety I am thinking of, darling. I will register for us, if you don't want to. Please, Willis. I would feel so much safer . . . Please."

The pressure of her hand made it hard for him to be stern with her. "Let me think about it for a while," he said. He started the car and got back on the highway.

"I know," she told him. "I'll use the name of an American girl I used to work with in Libya, before the oil companies were nationalized. We still correspond. She wouldn't mind." She put her hand back on his thigh.

They stopped at the Lamplighter Motel, on Cerrillos Road, near the southwest corner of town. Willis was very nervous about it, but he let her talk him into registering in her girlfriend's name while he waited in the car.

She came back out to the car smiling. "It was easy. Look." She showed him the key. "I paid in advance. You are now going to spend the night with Andrea Johnson, of Dallas, Texas." She gave him a lingering kiss.

They took the bags up to the room. She sat down on the bed and picked up the phone. "Now we will see what Saafi has to say," she told him. Sit here and rub my shoulders for me while I talk. He should still be at his apartment."

She dialed the number. Willis heard Saafi's voice answer. Samira greeted him in Arabic.

They talked for a while, and then Willis felt her relax. She turned to flash him a smile, then leaned back against him while she talked, pulling one of his hands forward to cup a breast.

She hung up and turned to face him. "Father has calmed down. There is no problem." She kissed him. "Let's take a little nap, before we go down to dinner."

Willis awoke with a start sometime in the small hours of the night, vaguely aware of noise and confusion, but unsure at first where he was and what was happening. They had gone to bed early, about ten o'clock.

The room was dark. He couldn't see, but he had the impression of other people being present. My God, were they being robbed? A muffled scream sounded in his ear. Samira!

He tried to untangle himself from the bed covers, to defend her. A tremendous blow struck his face. He recovered consciousness in agony. He was sitting up. He couldn't see. Something wet was in his eyes, stinging them. Blood? He tried to wipe them clear, but he couldn't get his hand out from behind him. Christ, he was tied to the chair! He tried to talk, but his mouth was full of something. All he could do was grunt.

"Shut up," a rough male voice sounded in his ear. Willis started at the sound, and lost consciousness again from the horrid pain that the movement brought with it.

When he came to the second time, his eyes were better. Across the room he saw Samira, also tied to a chair. A big man with a broad, dark face was standing beside her, a knife in his hand. Willis tried to go to her. He couldn't move at all. the pain of the effort made him moan.

"They are my half-brother and cousin, Willis," she whispered, cowering away from the knife. "Father has sent them. He has ordered my death for what he calls my adultery. Saafi lied to me. They were with him when I called him this afternoon."

Willis' mind revolted at the idea. This couldn't really be happening! They were in America, not some God-forsaken pesthole in the Middle East.

"They are going to kill us both, Willis." Tears poured down her face. "Forgive me for getting you into this, my love. I am sorry."

The big man's hand clamped over her mouth. The arm holding the knife tensed. Willis closed his eyes against the horror of it.

He heard her mumble, then burst into a torrent of choking, whispered Arabic and then suddenly stop. Oh, Christ, she was dead! His eyes flew open.

She was still alive, and she was looking at him. So was the man with the knife.

"They want to talk to you, Willis. Promise you won't shout when they remove your gag. Please, my dear. It is our only chance."

Willis didn't understand what was happening, but he nodded agreement. His gag was abruptly jerked loose from behind, and a rough hand reached around to pull a wadded-up handkerchief from his mouth. No wonder he couldn't talk.

"Forgive me, Willis," Samira said to him. I had to tell them that you work at Los Alamos."

"Huh?" He couldn't talk well, even with the gag out. What was she talking about?

I told them that you work with critical uranium assemblies. It was the only way I could save your life."

"What does that have to do with it," he croaked.

"Libya is desperate to obtain nuclear technology, Willis. My father is the Libyan Minister of Energy. My half-brother," – she gestured with her chin at the man behind Willis,—"works with him. I told them you would give them valuable information if they spared your life."

The idea shocked Willis. "I can't do that, Samira."

The big man pulled her head back and put the knife to her throat again. Willis instinctively tried to lunge forward to her rescue, and was brutally yanked back into his chair by his hair. "You must make the decision now," said the man behind him. "Talk, or she dies."

The big man began to pull the blade across Samira's throat. Willis was in torment. It might be treason, but how could he bear to watch her die? The see the blood gush from the slender throat, the final horror in her eyes?

"No, no," he heard himself saying. "No, please. Don't hurt her. I'll tell you anything you want."

Chapter Nineteen

August 17
Santa Fe

Prodded by questions from the Arab, Willis talked for two solid hours. The Libyan who questioned him, Samira's half-brother, wanted to know about the enriched research devices in Technical Area 18: Skua, Godiva, and Flat Top, and about Willis' experiments with them.

The Arab was particularly curious about all the security systems in Kiva 3, physical, human and electronic, and about the interior of Kiva 3 and its layout. His English was amazingly fluent and unaccented.

Revealing information he knew to be classified made Willis terribly uncomfortable, even if he had always regarded most of the LASL security regulations as having been designed for use by six-year olds. He promised himself that as soon as he got loose, he would tell LASL Security what had happened. Ed Adams could earn his salary, for a change.

Samira's half-brother seemed particularly interested in the details of Willis' forthcoming experiment with Skua: its date, the details of how many people were to be in the kiva, how long it took to prepare the device and who did what. He didn't look much like Samira, Willis noted, but of course, they had different mothers.

Willis comforted himself with the thought that the Arabs couldn't get by the security systems, no matter how much they knew about them. The systems had always seemed very efficient to Willis. Now, to discourage the Libyans, he tried to make them sound absolutely impenetrable. He thought perhaps he had succeeded. The Libyans didn't look very happy at the end of the debriefing.

"The Libyan government will evaluate the information you have provided," the half-brother told Willis. "Some time will be necessary for such an evaluation."

"Government? Hey, wait a minute." Willis tried vainly to get to his feet.

The Arab slammed him back down onto the chair. "Listen to me, Dr. Wilson," he snarled. "When we agreed to spare your lives in exchange for information on the nuclear devices you work with, this entire matter changed from a matter of family honor into an affair of the state. We are not through with you yet."

Willis felt betrayed. "You lied to me, you bastard," he hissed.

Without moving from his position, the Arab back handed him across the face.

It was the first time in his life that Willis had ever been deliberately struck. He fell back in the chair, trembling. He felt as if he were going to vomit. How dare they treat him like this?

The Arab continued as if nothing at all had occurred. "This room is hardly suitable for such a protracted wait. We will therefore take you to another place nearby, where you can stay in comfort, with Ibrahim,"—he nodded at the big man—"to keep you company."

The Arab got to his feet. "I will take my sister with me, as a guarantee of your good conduct in her absence."

He said something in Arabic to the big man, took Samira by the arm and pulled her to the door. She waved a frantic goodbye to him, and then was gone.

The big Arab, Ibrahim, motioned for Willis to pack his things. His scowling face and the memory of his knife on Samira's throat cowed Willis. When the bags were packed, he spoke to Willis for the first time, also in accented but understandable English.

"Now we must go to the car. I will be right behind you. Remember, her life depends on you."

Willis nodded miserably. He carried his suitcase painfully down to the lobby. With Ibrahim ten paces behind him, out of sight on the stairs, Willis walked past the desk on his way to the front door.

The clerk was dozing in his chair. Willis dropped the key on the counter and mumbled, "Paid in advance. No calls." The man barely raised his head. Willis went outside. He was startled to see that it was already getting light in the east.

He had barely gotten through the door when Samira's cousin was beside him. "Get into the back seat and lie down on the floor," he said. When Willis had done so, the Arab leaned over the seat and blindfolded him.

The only thing Willis could tell about the journey was that it was definitely uphill. They must be going up into the Sange de Cristo mountains.

After what he guessed to be about half an hour, the car stopped. The Arab pulled him out of the rear seat and led him, stiff and stumbling, inside a building of some sort.

When the blindfold came off, Willis found himself in the bedroom of what he guessed was probably a vacation cabin. The walls were of pine board, and the furnishings comfortable looking, if a bit rustic. The window of the room he was in had been boarded up. He could hear no sounds at all from outside.

"This is your room," the big man said. "That is a bathroom." He motioned toward a closed door set in one wall.

"There are some books to read. Do not make noise or be a problem to me. If you behave, you will see Samira again soon. If you try to get away, you will have killed her." He turned and walked out of the room. The door closed, and Willis heard the dead bolt snap into the frame.

August 17

Arlington, Virginia

"Link, wake up."

Link heard Barbara's voice as if from a great distance, but he could feel the warmth of her body against his in the bed, and her hand on his shoulder, shaking him.

"Link, come on. It's almost eight o'clock."

He groaned.

His old buddy from the New York field office, Charlie Hoover, had come to town late yesterday afternoon and called Link to see if they could have dinner together. It would be his first evening apart from Barbara since he moved in with her three weeks earlier.

The three weeks of living together had not been as blissful as Link had imagined, and he recognized that it was mostly his fault. He couldn't get over blaming himself for Leo's death, and that made him hard to get along with. On top of that, he and JJ feuded almost non-stop over the Libyan nuclear theft issue: Link had a very strong gut feeling that the Arabs hadn't given up. JJ absolutely refused to discuss it, and Link had vented his frustration at that situation on Barbara. They had two serious fights, both ultimately repaired with kisses and apologies.

Link really had wanted to talk over the good old days in New York with old Charlie, thinking it would get his mind off Leo and the goddam Libyans. He had checked it out with Barbara and she had agreed. She would eat supper with her parents out in Falls Church, and see Link back at her apartment about ten or ten-thirty. He had agreed to accompany her to church the following morning, which had now become this morning.

He and Charlie had had a great time. He HAD been able to get Leo and the Libyans off his mind, and it had done him a world of good. He'd had more beers than he should have, though, and before he knew it, the evening had turned into early morning. When he finally came in at two a.m., the reception he got from Barbara had been silently chilly.

Now that she was speaking to him again, he wished she weren't. The beers were still in his head.

"Barbara, have a heart," he mumbled. "I haven't had enough sleep."

"Link, you promised to take me to church." There was a hint of steel in her voice. It was a tone that he remembered hearing on occasion in his mother's voice, and, come to think of it, some of those occasions had been Sunday mornings, too.

Barbara was still shaking him. He decided that his best defense was to go on the offensive. Maybe he could get her to forget church. Eyes still closed, he rolled over suddenly and smothered her in a bear hug.

There was a yelp of surprise, followed by a lot of soft, silk-covered shoving and pushing. She finally slipped out from under his arm.

"Don't think you can change the subject, buddy," she told him, emphasizing the point with two sharp jabs to the ribs. "Get moving."

He groaned again. She could be as hard as nails, sometimes.

"Link, come on. It's not my fault you feel this way, and I shouldn't have to pay for it. You can take a nap this afternoon, but I want you to go to church with me. I'll fix us breakfast while you shower. Come on, up!"

He opened one eye, and hastily closed it again. The room was flooded with morning sunlight. Damn. He really didn't feel like getting up yet, much less like going to church.

"Link!" There was a lot of steel in her voice now. He dug himself out of bed and lumbered resentfully to the bathroom.

Showered and shaved, he sat morosely at the breakfast table. Barbara, who looked marvelous in a pastel flowered dressing gown, was in a polite, but not completely forgiving mood as she set his breakfast plate down in front of him.

She was a terrific cook, and she had obviously put a lot of effort into the breakfast. There was juice, cantaloupe, bacon, eggs, toast and a huge mug of black coffee.

Perversely, even though he knew it would make him feel better, he just toyed with it. What he wanted wasn't coffee, he thought, but about four more hours of sleep.

Barbara noticed that he wasn't eating. "What's wrong," she asked him. "Is your stomach upset? What did you drink last night, anyway?"

Her tone of voice irritated him. It implied that a slob like him probably drank paint thinner. Christ, he might as well be married to her, for all the hell he was catching.

"Come on, Barbara, give me a break," he said. "All that happened is, I didn't get here last night when I said I would. I got to talking to Charlie and drank too much beer, and time got away from me, that's all. Don't make a goddam federal case out of it."

"I haven't said a word about last night," she answered.

It was amazing how women could do that, he thought — tell the truth and lie all at the same time. She HADN'T said a word about last night, but her silence on the subject had been screaming at him ever since he woke up.

"After all," she went on in an infuriatingly reasonable tone, "I've been on earth long enough to know that men have to have a night out with the boys every now and then. I would like to have been warned in advance, but it's still OK. I just want you to take me to church this morning. I don't think that's unreasonable."

"Ok, Barbara," he snapped. "I'll take you to church. Can we just not talk so much about it in advance? My head hurts."

"Don't yell at me, Link," she said. "You don't have any right to be angry with me."

"OK, OK. I'm sorry," he said testily. "Let's get the show on the road." He got up from the table, took his plate to the garbage can and dropped the contents inside.

"If you don't care enough for my cooking to eat it," she said icily, "you might as least save it for Biff." Her silly-looking, bristly little black dog had been circling around Link's feet the whole time he had been sitting at the table. It wasn't a bad dog; in fact he kind of liked it, but the way he felt right now, it was bugging the hell out of him.

"I'm sorry," he yelled, dug a handful of scrambled eggs out of the garbage sack, and put it back on the plate. He put it on the floor in front of the dog. "Come on, dummy," he said. "Chow time."

Barbara recoiled as if he had struck her, turned on her heels and marched into the bedroom. The door made a very angry noise when it closed behind her.

Link knew he'd gone too far. If he knew what was good for him, he'd better eat some humble pie, but Goddamit, he was hung-over, sleepy and didn't like being bossed around over a dog that looked like a fucking porcupine.

141

The LIBYAN BOMB

He lay down on the couch and closed his eyes. He really needed some more sleep. Just a couple of minutes, until Barbara was ready to go.

He woke up three hours later. Barbara wasn't there. A note on his chest said, "I have gone to church and lunch alone. Please be out of here, permanently, by the time I get back."

Chapter Twenty

August 19
Mexico City

Abdallah-al-Sanussi arrived at the Pedregal safe house on Tuesday morning. Da'ud was waiting for him just inside the street door. At the sight of him, Abdallah recoiled slightly then peered more closely. "Is it you?"

Da'ud laughed. "The disguise technician you sent from Tripoli did a good job.

They embraced warmly. Abdallah had recruited Da'ud and been his mentor in his early days in the service.

"Where is our heroine?" he asked Da'ud, looking around.

Da'ud snorted. "If you mean the whore, she's still sleeping."

Abdallah smiled reprovingly. "Don't begrudge her the praise that is due her, Da'ud. The operation to date has depended on her."

"It is a good thing for Libya that I was on hand to order our heroine back into the United States after she destroyed the first mission," Da'ud snapped. "It was no thanks to her that we got a second chance."

Abdallah laid a hand on his shoulder. "Da'ud, both I and the Chairman know that nothing at all could have been done, or can now be done without your leadership. Come, let me eat some breakfast and we will talk about your plan. After reading your cable on Sunday, I felt I had to come here in person and get the full details, face to face, in order to properly brief the Chairman, who, of course, will make the final decision whether or not to proceed with the final phase."

It was almost one hundred percent a lie.

In the three weeks since Gaddhafi had ordered the Sleeping Lion team back into the United States, Abdallah had become progressively more frightened about the ultimate outcome of the operation.

Chairman Gaddhafi seemed to have lost all touch with reality. He was absent from Tripoli for days on end, out in the desert in his tent, communing with Allah. He had done that for as long as Abdallah had known him, but in the past, when he returned from those expeditions to his office in the al-Azizia Barracks, he was as politically aware and as calculating as ever. This time was different. Now he was indifferent, distracted, bored with affairs of state. He scarcely paid attention during briefings. It was if he had ascended to some higher level of consciousness.

Except for Operation Sleeping Lion. He demanded a full briefing on the status of the operation from Abdallah every day he was in Tripoli. Abdallah had seen more of him lately than he had in the previous year.

In the early days of those briefings, Abdallah had injected some commentary on the probable American response to the operation, but each time, he had been so ferociously rebuffed by the Chairman that he had had to desist. Gaddhafi was simply not concerned with the American response, and, rather than incur further wrath, Abdallah had been reduced to hoping that the American physicist would not succumb to the charms of Sabana, or that he would find the courage to defy Da'ud and refuse the recruitment pitch, if and when it came.

Da'ud's long cable from Mexico had dashed those hopes. Alas, the American had been recruited, debriefed, and the proposal for the action phase submitted in the cable under discussion.

Its contents had horrified Abdallah. In his view, the whole operation was madness. Whether it succeeded or not, the American response would be a national tragedy for Libya. This time the Americans wouldn't come with F-111s; they would come with B-52s, waves of them.

He had not dared show the cable to Gaddhafi for fear that the Chairman would approve it on the spot. Instead, Abdallah had decided to travel himself to Mexico—in alias, of course, and on the pretext that an operation this important required his on-the-spot supervision-—in a last-ditch effort to persuade his protégé

The LIBYAN BOMB

Da'ud of the deadly danger to their homeland of proceeding further.

"I have read and re-read your cable, Da'ud. So much of what you propose depends on the American. Can Sabana keep him in line? It will be up to her."

Abdallah's praise of Sabana still rankled Da'ud. "It is up to Allah, not the slut, and Allah is on our side."

The answer dismayed Abdallah. He grasped Da'ud's hand between his own. "You are a lion, Da'ud, but you must understand the situation. The Americans know the full story. They sent us a note, accusing Libya of the conspiracy against General Atomics and threatening overwhelming retaliation if anything similar happens again."

"What was the Chairman's reaction?"

Abdallah's tone was as grave as his face. "The Chairman was furious at the threat. He said, "Let them do their worst." Since the death of his daughter in the air raid, he thinks of nothing but revenge on the Americans, and completely disregards the consequences."

"Allah bless him," cheered Da'ud. "He does not fear them, and no more do I."

Abdallah tried not to let his face reflect his dismay. Allah save us all, he thought, Gaddhafi and Da'ud are two of a kind.

Aloud he said, "Well, let us go over your plan together. Again I ask: what of the American, Wilson? Will he betray you, once he is out of your sight? And if he does, what?"

146

Da'ud responded without hesitation. "If he does, then the operation is over, and we will be in danger. However, we have told him no details of the plan, and he does not know, nor will he know, where we are, so it will be some time before they can track us down, and we will be very alert for signs that a search is under way. If we see them, we are prepared to move fast."

"I think, however, that there is a better than fifty percent chance that the American will keep silent about us, in order to spare the whore's life, and in that case, we will be very busy, for our opportunity will come on the 27th, only eight days from now.

First, we have to determine if there is a way for Ibrahim and me to safely enter Technical Area-18 while the experiment is under way. That is the key. If we can get close enough to the blockhouse where the experiment takes place, we can seize it and get back out again by helicopter with the device. It is very heavy, but small in size, and Ibrahim should be able to carry it."

Abdallah interrupted him. "Yes, the helicopter! You mentioned that in your cable, but where will you get a helicopter, and who will fly it?"

Da'ud smiled ironically. "Once again, your Arab heroine will earn her pay. This time she will play the role of assistant to a foreign real estate investor. Aziz will accompany her, playing the role of her client, to assure that she follows orders, and also to control the pilot, when he is ordered to land at TA-18. Up to that point, he should have no grounds for suspicion. There is a helicopter charter company in Albuquerque. We have to act quickly to charter the aircraft."

Abdallah accepted the explanation with a nod, but protested, "Once out of Los Alamos, what next? It is a very long way to the Mexican border, and no matter how slowly the Americans react, they are sure to have fighter planes in the air before you can get across the Rio Grande in a helicopter. Are there U.S. Air Force bases in New Mexico between Los Alamos and the frontier?"

"There are three such bases, in fact," answered Da'ud, 'so "I will make a transfer from the helicopter to a small but fast plane, a business jet or turboprop, in Taos, which is not far north of Los Alamos, and has a small airport. That plane will be instructed to be ready for departure on a flight plan to El Paso. Once again, the pilot can be quite unaware that he is involved in anything illegal until the last minute."

"But can he out-fly the fighters to Mexico?"

"Possibly, but even if he did, the Mexican government would be pressured by the Americans to detain the plane and passengers when it landed for fuel, as it sooner or later must."

"So??"

"The plane is a decoy. Sabana, Aziz and Ibrahim will get on it, carrying a large suitcase. I and the device, however, will remain on the helicopter, which will immediately depart again to the south. As soon as we are out of sight of Taos, I will force the pilot to land in a secluded spot where I will have pre-positioned a car, rented with my new Texas identity. I will kill the pilot and transfer the device to the car, then drive with it to Albuquerque and put it in a self-storage unit, which we must also rent as soon as I return."

"You will drive back right past Los Alamos?"

"Yes. There are no nearby large cities in any other direction, and in any event, having seen the device taken away by air toward the north, and even if they learn of the plane in Taos, the Americans will not expect any of us to be returning to the south by road. Allah favors the bold."

"What then?"

"Once I have stored the device, I will return the rental car, and catch a bus to Canada. The storage unit will be pre-paid for a year, and a spare key mailed to you at a safe address. Insh'Allah, you can retrieve the device and exfiltrate it later, after the search dies down. As for me, even if I am captured, I will not be taken alive."

"But what of the others? Once they have been forced down, as you believe they will be, they will be interrogated. Sabana, and perhaps even Aziz, will break under interrogation."

"They will not know what I plan, not even Ibrahim. And in any event, when they are forced to land, Ibrahim will kill both Sabana and Aziz and will himself die fighting. He loves the idea of a holy death making Jihad against America." Da'ud's face and voice were both utterly emotionless.

Abdallah tried to keep his own emotions from showing. Da'ud had become as fanatical as Gaddhafi. He spoke of the death of his teammates—one of them a woman with whom he had slept for the past four years—as casually as he might discuss his plans for the weekend.

Da'ud continued his briefing for another five minutes, laying out details of the plan. When he had finished, Abdallah said, "The Chairman himself will, of course, have to decide whether to proceed, once I have briefed him. Remain here in Mexico until I advise you by cable through the Embassy." He wanted one final chance to dissuade Gaddhafi.

"I can't remain here", Da'ud protested. "The American has to be back at work in a few days. I must return to Santa Fe and make preparations so that we can move immediately once we have received approval."

Abdallah could think of no valid counter-argument. "Very well. I will stay here myself, and submit the final briefing by cable. We will arrange for both a telephonic message and ring signals at a pay phone to tell you yes or no, and pass any last minute instructions. You have numbers you can give me?"

Da'ud nodded.

"All right. How will you get the weapons into the United States, if the operation is approved?"

"They are illegal types of weapons, so I don't want to have them on hand until the last minute. Abdul will have to drive them to Ciudad Juarez and meet me there. He can pass me any last-minute instructions at the same time."

At the door, Abdallah kissed Da'ud on both cheeks. He had, after all, at one time loved him like a son, and there was little doubt in his mind that they wouldn't meet again in this life. On his way back to the Embassy in a cab, he made a mental note to send every bit of money he could get his hands on to his account in Cairo, just as soon as he got home. He had done his best here, but now he had his family to think of.

Chapter Twenty-one

August 20
Santa Fe

Willis was on the bed, reading one of the ten books in the room for the third time, when the sound of voices in the living room brought him upright. It was the middle of the fourth day of his captivity.

The door to his room opened, and Samira came in, followed by her half-brother and Ibrahim. He rushed to her and pulled her into his arms with a passion that made her wince.

Her brother pried them apart, and pushed Willis back onto the bed. "You see, Dr. Wilson," he said, "I have brought my sister back, as I promised. Would you like to know what has been decided?"

"When can we get out of here?"

"The information you provided was found to be of great interest," the Arab stated, ignoring his question, "but by itself, it is useless. The material is so highly guarded that we cannot obtain it, even with full knowledge of the security systems."

"I told you so, didn't I," said Willis. "Please let us go. I can't do any more for you."

"That is not so, Dr. Wilson. There is something else you can do."

The Arab looked at him dispassionately. "You can help us steal the Skua critical assembly."

The man's calm assumption that he would agree to an act of treason which might ultimately cost the lives of millions left Willis stunned.

The Arab continued as if he were discussing the weather. "Let me make this matter quite clear to you." He ticked off the points on his fingers as he made them.

"One: If you agree to keep silent, and continue with your scheduled experiment as if nothing had happened, the theft will be so arranged that no suspicion will fall on you. You will appear to be a victim, not a conspirator."

"Two: Upon your agreement, you will be released from confinement. After everything is over, you can marry Samira without any further claim on you by either my country or our family."

"Three: If you wish, you will receive the sum of three million US dollars or the equivalent in the currency of your choice."

The man must be crazy, to think that he could buy Willis! He tried to interrupt, but the Arab raised his hand. "Before you refuse, Dr. Wilson, listen to the other side of the coin."

The Arab took a miniature cassette recorder from his pocket and switched in on. Willis heard his own voice, describing the protective measures in Kiva 3. They had recorded what he told them in the hotel room!

His tormentor switched off the recorder and handed Willis a three by five inch card. On it was written, in what appeared to be his own handwriting, "I acknowledge receipt of the sum of $200,000.00." The signature likewise appeared to be his.

The Arab retrieved the card from his numb fingers. "Do you see the position, Dr. Wilson? It would appear that you have betrayed your country's nuclear secrets in exchange for money."

Willis felt a chill in the pit of him stomach. Could he prove that the receipt was false, when the voice on the tape was clearly his? Would LASL administration believe that he had not sold the information? Would Ed Adams believe it? He knew the answer to that.

The Arab pocketed the recorder and card. "Finally," he said, "if you refuse our offer, you will be compelled to watch the execution of your beloved, here and now, after which you yourself will be killed. You have three minutes in which to decide."

His voice was absolutely calm, and his expression was composed, almost detached, as if he were actually thinking about something else. That complete lack of emotion was far more terrifying to Willis than the violence which had accompanied his previous threats in the hotel room. There was no possibility at all that the Arab was bluffing.

The LIBYAN BOMB

In the end, that was what decided him. He couldn't see Samira die. Not for LASL, not for the United States, not even to save his own life. She meant more to him than anything else in the world.

He nodded his surrender.

Willis spent the rest of Wednesday talking with Da'ud. The Arab had invited him to call him by his first name, since they were to be brothers-in-law, but Willis refused to do it. In contrast with all that he had been coerced into doing, it was a very small act of defiance, but it was the only one he had available.

Da'ud interrogated him all over again on the layout of TA-18, with special reference to Kiva 3, and in enormous detail. He had Willis draw sketches of the door and vault locations, the radiation sensors and closed-circuit television camera locations. He asked about the precise location, size and weight of the Skua reactor and the location of every other item Willis could remember inside the kiva.

He wanted details that Willis didn't have any idea about, such as power supply and circuit breaker locations, and the position of the alarm and light switches. They went over it again and again, re-doing and correcting the sketches until Willis' eyes and fingers ached.

The whole business terrified Willis. These madmen really intended to steal Skua during his experiment! He had visions of truckloads of armed LASL guards bearing down on the kiva, shooting at everything that moved. He was a physicist, after all, not a security expert. It could well be that there were alarm systems protecting Skua of which he was not even aware.

As frightened as he was for his own safety, he was even more fearful for Samira's. After committing treason to save her life, it would be unbearable irony for her to be shot to death by a LASL guard. "How close will Samira have to be to Kiva 3 during this thing you're planning?" he demanded of Da'ud.

The courtesy the Libyan had shown him since his agreement to help them disappeared in a flash. "That is none of your business."

Despite his fear of the man, Willis held his ground. "It is, too," he answered. "I've only agreed to help you because of her. Unless you promise me that she won't be anywhere near TA-18, I won't do anything more to help you. You can kill me, but that's the way it's going to be."

The Libyan fixed him with a look that made Willis' heart shrivel. For one awful moment, he thought the man was going to take him at his word. Then, with a visible effort, Da'ud mastered himself.

"You are a braver man than I took you for, Dr. Wilson," he said. "I admire courage. I promise you, Samira will not be near TA-18."

Willis' relief was almost immediately replaced by another fear. Was Da'ud going to involve her in transporting Skua, if they actually succeeded in stealing it? "I don't want her anywhere near the device afterwards, either," he blurted.

This time, the look Da'ud gave him was thoughtful, rather than angry. "Why should she not be near the Skua?" he asked Willis.

"Damn," thought Willis. He shouldn't have said that. If he could be sure that Samira would be nowhere around, he might well be able to put the two men in position where Skua itself would kill them.

He was fleetingly shocked by the thought. It was a reflection of what this ordeal had done to him. He had never before in his life even remotely contemplated killing another human being.

"I asked you a question, Dr. Wilson. I want an answer NOW." Da'ud's voice was like a dagger. He took a step toward Willis.

"Skua is a critical assembly," Willis heard his frightened voice saying. "That's why you're trying to steal it, isn't it? If you toss it in the back of a pickup truck like a tool box, it's likely to kill you and everyone else around."

Willis thought he saw a flash of alarm in the Arab's eyes. But how could be exploit it?

"You have assured me that Skua cannot explode," Da'ud said. "Isn't that true?"

"Probably. Not a nuclear explosion, anyway, but it can certainly go critical, and the results for you would be as deadly as a bomb."

The Arab looked at him sharply, as if suspecting deceit. Then his brow cleared. "Samira will join us once we have Skua in our possession," he said. "If she is to be safe, you had better tell me how to protect ourselves from it."

He smiled broadly, pleased with his cleverness in having assured Willis' honest reply.

Willis mentally cursed both the Arab and his own slow wit. If only he knew more of their plans! As it was, Da'ud was right. To protect her, he had to protect them all.

"All right, listen," he told Da'ud. I'm going to give you a thirty-second course in the physics of a U-235 assembly."

"Highly enriched uranium is naturally unstable. It constantly leaks alpha, beta and gamma particles. In other words, it's radioactive. On top of that, it's fissile. That is, its molecules can be split." It was comforting to revert to the role of teacher. The lecture let him escape for a moment from the nightmare he was trapped in.

"If an atom of U-235 is struck squarely by a neutron, it will split, releasing two or three additional neutrons in the process of fission. These can strike and split other atoms and so on, starting a chain reaction. If the process goes far enough, fast enough, you get a nuclear explosion."

"Whether criticality is achieved depends on the mass, purity and configuration of the device. Now, in terms of mass and purity, Skua is already a critical mass. What keeps it from going hot is its configuration – the fact that it's a hollow ball. That, plus the safety chain inside it and keeping it well away from neutron sources and reflectors."

"However, if you put it in surroundings where enough of its escaping neutrons are either reflected or moderated, it will initiate a chain reaction, and release a massive burst of gamma radioactivity, fatal to everyone nearby."

The Arab was silent for a moment following Willis' lecture. Then he pointed at Samira and asked, "How do you recommend we keep it from killing her, then?"

The son of a bitch! Willis had never dreamed that he could hate anyone the way he hated this man. Even his anger at his wife paled by comparison.

The LIBYAN BOMB

"Keep the safety chain in it, and pack it in a neutron-absorbent material such as carbon, or better still, cadmium. Keep it dry. Water moderates neutron flux. And since you're a devout Muslim, you can pray."

Da'ud accepted the sarcasm with a frigid smile.

"Thank you for your advice," he told Willis. "If it is valid you may well have saved your beloved's life. If it is not —well, that is something you will have on your conscience, isn't it?"

Willis could think of no retort to that.

After dinner that evening, Da'ud blindfolded him and drove him away from the cabin in Willis' own car. When the blindfold was taken off, Willis saw that they were in the empty parking lot of the Santa Fe Opera, off the highway to Los Alamos, on the north side of Santa Fe. He saw Ibrahim parked nearby, in another vehicle.

Da'ud handed him a scrap of paper with a number written on it. "That is the number of a pay phone somewhere in Santa Fe. Once you have memorized it, destroy the paper."

"Tomorrow afternoon between five-fifteen and five-thirty, one of us will be close enough to that phone to hear it ring."

"If there is some danger for yourself or for us, you are to call that number, let the phone ring just two times, and then hang up. That is a signal to us that at seven o'clock the same evening, you will be at the main entrance to the Santa Fe Village Shopping Center. Do you know where that is?

"Yes."

"You will make certain that you are not followed. One of us will meet you, and you will tell us what the problem is."

"I understand," said Willis. "Suppose there is no problem? When do I see Samira again?"

"You will come back here on Friday at 7:00 p.m. One of us will meet you and take you back to her. Again, be careful that you are not followed."

"You may go now, Dr. Wilson, but remember; only you are responsible for Samira. If you betray us, the hand that holds the knife will be mine, but the decision to kill her will have been yours.'

Chapter Twenty-two

August 21
Santa Fe

Early the next morning, as they had every day while in Mexico, Da'ud and Ibrahim ran a quarter-mile though the woods around the cabin. Ibraim carried a heavy stone in a backpack, to simulate at least some of the 143 pound weight of Skua.

They always kept themselves in excellent condition, but running for the helicopter from Kiva 3 in Pajarito Canyon at over 7000 feet above sea level, was going to require a physical effort that would tax an Olympic athlete. They had to prepare for it. At the even higher elevation where they now were, the run left them both gasping.

After breakfast, he and Ibrahim drove Sabana to town, and left her in the company of Aziz. Da'ud directed the two of them to take Aziz's car to Albuquerque airport, and charter the two helicopters—Da'ud had realized that there would have to be two flights, the first for a radio check—and the turbo prop for the flight from Taos to El Paso. He passed Aziz five thousand dollars for the purpose, with strict orders to bring back receipts.

Sabana was silent and sullen, as she had been ever since they had brought the American to the cabin. Da'ud didn't care how she felt, just as long as she feared and obeyed him. He fully intended to keep her with another member of the team from now on. He didn't trust her a millimeter.

He and Ibrahim drove north from Santa Fe, across the twenty-five or so miles of valley and back up the steep grade of Highway Four toward Los Alamos. They spent most of the day in the general area, thoroughly familiarizing themselves with the terrain, and locating a site off highway 285 toward Taos, where Da'ud could safely leave the rental car, and where the abandoned helicopter and its dead pilot might not be immediately discovered.

The latter proved to be harder than Da'ud had imagined, but they finally located a relatively flat area in a small valley at the end of a dirt track four miles off the Taos highway. It wasn't ideal, but it should work, insh'Allah.

In the course of the day, they drove twice past the entrance to TA-18, off Route 4. They could see no sign of unusual activity—a good omen.

Before returning to the cabin, they sat in the car outside the convenience store where the pay phone was located, drinking soft drinks and listening for a call from Willis Wilson. None of the phones rang.

The LIBYAN BOMB

Encouraged, they drove to Aziz's apartment to pick up him and Sabana. They had good news: both helicopters were chartered: the two-place machine for Monday and the Bell Jet Ranger, big enough to hold all of them, for Wednesday, the day of the experiment.

The turboprop Beech King Air was likewise chartered for Wednesday, and would be at Taos airport from 9 a.m. on, with a flight plan filed for El Paso, Texas. Aziz duly accounted for the money. He and Sabana were both more subdued than they should have been after such a successful day. They were both frightened to death for their own miserable skins, thought Da'ud, now that the action phase was approaching. He'd have to keep them together to watch each other.

They all went back to the cabin for dinner, and later that night, they ran through a dress rehearsal of the approach to the kiva. The route to and from the highway to the kiva had to be found and marked prior to the operation, and the accessibility of the kiva area determined. In addition, Da'ud reasoned that if Wilson had betrayed them upon his return to LASL, a dry run tonight might let them see preparations being made to ambush them.

At 11:00 p.m., with Sabana at the wheel, and Aziz—irritated at having had to take a night off from his job at the Staab House—in the front seat beside her, they drove across the bridge over Los Alamos Canyon, through the LASL administrative area, and turned left on Pajarito Road, past the plutonium recycling facility and various other technical areas.

When she drew abreast of TA-51, Da'ud checked behind them, and seeing nothing, directed her to pull to the side of the road and shut off the lights.He and Ibrahim got out, pulled the ladder from the trunk, and scrambled off the road. As soon as they were out of the car, Sabana turned the lights back on and she and Aziz drove off down the hill.

Ibrahim carried a segment cut from the center of an aluminum extension ladder with him. They had bought it earlier today at a hardware store in Tesuque, on Route 285. They had hacksawed it to size, so it would fit in the trunk and spray-painted it black after dinner. The two men crossed the road, walked down the power line right of way between TA-51 and TA-18, finding their way with hooded flashlights, then turned right along the rim of the lava-rock canyon above TA-18, toward Kiva 3.

They bent down branches on pinon bushes as they went, to mark their trail back. After two false starts, they found a draw, and climbed carefully down the hundred or so feet to the canyon floor, removing loose rock and debris as they went.

Once on the floor of the canyon, they approached the perimeter fence, and waited near it for twenty minutes to see if there were roving foot patrols. While they waited, they examined the fence carefully, looking for sensors, or electrical wires. Finding none, they put their ladder against one of the fence posts and tossed the length of rope tied to the top rung over the top wire of the fence. Then, one after the other, they climbed up and dropped over on the inside.

They pulled the ladder over to the inside of the fence, and then lay flat on the grass for three minutes, frozen in nervous anticipation. No alarms sounded, no lights went on, no one came to investigate.

They set up their ladder and went back out again. The perimeter could be penetrated!

They hid the ladder near the mouth of the draw down which they had climbed, and moved north along the outside of the fence until they were even with Kiva 3. The moon had begun to rise, and visibility was better. They could see that Willis had not lied when he told them that there was a good deal of flat, open space near the kiva. The helicopter should have no trouble landing.

The huge bulk of the building loomed in the night less than fifty meters away. It was illuminated only by a floodlight mounted on the roof at each corner. Da'ud made careful note of the point at which the power line entered the kiva. It agreed with the information given him by Wilson. Another good sign.

They scouted the fence line to the north for another two hundred feet, looking for a site at the base of the canyon wall which gave them both concealment and an unobstructed view of the kiva door. Finding one that suited them, they settled into it and waited.

The night passed. At hourly intervals, a guard truck from the gate area of TA-18 rattled down the macadam road toward them, paused with its headlights on while the guard dismounted and unlocked the gate to the kiva area, then drove up to the building.

Each time, he left the lights on and engine running while he checked both the vehicle and personnel doors of the kiva— both of them massive steel affairs–and then he drove off again. There was no inspection of the fence line, and no foot or dog patrols appeared.

At four o'clock, the two men got stiffly to their feet, checked the area where they had been sitting for any tell-tale litter, then moved back up the base of the canyon wall to the foot of the draw.

They recovered their ladder, climbed the draw and ran back to the power line right of way, trying to combine maximum possible speed with silence. Da'ud wanted to see what a foot exfiltration would be like, if the helicopter failed to arrive. They arrived at the edge of Pajarito Road gasping for breath and flopped in the sand beside a juniper. Da'ud checked the luminous dial of his watch. "Nine minutes," he panted. "Good."

It was almost four-thirty when the whisper of tires and the hum of an idling engine brought them out of the shadows onto the road. Sabana and Aziz pulled up, lights out. The two men loaded the ladder into the trunk, got in the back seat, and the car pulled away again. It had paused only a few seconds.

As they drove past the main entrance to TA-18, there was no sign of activity at all. Forty minutes later, they were at the outskirts of Santa Fe, and jubilant. Wilson had not betrayed them, and they could do it!

August 22

Santa Fe

On Friday morning, after a few hours sleep, Da'ud drove to town to wait by a public phone outside a grocery story. At nine o'clock precisely, the phone rang three times, then fell silent. He drove back to the cabin.

The LIBYAN BOMB

"The operation has been approved by Tripoli," he told Ibrahim and Sabana. "I am going to Ciudad Juarez to meet Abdul for any final instructions and to receive the special equipment from him. I should be back tomorrow morning."

He threw a few toilet articles in a small bag while he gave instructions. "Ibrahim, take Sabana to town and let her rent a car as Samira. We will need another vehicle. Trail her back here to the cabin. Take her with you when you go to get more supplies."

"Sabana, this evening, go meet Wilson at the opera parking lot. Keep him happy until I return. Ibrahim, take another car and trail her to and from. Watch your mirror carefully on the return route to be sure they are not being followed."

✧ ✧ ✧

At six fifty-five that evening, Sabana and Ibrahim's cars arrived in the opera parking lot. Three minutes later, Willis arrived. She was overwhelmed by a tidal wave of happiness at the sight of him. He parked, locked his car, and got in with her, pulling her into his arms. She kissed him, frantically.

"Is everything all right," she asked, between kisses. She was healing. Her ribs didn't hurt nearly as much now.

"Wonderful, now that I'm with you again." He pulled her back to him.

"No, silly," she said when she came back up for breath, "I mean at Los Alamos."

"Oh, fine. The neighbors invited me over for dinner. I went into the office for a while this morning. They all seemed happy to see me again. It was really sort of surprising how friendly everyone was. Sort of like the Prodigal's return."

"I'm so glad for you," she said. "Then there are no suspicions, there is no danger?"

The happiness fell from his face. "No," he said mournfully. No suspicion." He looked around the parking lot. "Where's Da'ud? Where's Ibrahim?"

"Da'ud has gone to get some of the equipment they need. Ibrahim is watching us from his car." She jerked her head at the high ground behind them.

Willis' shoulders sagged. "Hell. I thought we might have a chance to make a run for it."

She felt her heart leap at the words. She had thought of little else all week, but she had not had the slightest opportunity. "Love, I haven't been left alone for a minute, and now that we are together, and I have a car, they will watch us all the more closely. We will watch for a chance, but they will kill us if we try it and fail. Don't do anything foolish."

He turned a wounded face to her. "I would never expose you to danger, darling. Never."

She kissed him. "I knew you wouldn't. Come on, let's get back to the cabin so I can welcome you properly. Here, put this handkerchief over your eyes. Ibrahim is watching, to make sure you do.'

She checked the mirror constantly as they drove toward the edge of town. She could always see Ibrahim's car in the mirror, and the closer they got to town, the more he moved up on them. No chance.

"Is your experiment on schedule?" she asked him, as they turned on to the road toward the ski basin.

"Oh, I meant to tell you before. When I showed up at the office this morning, Tim Downs asked me if I'd mind advancing the date, since Dr. Lundquist has all his work ready. There wasn't really any reason for me to object, and besides, I figured, the sooner we get this insanity over with, the sooner you and I can go on with our lives."

Sabana very nearly lost control of the car. "Willis, what do you mean, advancing the date? When is it scheduled?"

"Monday morning."

She was so shaken that she couldn't drive any more. She brought the car to a stop in the middle of the road. "Willis you can't mean it! This Monday? Three days from now? You can't. They are not ready."

He snatched off his blindfold and looked at her with near-sighted bewilderment and irritation. "Not ready? Da'ud didn't tell me there was a specific time frame. I told him the experiment was set for next Wednesday, but he didn't tell me it had to be on that date. I'm a scientist, not a mind reader."

Fear pounced on her. She wanted to scream. How would Da'ud react? The helicopters and the turboprop were chartered for Monday and Wednesday. Would it be possible to advance the dates? Her fear of Da'ud kept her from telling Willis about the airplanes. "I heard Da'ud tell Ibrahim they need three or four days to get equipment here. You have to get it postponed."

"I can't, Samira. The whole schedule has been revised. Even if I could get it cancelled for Monday, we couldn't re-set it now in less than two or three weeks."

His tone changed from petulance to pleading. "I can't live like this for that long, Samira. Look, we can get away from Ibrahim. Let's go to the FBI. Surely they can protect us."

A glance in the mirror showed her Ibrahim's car coming up on them fast. "Do not underestimate Ibrahim, Willis. He is not as slow-witted as he looks. He is right behind us now. Put your blindfold back on."

She put the car in gear again, her mind in a whirl. Da'ud would suspect that Willis had deliberately sabotaged the operation, or was setting some kind of a trap. Oh, God! He would be furious! What would he do?

She patted Willis on the cheek. "Don't worry, darling. It's not your fault. Da'ud should have told you more of his plans. When he comes back, I will try to talk him into giving up on their scheme and letting us go." In her heart, she knew it would not happen. Not that easily.

Back in his bedroom in the cabin, they made love. The delight they derived from each other's bodies overcame their apprehension, and they came together in a gasping, trembling convulsion of flesh. Her ribs still hurt, but she didn't care.

Afterwards, Willis slept, and she lay close beside him, watching his face. She felt as if her soul had been cut down the middle with some great scimitar. Half of her had never been happier: for the first time in her life, she was loved by a good, honest, decent man.

Her ten days on the road with Willis had become the romance she had dreamed of all her life. At first, even though she had liked him for his naivete and the pain he was in over the loss of his daughter, the memory of Da'ud and his knife had let her remain cynical and detached from what she was doing to him. Then, as the days went by, little by little, the power of his love for her, and his basic kindness had overcome her, and in the end, she had fallen in love with him. He had become the man of her dreams.

In the other half of her mind, shame and fear jostled with doubt and terror. She was so ashamed of the role she had played in what was happening to him. Would he learn about it? If he did, could he possibly forgive her?

There was no realistic way she could imagine that would result in a happy ending. Da'ud had told her and Ibrahim that the Americans had learned that Sabana al-Murtada and the Salvadorian Maria were the same person. Would she have to go to jail for that? Could she ever legally remain in the United States? She couldn't be sure. She couldn't be sure of anything. Indeed, she couldn't even be sure that the two of them would be alive at this time tomorrow.

She saw moisture on Willis' sleeping face, and realized that is was her tears falling on him.

Chapter Twenty-three

August 22
Mexico City

Two hours later and thirteen hundred miles south, Johnny Rodriguez finished tying his tie and inspected the results in the mirror. He had a date tonight with Marta Mendoza, a really sweet Mexican girl.

Johnny had been baptized Juan Jose Rodriguez, and the first language in his San Antonio home was Spanish, but despite that, and despite his obsidian eyes and dark skin, he was an American to his toes. He had a CIA Top-Secret/Codeword clearance to prove it.

As he reached for his suit coat, the phone rang. He threw the coat over his shoulder and walked into the kitchenette of his apartment to answer it. "Bueno?"

"Johnny, this is Zak." Bill Zakarewsky was the duty communicator this evening. "You have a call from a Mr. Murphy about his consular matter."

"Thanks, Zak. Appreciate the heads-up."

"Mr. Murphy's consular matter" was the open code for an emergency contact signal from Johnny's most sensitive agent. He wanted to be met in one hour from right now.

In the six months since Johnny had recruited him, this was the first time the agent had signaled for an emergency contact. Johnny felt adrenaline surging in his veins. This had to be something big! The senorita would have to wait.

An hour later, Johnny looked up into the mirror behind the bar at the man who had just entered the El Mexicano Bar of the Presidente Chapultepec Hotel.

The man looked perfectly normal in those surroundings. He had Mediterranean features, wavy hair and dark brown eyes. There were at least ten other men in the room who looked something like him.

The thing which distinguished him from the others wasn't visible, but it was very real, and Johnny was responsible for it: if this man's employers ever found out what he was doing in the El Presidente, they would kill him.

The man stood in the entrance for a moment, surveying the crowded room as if looking for a friend. For a micro-second, his eyes met Johnny's in the mirror.

Apparently not finding the person he was looking for, the man made his way across the floor to the men's room, located just off the bar. A few minutes later, he came back into the bar. His friends had apparently still not arrived. After another look around, he left El Mexicano and went into the lobby.

Johnny observed his departure in the mirror. He was pleased to note that no one else in the room paid the slightest attention. He finished his own drink, paid the tab and went to the men's room himself.

He entered the toilet stall farthest from the door, entered it and slid the bolt shut.

He lifted the top off the water reservoir on the toilet, and laid it upside down on top of the toilet seat. Taped to the inside of the heavy porcelain top was a small envelope.

Johnny removed the envelope, tore off the tape, and put the envelope in the inside pocket of his coat. He replaced the top on the toilet, flushed it for the benefit of anyone else who might be in the room, and left the stall. He washed and dried his hands, combed his hair and re-entered the bar.

A few minutes later, he left the hotel. Coming out onto Avenida Campos Eliseos, he turned right to the first corner, then right again into the side street. He walked along the sidewalk near the curb, next to the parked cars. His eyes scanned the make and license tag number of each car as he came to it, while at the same time he listened for the sound of footsteps on the sidewalk behind him. He could hear none.

Three-quarters of the way up the block, he saw the car he was looking for. It had diplomatic tags, and he knew the number. He looked ahead down the sidewalk. No one was approaching. There was still no sound of footsteps behind him.

The front window on the curb side of the car was down about an inch. From the left pocket of his raincoat, Johnny fished a small dark package. As he passed the car, he flicked the envelope through the cracked window. It landed on the floorboards, completely invisible in the darkness. It contained U.S. one hundred dollar bills. Lots of them.

Johnny walked on to the corner, turned right again and walked on for two more blocks. He stopped in a tiny café for a quick cup of coffee and a yarn with the owner.

No one passed the door while he was inside. When he went back out on the sidewalk again, he saw no one. He heard no footsteps behind him as he continued on to the corner and turned back toward Campos Eliseos.

He paused for a moment on the curb of the avenue, looking at the almost constant stream of traffic. A light rain was falling. He suddenly made a dash across the avenue into the darkness of Chapultepec Park. A few cars braked for him, several people cursed, but no one stopped. No one followed him across the boulevard.

A quarter of an hour later, he knocked on the front door of the American Embassy, on Avenida Juarez. He was examined through the barred door and then admitted by one of the Marine Security Guards. "Good evening, Mr. Rodriguez. Got you working on the weekend again?"

"That's it Willy. No rest for the wicked." Johnny signed the night log at the desk and took the elevator up to the top floor. He worked the cipher lock on the heavy door which barred the hall leading to the group of offices at the rear of the building, and went through. The door closed automatically behind him.

Seated at his desk, he pulled out the envelope he had taken from the toilet tank and opened it with great care.

The only thing in it was a blank sheet of paper. He left his office and walked down the hall to the restroom, carrying the paper with him.

He turned on the cold water tap at one of the lavatories just a tiny bit, and, holding the paper tautly in both hands, held it under the thin stream of water.

He moved the paper back and forth under the water, tipping it one way and another to assure that all of the paper was wet. Then he pulled it out from under the tap and held it above the basin to drip dry, shaking off the water droplets.

Holding the sheet gingerly in the fingers of one hand, he shut off the water and walked back down the hall to his office blowing on the paper as he went.

Back at his own desk, he laid it on his blotter pad, pulled his desk lamp closer and squinted at the faint writing which was beginning to appear on the paper.

It was upside down. He turned it around and read it. He suddenly sat up quite straight in his chair, shook his head in disbelief and read it again, very carefully. Then he reached for the telephone.

Forty-five minutes later, the CIA Chief of Station joined him. "What's happening, Johnny?"

"Sorry to spoil your evening, Sir."

"It was a deadly dinner party," his boss answered with a smile. "I owe you. What have you got?"

"Emergency contact from my asset in the Libyan Embassy, Sir. I think we've got a big problem."

He held out a typed sheet of paper. The original was in the burn bag in his safe, the water-developed writing on it faded into nothingness.

The COS perused the brief message.

"Jesus Christ," he said after a moment. "Persistent bastards, aren't they? Well, let's tell Washington." He sat down at the word processor at the next desk and turned it on. "As I recall, you can't get back to this guy for any further details. Is that right?"

"Correct, sir. Communications are all impersonal, emergency contact is one-way only, him to us."

"Well, I can't say I blame him for that. In his shoes, I'd do exactly the same," said the COS, tapping briskly on the word processor as he spoke.

In less than five minutes he had drafted the cable, reviewed it on the monitor in front of him and edited it to his satisfaction. He scrolled it back up to the heading and typed in, "TO FLASH DIRECTOR, NIGHT ACTION, EYES ONLY," then pushed the button that sent it to the communication vault for transmittal.

The COS sat back in the chair and looked somberly at Johnny. "You know," he said, "when I was a young case officer fresh out of training, I used to day-dream about waking up the Director in the middle of the night with some red-hot flash message."

He poked absently at the word processor. "In twenty years, this is the first time I've ever done it, and I wish I hadn't had to. In about two minutes, the shit is going to hit the fan in Washington."

Chapter Twenty-four

August 23
Washington, D.C.

It hit Link's fan at precisely 4:06 on Saturday morning. The telephone finally dug him out of bourbon-induced sleep on the fifteenth ring. It took him another three or four rings to find the damn' thing and pick it up.

"Hello," he snarled.

"Good morning, Mr. Rowe." Link recognized the voice. It was the Criminal Division's Duty Secretary.

"Jesus, Betty, do you know what time it is?"

"You bet I do, buddy," came the crisp retort. "I've been up since three. Get up and get in here, Link. Report to the Division Chief's office."

Link felt as if he were trying to get dressed in a vat of molasses. He just couldn't get his body moving. The drive into D.C was downright scary. His eyelids kept closing on him.

He made a resolution to drown his sorrow in something besides whiskey. Life without Barbara was grim—she hadn't spoken to him since the day of their bust-up—but her absence plus a daily hangover was too much for him to carry and do his job at the same time.

JJ had beat him in. By over half an hour, according to JJ, who wasn't in the best of moods himself. Link didn't give a shit. Since JJ's remark about Link's failure to order backup for Leo, Link had barely spoken to him except to argue about whether or not the Libyans had given up and gone home.

There were three of them slumped in the chairs in the outer office of the Division Chief's suite. The last member of the trio (or the first, if you counted according to rank), was the Deputy Chief of the Criminal Division. He claimed he didn't know any more than Link and JJ about what was going on, but whatever it was, it was obviously Bad News. They waited.

It was after five-thirty when the Division Chief came in, looking every minute of his age. He crooked a finger at DC/CD. They went into the inner office together. Two minutes later, DC/CD came back to the door and waved Link and JJ in.

The Chief/CD was seated behind his desk. Fatigue and strain had made the color of his skin match the gray of his hair.

"I've just come from the Director," he told them, "and he had just come from the White House. Our Libyan buddies are back.

They have apparently recruited or suborned some employee of Los Alamos Scientific Laboratory."

No one said anything, but Link did some hard thinking directed at JJ. Los Alamos, huh? Well, now they knew what had happened to that fourth guy, Aziz; the one Link hadn't found any trace of in California. He tried to catch JJ's eye. JJ was not looking his way.

"How did we find out?" DC/CD asked the Director.

"CIA apparently has a penetration of their Embassy in Mexico City." The Director explained. "The head of the action arm of the Libyan intel service made a flying visit to Mexico this week, and sent off a report to Tripoli through the embassy code room. The CIA asset filched part of it out of the burn bag."

He looked wearily at JJ and Link. "You two hunted them down before, so you get the duty again. Only this time, both of you go to the field. The Director wants me to report directly to him, blow by blow, and that's the way I want to hear it from you, too. Coordination and support at this end will come from my front office."

Link's heart sank. How could he operate with JJ tied around his neck like a millstone? JJ probably wasn't too happy about it either. He hadn't been on the street in a century.

"As a practical matter," C/CD went on, "John will handle liaison with the Department of Energy and LASL Security, and keep me advised of your progress. Link will direct the field activity of the task force."

That was a little better, thought Link. At least JJ wouldn't be countermanding his orders on the street.

"We don't have any idea at all of the Libyans' timetable," C/CD continued, "so you have to move fast. DoD has put Air Force Two at our disposal. It is being set up at Andrews AFB right now to fly you to Albuquerque, where you'll get a courier flight up to Los Alamos."

"You can take any or all of your own staff from here if you like, but we're calling in agents from all over the southwest for your manpower. The President has directed Delta Force to deploy from Fort Bragg to provide firepower. Their commander will take orders from you."

The Director looked directly at Link. "You had a bad experience with these people in California, Link. Am I correct in thinking that you'd like to get even?"

"Yes, Sir!" Link's reply was emphatic. He found himself these days feeling about the Libyans the same way he used to feel about the North Vietnamese 365th Regiment. "They won't catch me by surprise this time."

"Be sure they don't, Link. There isn't any prize for second place in this race." He nodded his dismissal, and they all stood up to go.

The Chief/CD motioned for JJ to remain behind.

✲ ✲ ✲

"There are a couple of things I want to say to you in private, John," he said, when the door closed behind the others.

"First, the Director says the President is fighting mad. He wants these people put out of business at any cost. On the other hand, absolute secrecy is a must. A civilian panic is the last thing we need.

Also, we can't reveal the source of our information on this to anyone. CIA doesn't want their agent to go the way of that Mossad source. It took a direct Presidential order to get them to tell us the details of how they got this information."

"I want you two to charge hard on this case, but Rowe is still inexperienced in the political side of things. This fall is a mid-term election year, and the President is very heavily involved. We do not want to create a problem for him.Keep an eye on Link. Make sure he doesn't charge too hard in the wrong place."

"JJ's reply was as emphatic as Link's had been earlier. "Yes, Sir!"

Santa Fe

August 23

Blind, red rage flooded Da'ud's mind. "You betrayed us, you son of a whore," he shouted, and swung a furious fist at Wilson's pallid face.

The American ducked, and fell to his knees. He grasped Da'ud's legs. "Please. Please don't hit me," he begged. I swear I didn't betray you. It's not my fault. You didn't tell me you needed a specific date."

Da'ud had returned from the border, just after sunrise, worn out from lack of sleep and nervous tension. A New Mexico State Police car had been behind him for almost three hours on the way back, and he had arrived at the cabin only to hear Sabana's news of the advanced date of the experiment.

He looked down at the wretched Yankee, groveling at his feet. With all his heart he wanted to kick the pale, frightened face into a pulp of blood and brains. He took a step toward him, and then was struck from behind by the full force of Sabana's body. Her arms pinned his own to his sides.

"Don't you dare hit him!" she shouted in Arabic. "He has done nothing wrong. It's not his fault."

Da'ud instinctively wrenched himself out of her grasp and whirled around to face the assault. Sabana's face was inches from his own, contorted with anger.

Da'ud's mind caught up with his instinctive reflexes just before he hit her. What in the name of all the djinns was going on? This was kilometers beyond Sabena's role as Samira. Why was she speaking Arabic? What was she thinking? He realized that his mouth was hanging agape, and closed it. She was still shouting.

"He isn't lying. He hasn't betrayed us. He is good and honest, nothing like you."

Then he understood. He felt his mouth drop open again with the shock and surprise of it. She meant what she was saying! She had fallen in love with the American! The whore was in love!

His first instinct was to laugh, instantly overcome by the realization that he was faced with a deadly threat to the operation. Sabana wasn't part of his team any more; on the contrary, she had gone over to the other side.

This was far more dangerous than the possibility that she would run away again to save her own skin. He fought down the wave of rage he felt flooding into his brain. He needed to think. He dared not make a mistake with this. He pushed the woman off, and backed away, making placating gestures with his hands.

"Watch them," he said to Ibrahim, who was standing by with anger and perplexity on his dark face, and ran out of the rear door of the cabin and into the cool, dawn forest. He walked through the tall trees, trying to wrap his mind around this new, potentially mortal situation.

His initial thought, when he heard Sabana's news, had been that it was a trap; that the American had told LASL Security or the FBI about the Libyans.

He now discarded that idea. The FBI would never have risked Wilson's life by sending him back to them. Well, perhaps, to find out where the team was hiding, but in that case Sabana and Ibrahim would have been attacked in the Opera parking lot, which was a perfect place for an ambush, and Da'ud would have driven into a hail of bullets when he arrived at the cabin. It didn't make sense.

And then, the shocking reaction of Sabana in defense of the American was too dangerous for her to be anything but real. She had truly fallen in love with Willis Wilson, as improbable as that might be. Now, how was Da'ud to deal with that?

If he killed them both, the operation was lost. If he killed Sabana, the American would betray him the instant he was back at LASL. But what could he do to get her back under control? Her assault on him just now was proof that simple fear of him and his knife would no longer suffice; yet, if there was to be any hope of salvaging the operation, he needed her participation.

He remembered Abdallah's praise of the woman, when they met in the safe house in Mexico. Would honey work, instead of vinegar? He weighed the question for an instant. He could not trust her at all, now, and she could never be left alone, not even for a minute, but it was the only option he had left, if he wanted to go ahead.

But could they continue, even if he got Sabana's cooperation, and she got Wilson's? The King Air turboprop and pilot they were going to use to fly as the decoy from Taos to El Paso was chartered for Wednesday; and so, even more importantly, were the helicopters. Could they get everything moved up two days on such short notice? And could they cram in all the other preparations in the time they had?

There wasn't any time to ask Tripoli, either, not with the experiment to take place in less than forty-eight hours. Da'ud was on his own.

Once he faced that prospect, however, he found it curiously liberating, even comforting. He didn't need Tripoli! Sleeping Lion was his operation. Everything he had done, every place he had ever been for the past five years had combined to put him here, for this purpose. He could, and would, carry it out in spite of the treacherous, love-sick bitch and her God-damned American boy friend.

Insh'Allah. First he had to deal with Sabana.

He found the physicist still trembling on the cabin floor. The bitch was fussing over him. Da'ud squatted down in front of them.

"I apologize to you, Dr. Wilson," he said. "Of course you would not put my sister in danger. It was unforgivable of me to strike at you. I beg your pardon."

The pathetic fool accepted the apology, as Da'ud knew he would. Out of the corner of his eye, he saw Sabana's look of surprise.

He turned to her. "Come with me into the other room, sister," he said softly. "I have to talk to you."

Fear replaced surprise in her eyes. He smiled at her. "Have no fear," he said in Arabic, "I mean no harm to you, nor to him." He led her into the bedroom the three of them had been sharing and closed the door behind them.

"Lie well, Da'ud," he said to himself. "If you have ever lied well to anyone in your life, lie better now."

To Sabana he said, "I now understand what has happened. You are in love with the American."

Terrified, she shook her head. Her eyes were huge with fear. He smiled again.

"It's all right," he told her. "I should have realized that it could, probably would, happen in these circumstances. Why not, after all? He is a good man, and we are putting him in a terrible situation. Is that not so? Do you love him?"

His reasonable tone and the distance he kept himself from her emboldened her. She squared her shoulders to him. "Yes, it is true. No matter what you do to me, I love him."

He let her declaration hang in the air between them for a time. "well then," he finally said, "let us speak very frankly to each other. First, I have nothing against Dr. Wilson. I have no reason to kill him, or, for that matter, you. What I want is for this operation to go forward, and to get away from Kiva 3 with the nuclear device, Skua." Her eyes were glued to his, listening.

"What you want," he continued, "is for Dr. Wilson and yourself to come out of the operation alive; he with his reputation intact and you with some possibility of making your peace with the American government so that the two of you might some day have a future together. True?"

Sabana slowly nodded assent, her eyes never leaving his.

"I therefore propose a bargain," he said. "I solemnly promise you that, if he continues to cooperate with us, Dr. Wilson will come to no harm, and there will be no evidence that he was anything but a victim. I further promise you that when we leave TA-18 in the helicopter, you may jump out of it, as if you have escaped, and turn yourself in to the FBI. You can tell them everything, to buy your peace with them."

He saw her mouth drop open in amazement. "Excellent!" he thought. "I have hooked her!"

"How can that be?" she stammered. "How can you say that? Abdallah will never honor that promise."

"Of course he will," he responded, his tone as reasonable as he could make it. "Why not? You don't know what will happen after we fly away from the kiva. I will either make my escape with the device or not, but either way, all you will be telling them will be history. You can easily convince them that you were coerced into your part of the operation. After all, it's true, and the circumstances will persuade them that you came to them at your very first opportunity."

He could read in her eyes her intense desire to believe him. It was time to put the icing on the cake.

"Finally," he said gently, "I swear to you that all violence and threats of violence, toward both you and Dr. Wilson, will cease as of this moment. Henceforth, we will be partners, not adversaries. Have we a bargain?"

"You intend to go ahead then?"

"She is stalling," he thought, "to gain time while she thinks it over." Aloud, he said, "We will try. Perhaps it will not be possible. If the helicopters or the turboprop are not available on short notice, it is finished. The team will leave the country. You may stay or go with us, as you choose. That is another promise I will make you."

He saw the light of hope begin to flicker in her eyes, and held up a cautionary finger. "However, if the airplanes are available and no other impossible hurdles arise in the time we have remaining, yes, we will go ahead. Are you willing? Do we have a bargain?"

Slowly, then decisively, she nodded. "Yes, we have a bargain."

"He nodded, too. "Good. We can both get what we want." They solemnly shook hands on the deal.

It was, of course, a lie, or part of it, at any rate. He didn't care what happened to Wilson, once he had Skua, but he had no intention of letting Sabana leave the helicopter alive.

And now, he had to take her to town to call the helicopter and turboprop charter people.

Chapter Twenty-five

August 23
Los Alamos

Waiting for his visitors to appear, Ed Adams stood looking out the window of his office on the top floor of the LASL administration building. They should have arrived long ago, but the courier plane had developed engine problems in Albuquerque.

That was just as well. Ed had needed all the time he could get to round up the weapons-grade material from the outlying sites and concentrate it where it could be better protected.

He had been awakened this morning with the news of the new terrorist threat. The news had hit him like a thunderbolt. It had been bad enough when Los Alamos was just one of a large number of possible choices for the Libyans. According to the information in the classified cable he'd been handed before dawn, LASL was now believed to be the primary target.

And the business about a LASL employee having been sub-verted! He couldn't quite make up his mind if he believed that or not. No Libyans had been in Los Alamos. He damn well knew it when foreigners were on his turf.

On the other hand, however, he could think of one LASL employee who had been out of town, and thus available to foreign contact, for the last few weeks; an employee who was personally unhappy, who had been drinking a lot, and who might be vulnerable to any one of a number of approaches by a foreign intelligence service.

While Ed had been out in the technical areas dealing with the material, his staff had pulled the personnel files of all LASL employees for review by the FBI group when they arrived.

Downstairs on the conference room table were the files of employees who didn't have routine access to weapons-grade material. On Ed's desk were the files of those who did.

The latter were sorted into two stacks, one much larger than the other. Ed thought of the larger stack as the Good Guys. The small stack contained the folders of employees about whose personal lives there might be some question.

As far as Ed was concerned, that stack contained only one file.

His secretary alerted him that the visitors were on their way in from the airport. He went down to meet them on the sidewalk.

After introductions and handshakes, he told the FBI Special Agent in charge of the group, "Mr. Maloney, my staff and I are at your disposal. Do you want to proceed in any particular order?"

"Call me John," Maloney replied. "We're going to see too much of each other to stand on protocol. To answer your question, no. You tell us what we ought to do first."

Ed was impressed. He had fully expected the Bureau people to barge in and start giving orders.

"Fine," he said. "Let's go first to the technical areas where the enriched material is stored and look at the security set-up."

For the next three and a half hours, he led them through the facilities where the weapons-grade uranium and plutonium was stored. They viewed the sites with particular attention to their security: the fences, gates, building entrances and alarm systems.

Ed explained the pass systems, what human, physical and electronic security systems were in use at each site, and how they interfaced with each other.

It was an impressive presentation, if he did say so himself. He and his predecessors had developed it over many years, based both on LASL regulations and on their accumulated experience.

Technical Area 18 was the last site they visited before dinner. It was remote from the main LASL areas for safety reasons, and Ed had considered moving the devices out of it, but aside from its location, there really wasn't any more secure site at LASL, so he let them stay.

"These blockhouses—we call them kivas, after the Hopi Indian ceremonial chambers—are made of four-foot thick ferrous concrete," he explained to the visitors. "There are no windows, and the doors are of heavy steel, with two locks."

"The staff here is divided into two teams, the members of which have access to only one of the keys. They have to sign them out in the control room before each opening of the kiva."

"Once they're inside, they still need a member of each team, because one team knows the combination to the steel cover over the vault dial, and the other has the combination to the vault itself."

Ed had always enjoyed giving this briefing. TA-18 was his baby. "When the kiva is open," he continued, "closed circuit television cameras monitor the activity. When the kiva is empty, an ultrasonic intruder alarm is activated from the control room. A moth flying in the kiva will set it off."

Link was impressed. This Adams was a pompous old goat, but he knew his physical security, no doubt about it. Nonetheless, it had been a real effort for Link to keep quiet and pay attention. It was all very well to look over the lay of the land, and he had to admit that JJ was doing a great job of buttering up Adams, but dammit, they needed to start searching for this bent LASL employee.

There was a clock ticking out there somewhere, and no one in Link's camp knew what time the alarm was set for. For all they knew, the Libyans could be planning to make their move tonight.

Santa Fe

After a Spartan dinner, Willis and Sabana went into Willis' bedroom. When they had gone, Da'ud and Ibrahim inspected the items that Da'ud had brought across the border, and that he and Sabana had bought in Albuquerque after paying the Sunday-flight fee for the helicopter.

There was a heavy-duty, aluminum frame backpack, black overalls, stocking caps and rubberized gloves for himself and Ibrahim, and four dozen nickel-cadmium batteries, on which Ibrahim had worked all afternoon, prying out the cadmium.

In addition, there were three General Electric walkie-talkie radios, all set to the same VHF frequency, with a privacy mode which masked the transmissions from casual eavesdroppers.

Finally, they retrieved the weapons, in three waterproof boxes, from the cache they had built under the kitchen floor. The smallest box contained three automatic pistols: one Walther PPK .380, small enough to be hidden in Aziz's pocket, but powerful enough to kill with one shot at close range. The other two guns were Woodsman Colt .22 automatics, silenced. These they disassembled, inspected closely and reassembled.

The guns' ammunition was with them. The .22 Devastator explosive rounds which Da'ud and Ibrahim now carefully inspected and loaded into the clips were very small, but they were capable of inflicting instant death if well placed. At the ranges Da'ud contemplated, and in his and Ibrahim's hands, there was no question about the placement of the shots.

The longest of the containers held an M-79 grenade launcher. It looked like a stubby, fat-barreled shotgun. In the final box was its ammunition, four rounds of 40mm. rifle grenades: two rounds of high explosive, and two of white phosphorous. Despite its single-shot capacity, the M-79 was a formidable weapon. At a hundred yards it would turn a car into an inferno. Ibrahim was an expert with it.

Satisfied with the state of the weapons, they put them back in the cache, moved the kitchen table back over it and went over the maps and diagrams one last time. At nine o'clock, Da'ud told

Ibrahim, "Stay here with them. I've got to go to town and make a call to Aziz. He needs to know of the change in our situation, and be ready to fly with Sabana on Monday."

In the bedroom, wrapped in each others' arms, Willis and Sabana held an intense conversation. Her great hope, that the helicopters and turboprop airplane would not be available on the earlier dates, had evaporated this morning. With Da'ud beside her at the public phone, she had called both companies, and learned that the advance in date could be managed.

Throughout the day, buoyed by Da'ud's optimism and decent treatment of her, she had accustomed herself to the idea, but Willis took it very badly.

"Oh, no, oh God," he moaned. "It will never work. We'll be killed, or they'll find out that I'm involved in it. The security chief at LASL hates me, you know."

She didn't know, but it was too late to worry about that now. Poor baby. He had so much to lose. She did the best she could to encourage him with the prospects opened up to them through her bargain with Da'ud. Him. It wasn't easy. She was severely constrained by the huge tissue of lies which she had woven around herself and Willis from the day she'd met him.

She desperately wanted to reveal the entire story, to be totally honest with him, but she dared not do it, for fear that his love for her could not withstand his understanding of the true role that she had played in the plot against him.

"No, love," she reassured him. "Da'ud will honor his promise to make you look like a victim. He is brutal and medieval, but he has a code of honor. He will keep his word to you, and to me. It does not hurt him for me to go to the FBI after it is all over. I don't know what he plans to do after they take the device, so my ostensible escape at the Kiva cannot hurt him, either."

She realized, of course, that Willis would at some point learn that she had been Da'ud's wife for four years in Houston, and posed as Maria in San Diego, but she had to trust that his love for her would overcome that deception.

Even if it did not, all that was in the future. For now, he would have survived, with his reputation intact, and that was, for her, the most important thing in the world; that Willis not be harmed, either physically or professionally, as a result of his love for her. It was the least she could do for him, after the awful trap she had lured him into.

"I don't know if I can carry it off," he told her, almost weeping, "I've scarcely slept for the past three nights; I keep thinking of all the horrible things that might happen when they fly into the kiva. There may be security systems that I don't know about; there probably are."

That thought frightened Sabana, too, but what could they do? What was written was written. Da'ud was determined. The promise he had made her was their best, indeed their only chance for survival.

In the end, Willis let himself be reassured. He still felt as if he were caught in a maelstrom, being pulled inexorably downward toward Monday morning, but of all the possible scenarios he could envisage, Da'ud's bargain seemed to offer the best chance for Samira's survival, and his own. All he could do was hope.

Los Alamos

At ten-thirty that night, Link, JJ, Adams and half-a-dozen Bureau and LASL security types were still seated around the long table in the conference room, where they had been since right after their brief dinner.

They had skimmed through the personnel file of every LASL employee with no routine access to weapons-grade material, and read very carefully the files of those who did.

Link had tried to speed up the process, but no dice. JJ wanted to start over from scratch, and Adam's supported him. Old JJ was a hell of a politician; you had to give him that. Link could see how he'd done so well for himself in the Headquarters bureaucracy. He and Adams were getting along like a pair of brothers.

They looked enough alike to be brothers, as a matter of fact, with the same mane of white hair and high skin color. They sounded alike, too. It wouldn't have surprised Link a bit to learn that they'd graduated from the same Boston high school.

JJ finished reading the final file, laid it down on the table and yawned hugely. "Okay, Ed," he said. "I agree with you. The only guy with routine access who seems to have had some problems recently is this Dr. Wilson."

He re-opened the file. "The last thing in here is your memo dated August first, stating that you recommended physical and psychiatric evaluation of Wilson to Dr. Timothy Long, his supervisor, and that he didn't agree with you. What happened then?"

"Wilson went off on leave the same day," said Adams. "I called his next door neighbor this morning, to see if he's back. According to her, he came in Wednesday night, and he's a new man. No drinking, worked on the house and yard all day Thursday and Friday, looks and acts like his old self, only nicer."

"Sounds like he's over his problems," remarked Link.

Adams favored him with a brief stare. "Maybe he is, but nonetheless, he has to be checked out. After all, he was vulnerable. His wife had ditched him, his morale was at rock bottom, and he was drinking."

"Okay, let's go talk to him."

"We can't," Adams answered. "He's out of town again, for the weekend. The neighbor lady said he left right after work on Friday. She says she'll call me when he comes in, but I thought I'd ask the Sheriff to put one of his deputies down by the Route 4 Bridge over the Rio Grande, in case Wilson comes home after she's gone to bed."

"Good idea," JJ said. We want to talk to him whenever he comes in, day or night. Tomorrow I'll try to get authority to tap his phone, too. We'll pull the photo from his file here and run off a hundred copies or so. Link's troops can show them around Santa Fe tomorrow."

JJ waxed philosophical. "You know, a change of scene can make a big difference in a man's outlook. Maybe a little leave was all he needed."

"Or," he went on, "maybe he met some woman while he was on leave. Nothing like the influence of a good woman to put a man back on the straight and narrow." He winked at Ed.

"Maybe," grunted Adams, "but if he did meet a woman, I want to make sure she doesn't speak Arabic."

It was the first thing Link had heard Adams say that he really liked.

JJ looked at his watch. "By Washington time, it's now one-thirty a.m. on Sunday. Let's knock it off and get some sleep. Tomorrow's likely to be another long day."

Chapter Twenty-six

August 24
Santa Fe

By the time Link came in to take charge on Sunday morning, the command post in the Federal Building in Santa Fe had taken shape. FBI agents from all over the central part of the country had converged on the city by car and plane during Saturday. Duty watches had been established, and every telephone, telex machine and radio now had a full complement of operators.

A telephone and radio net was in operation, linking this command post with the one in the Security Office at LASL, with FBI headquarters in Washington, and with the communications center of Delta Force, now bivouacked in the Jemez Mountains above Los Alamos. From their location in the Big Meadow, they could get to any technical area at LASL by helicopter in less than ten minutes.

The LIBYAN BOMB

Kirtland Air Force Base in Albuquerque was on the net, and in another hour or so, a secure-voice line to the White House Situation Room would be in operation as well.

Link stood before a wall map of Santa Fe covered with acetate, and drew pie shaped sectors on it with a grease pencil, starting at the Plaza and proceeding outward in a clockwise direction. He assigned five Special Agents to every sector, and gave them all the composite drawings of the Libyans, plus the photos of Willis Wilson he had brought from Los Alamos.

He directed them to show the pictures to the employees of every hotel, bar, restaurant or other place of business they found open today in their sectors, and to make a list of the places that were closed, so they could go back to them on Monday.

He just couldn't have had any worse luck with the timing of this manhunt, thanks to JJ's love feast with Adams all day yesterday up at Los Alamos. Starting on a Sunday meant that they had given the Libyans an extra 24 hours right up front. All he could do was hope that he got lucky.

When the hundred or so agents had left to start canvassing the city, Link sat back at a desk in the center of the CP, coffee mug in hand, and waited for his appointment with the judge.

Physically, he felt about a million times better than he had yesterday. The hangover he had brought to New Mexico was history now, he was away from the mutual admiration society that JJ and Ed Adams were running up at LASL, and best of all, he was on the street, doing what he liked to do. All he needed was more time. He hardly thought about Barbara at all.

At ten-thirty, he appeared before the presiding U.S. District Judge for the northern district of New Mexico, who had agreed to meet with Link in his chambers, following the judge's receipt of a cryptic but very sincere telephone call from the Attorney General of the United States.

Link gave his testimony on the circumstances of the case (which in the absence of the Attorney General's call wouldn't have begun to justify the ruling), and the judge signed an order authorizing the placement of a tap on the phone in the Camino Cereza residence of Dr. Willis Wilson. Link gave it to one of his agents to hand-carry to the offices of the Mountain Bell Telephone Company in Los Alamos, and sat back again to await developments.

At a little after eleven, Jerry Smolenski, the Special Agent in Sector Two, interviewed the cashier behind the desk of the La Posada de Santa Fe Hotel. She immediately recognized Willis Wilson from his LASL photo.

"Sure, I know him. It's an old picture, but he still looks sort of like that."

"That's right, Miss, the photo is about fifteen years old. Was he a guest at the hotel?"

"Oh, sure. Every weekend for — oh, five or six weeks."

"Do you remember ever seeing any foreigners with him?"

"Foreigners? No. —Oh, well, he seemed to spend a lot of time in the Staab House Bar, and the bartender there is a foreigner."

"The bartender? What kind of a foreigner?"

"Gee, I don't know. I only knew him to say, 'hi' to."

"Is he working now?"

"No. On Sunday the bar doesn't open until five."

The Agent showed her the composites. "How about these people? Ever seen any of them?"

"Sure. That's Saafi, right there."

"Who?"

"Saafi, the bartender in the Staab House."

"It is? Are you sure?" The girl nodded. "Let me use your phone for a minute, please."

She passed the phone over the lobby counter. Smolenski kept talking to her while he dialed the CP number. "How about the others? The woman, in particular. Ever seen her?"

She shook her head. "No. I don't think so."

"Okay. "Would you please ask the manager to come out here, and bring the employment record of this Saafi with him?"

"Hello, Mr. Rowe? This is Smolenski, in Sector Two. We just got a hit. The bartender in the hotel where Wilson spent his weekends this summer is the Aziz guy from Houston."

Link's howl of glee made Agent Smolenski wince and hold the receiver away from his ear.

"Hang on a second, Mr. Rowe. Here comes the manager with the guy's employment record." Smolenski showed his badge to the manager, and took the sheet of paper he held in his hand.

"Okay, here's the local address." He read it over the phone to Link. "He's probably there now. He doesn't work until five today. Sir? . . .Yessir, I will . . .Thank you, sir."

He handed the paper and the phone back across the counter with a grin. "He said I done good," he told the manager.

His gun drawn, Link flattened himself against the wall beside the door. Another agent was on the other side of the door, his own weapon at the ready, and there were six more armed men in the hall with them. Two more men were outside, in case Aziz tried to exit via the window. Link looked inquiringly at each man with him in turn, and when everyone had nodded readiness, Link reached out with his left hand and rapped on the door.

There was no response. He knocked again, and then again. After three minutes, he went off looking for the apartment manager.

He left the hall full of men. No more singleton operations against this crowd, not after losing Leo. Just thinking about that was like being kicked in the balls.

"Yeah," the manager said, handing back the composite. "That sure looks like Saafi, all right." Her gray hair was up in massive curlers. "He moved out this morning, real early. Left the place neat as a pin, too. Wish all my tenants were like him."

"Did he say where he was going?"

"Oh, back east somewhere. Chicago, maybe. Said he was going to get married. Nice little fella, he was. I wish him luck... Huh? No, he didn't leave a forwarding address."

"Shit!"

The startled manager spilled some coffee from the cup in her hand.

"Sorry," said Link. "Just thinking out loud." He gave her his card. "If you see or hear anything further about him, please call me immediately at this number. It's very important."

"I'm going to fry JJ's ass for this," he thought, driving back to town. Last night, while they were waltzing Ed Adams around up in Los Alamos, Aziz had been serving drinks at La Posada.

No wonder they hadn't found any trace of him in San Diego. The bastard had been in Santa Fe all summer, and had got in contact with Willis Wilson.

And now he was gone. Gone away to "get married". Wasn't that nice? No deaths in the family this time. Chalk up another one for the Libyans. With just a little more practice, Link reflected, he could get to where he really hated these fuckers.

What was this about, he wondered. Did this Aziz guy know something he didn't know? In his mind he could hear that clock ticking away, louder than ever.

☆ ☆ ☆

At a little before one p.m., Sabana parked her rental car beside the Cessna dealer's hangar at the Santa Fe airport. There was a small yellow helicopter in front of the hangar. She supposed it was the one she had chartered. It was to pick her up at this hangar in Santa Fe.

She looked around for Aziz. He was to meet her here, not that there would be room for him in the helicopter, which was a two-place model, but Da'ud said it would add credibility to have the ostensible client on site. Sabana understood that his real motive was to keep an eye on her, but that didn't bother her. She had made her deal with Da'ud, and Aziz didn't enter into it, one way or another.

She scanned the parking lot for his rental car. No sign of it, either. Aziz had been very much off-form during their joint visit to the airplane rental companies in Albuquerque; not his normal humorous, agreeable self. He no doubt was feeling the same forebodings as she, as the date of the operation grew nearer. She could scarcely blame him for that. Still, it was curious that he wasn't here. His fear of Da'ud normally assured his promptness. Well, no matter. She didn't need him today. She entered the office in the hangar.

The two men in the office watched her walk toward them in wide-eyed silence.

Hungry male stares were Sabana's bread and butter. She marched up to within a foot of the man in flying clothes and gave him the full force of her warmest smile. "Are you Mr. Blankenship?"

He stammered an acknowledgement, led her out to the helicopter and helped her in. She declined his offer of assistance with her bulky shoulder bag. He started the engine and called the tower for takeoff instructions.

When they were in the air, she pulled out a copy of the National Geologic Survey map of the area north and east of Santa Fe, and leaned toward the pilot. He took off his earphones and put the radio selector switch in the "speaker" position.

She put her mouth very close to his ear. "As I told your office in Albuquerque," she shouted over the noise of the rotors, "I work for a wealthy individual who is interested in buying a large tract of recreational land in New Mexico. I want to survey this area for him.

Let's start close to town and work our way north along the Sangre de Cristos, okay?"

Blankenship nodded enthusiastically. Sabana noted that he seemed to like having her breathe in his ear. This part of it, at least, was going to be easy.

Special Agent Smolenski interviewed all of the staff on duty at La Posada, in an effort to learn more about Willis' activities and anything he could about the bartender.

There was only a skeleton crew working on Sunday, and he finished in a little over an hour. He called in his findings to Link.

"I'll have to come back tomorrow to get most of them," he said, "but I did come up with one interesting thing. The bartender told one of the waitresses that his sister was coming to Santa Fe to visit him, and sure, enough, she checked in on the 30th of July. Samira Khalid is the name. Home address, Casablanca, Morocco.. . . . .No, sir, I already tried, but no one on duty here today ever saw her. Here's a little coincidence for you, though. She checked out on the morning of August 5th, about the same time Willis Wilson did."

At one forty-two, Link got a call from an agent in Sector Fifteen, on the southwest corner of the city. "I'm at the Lamplighter Motel on Route 85," the agent told him. "Wilson may have been

204

here. The desk clerk thinks he recognizes the photograph as a man who checked out very early Sunday morning, a week ago. However, Wilson was not registered at the hotel."

"However again, the key that Wilson turned in – if it was Wilson – was to a room rented by a woman named Andrea Johnson, of Dallas, Texas. In fact, that's why the clerk remembers the guy, because he figured it was a shack job. He dug out her address for us."

He read Link an address on Turtle Creek Drive, in Dallas. "The clerk who checked her in is off today. No one here now either saw or talked with her. I'll have to come back tomorrow."

As soon as the agent hung up, Link called JJ, at the Los Alamos CP, and told him the story.

"It's Sabana, JJ! I'll bet you a zillion bucks. Huh? Hell, yes, I'm having the Dallas address checked!"

An idea occurred to him. "Listen, JJ, why don't you have Adams check with Wilson's co-workers at TA-18, just in case he mentioned to someone after he got back last week that he had a girlfriend. Maybe he's one of these guys who kisses and tells."

Ten minutes later, JJ called him back. "Link, Ed called Dr. Timothy Long, the TA-18 director, who is an old friend and former student of Wilson's. Wilson came into the office for a while on Friday. Long said he hadn't mentioned a woman to him, but he said he'd ask him about it just as soon as Wilson finishes his experiment tomorrow."

"What kind of an experiment is that?"

"Long called it a routine Skua neutron flux experiment. Remember Skua?"

Link almost dropped the telephone "Holy shit, JJ! Why didn't Adams tell us that yesterday? We've got to shut down that experiment. That's got to be when the Libyans plan to make their move!"

"I agree, in light of what we've learned this morning. We've got to brief Long on what we've learned today. Since you're up to date on all that, I'd like for you to come back up here and go see him with Ed and me."

"I'm on my way."

Chapter Twenty-seven

August 24
Santa Fe

Sabana flicked a glance at her watch. She wasn't going to be able to test the radio on time. The pilot was in the midst of telling her a story, and she didn't want to attract his attention to the shoulder bag by reaching down to it when his eyes were on her.

He finished his tale, Sabana laughed, and when he returned his attention to the horizon, she slipped her hand into the bag and gripped the radio.

She found the mike button and held it down while she asked Blankenship a series of questions about the area they were flying over. She talked loudly, ostensibly to be heard over the engine.

When she judged that sixty seconds had elapsed, she released the mike button, and turned the volume all the way down. An instant later, she heard two faint clicks. She pushed the mike button two times in quick succession in answer.

The radios worked. Another hope that they would not be able to carry out the operation had evaporated.

The pilot wasn't going to be a problem either. She could keep his attention, and Aziz could easily menace him with the pistol from the seat behind him. She pushed that thought from her mind and smiled again at the pilot.

☆ ☆ ☆

Ibrahim had been in the Los Alamos area since noon. He had killed some time by driving over to Bandelier National Monument. Now he was in the car again, heading up Pajarito Road from its junction with Route 4 at White Rock. The walkie-talkie was in a flight bag on the seat beside him.

He had turned the radio on at 3:40. He had synchronized his watch with Sabana's before leaving the cabin. She was to have tested at 3:45 precisely, just as he drove by TA-18.

It was 3:49, and he had almost reached the LASL administrative area, when the radio emitted a click and crackle, followed by the faint but clear sound of Sabana's voice.

He muttered a muttered, "God is great," and turned up the volume. He could hear a man — the pilot — talking to Sabana and the engine sounds as well. Good.

He pressed the "push to talk" button twice to let Sabana know that he had heard her. A short moment later, he heard her two answering clicks.

He turned around and started south again. As he passed the turn-off to TA-18, he was surprised to see vehicles and people in the parking area. On a Sunday afternoon? Why? He'd better get over to Pojoaque, and tell Da'ud about this. They had agreed to meet there, and drive together up Highway 285 to the site where Da'ud would leave his new rental car for recovery tomorrow morning.

The Special Agent in Sector 15 called back twenty minutes after Link left for Los Alamos. He had the Santa Fe CP record his call to play back for Link when they could reach him.

"I am at the Ramada Inn on Route 85," he recited into the phone, "just a couple of hundred yards down the road from the Lamplighter, where Wilson and the woman spent the night."

"According to the hotel register, two Arabs stayed here from the 14th to the 17th of August. They gave Meknes – I guess that's a city –, Morocco, as the home address."

"Now, the cashier in the coffee shop remembers that on the last morning they were here, one of them had breakfast in the coffee shop with a woman, and guess what, her physical description is the same as that of the woman who spent the night with Wilson, down at the Lamplighter."

"Furthermore, the woman was probably another Moroccan, because she and the guy were speaking some foreign language together. The cashier is Hispanic, and he knows it wasn't Spanish."

"I showed him the composite of the Libyans, and he thought the woman looked a lot like Sabana, Da'ud al-Musa's wife. That's where the coincidences stop, though. He couldn't ID any of the men, although one of them was a big dude, like this Ibrahim guy we're looking for. Anyway, the name of the guy who registered here is "A-b-e-l K-a-d-e-r," and I've got a license plate number for you, too. New Mexico plates. Probably a rental. Run it by the computer and see what happens. Tell Mr. Rowe as quick as you can, okay?"

The information was waiting for Link when he got to the Los Alamos CP. "This is amazing," he said to JJ and Adams. "Santa Fe probably hasn't seen a Moroccan in fifty years, and all of a sudden, the town in crawling with them."

He thought for a moment. "It bothers me, though, that we aren't able to get a good ID on these guys from the composites. Either we've got bad pictures or they've brought in replacements." He looked bleakly at JJ. "We'd better all pray they haven't. If we're dealing with a whole new bunch, we may have just run out of both time and luck."

"Tim, could I see you for just a minute?" Surprised, Tim Long looked up from his conversation with Ed Adams and the two FBI men to see Linda beckoning to him from the kitchen door.

"Excuse me, gentlemen," he said, and joined her in the kitchen.

"What is it honey," he whispered. "Can't it wait? What I'm talking to these people about is really important."

"I know what it's about, Tim. I eavesdropped from out here."

"Linda!" Tim was really shocked. It was the first time in their marriage that he'd ever known her to do anything sneaky.

"Tim, listen. You've got to do what they're asking. You've got to postpone that experiment tomorrow."

Now Tim was not only shocked, but irritated, too. "Linda, that isn't any of your business, and anyway, there isn't any reason to postpone it."

She stood her ground. "It is, too, my business, because you're my husband. Tim, this is deadly serious. The FBI thinks Willis Wilson is somehow involved with these Libyans. You just cannot let yourself get caught in the middle."

"Linda, if you overheard them say that, you know how absurd it is . . ."

"I know that you haven't seen Willis Wilson for more than ten minutes in the last three weeks," she hissed, "and when you saw him before that, he was in damn' bad shape. You don't know where he's been or what he's done while he was gone . . ."

"I do too, Linda. He sent me a card from Colorado."

She clenched a fist in frustration. "Dammit, Tim, that's the FBI out there, and they're talking about a plot to steal nuclear material! I don't care how much you think you owe Willis Wilson. You do what they want you to do, and let them and Willis sort out the right and wrong of it among themselves!"

He turned his back on her and stalked back into the living room, both angry and puzzled that she so obviously believed the incredible story the three men waiting in his living room had just laid before him. He knew that she had never cared for Willis Wilson, but this was too much.

To Tim's ears, their story made no sense at all. For openers, the idea of Willis as a traitor was ludicrous. Further, the presence of Ed Adams cast serious doubt in Tim's mind on the validity of their allegations.

Linda might be upset with him about this, but he wasn't going to let Adams kick Willis when he was down, with or without the assistance of the FBI. Not without a lot more proof than he had heard so far.

He took his seat again and looked at the heavy-set younger man opposite him. "I apologize for the interruption, Mr. Rowe," he said. "Of course I share your concern in this matter. I am, after all, personally responsible for the contents of TA-18. Nonetheless, I don't accept your view that one of my most eminent colleagues is involved in a foreign conspiracy to steal those contents. I spoke with Willis on Friday and he was fine; better than I have seen him for several weeks."

"I'll agree that Willis might have been vulnerable to an attractive woman," he continued. "Possibly he met one while on leave, and spent a night with her in a motel in Santa Fe. That's not a crime, and anyway, the woman he might have been with in the motel was an American."

The look on the FBI man's face indicated that he didn't much like what he was hearing, but Tim wasn't going to be deterred by that. "You haven't proved to me that Willis has met any Arabs at all, except, apparently, the bartender at the La Posada. I'll admit that there does seem to be an unusual number of Moroccans around, too, but you haven't proved to me that the Moroccans are really Libyans." He looked at the three men opposite him. "Is that a reasonable summary of the situation?"

Link nodded reluctant agreement. "Well, then, gentlemen," Tim concluded, "I will be happy to talk to Willis about this woman, or about any other subject you suggest to me, but I will not postpone tomorrow's experiment unless you can give me more proof than I have heard so far that he is presently in contact with some real, live Libyans."

The telephone in the kitchen rang. Linda answered it and came to the door of the living room. "It's for Mr. Rowe," she said. The look she shot at her husband was frigid. Link saw it, and wondered, "Now what's that about?"

He went to the kitchen, talked on the phone a while, then came back into the living room, a look of excitement on his face.

"That was a report from our office in Dallas, Dr. Long," he said. "There was a listing in the name of Johnson at the address the woman gave the hotel, but no one answered the phone."

"They sent an agent out to talk to the neighbors, and it turns out that the lady is indeed on vacation, only she's in Canada, and with her husband."

"The physical description of the Dallas woman doesn't match that of the woman in the hotel, either," he went on. "The Houston woman has black hair, all right, but it's cut short, and none of the neighbors thought she looked anything like the composite of the woman we'd fax'd them."

Tim was on the verge of re-considering his position, but the combination of Ed Adam's presence and Linda's portentous cough out in the kitchen convinced him to stick to his guns.

"Have I not heard correctly, Mr. Rowe," he said, "that eye-witnesses are notorious for their inability to provide accurate physical descriptions? And as for this lady being in Canada with her husband, if you and your wife weren't getting along and decided to take separate vacations, would you let the neighbors in on it?"

Rowe's exasperation was written all over his face. "I'm not being difficult just for the fun of it," Tim said to him, "but I know something that you may not know, which is that Mr. Adams here harbors a grudge of long standing against Willis Wilson."

Adams half-rose in protest, and Tim lifted a placating hand.

"I'm not accusing you of fabricating anything against Willis, Ed, but I am going to have to see some real, hard evidence before I take action. Now, if you gentlemen want to appeal my decision to the Director of LASL, that is, of course, your prerogative."

The three looked at each other, shrugged, thanked him for his time, and took their obviously unhappy leave. Tim saw them off from the porch of the house, and then went back in to face Linda.

Chapter Twenty-eight

August 24
Los Alamos

During the drive back to the administration building, Adams told Link and JJ the story of his earlier run-in with Willis Wilson. He apologized for not telling them about it earlier, saying that he hadn't thought it was relevant.

Link would have loved to be able to blame him for the problems they'd just had with Dr. Long, but he really couldn't. Maybe Ed WOULD like to see Wilson's head on a plate, but the evidence that linked Wilson with the Libyans was all independent of Adams. It was just hard luck that Dr. Long's knowledge of the bad blood between the two men had made him unwilling to cooperate.

Wilson was still their prime suspect—the only suspect, in fact— and for good and sufficient reasons. They HAD to talk to him before that experiment got under way tomorrow. They were just going to have to go over Long's head to the Director of LASL, that was all. He said so to JJ, as soon as they were alone.

JJ absolutely refused.

Link couldn't believe his ears. "What do you mean, we can't," he demanded. "We can't do anything else! You know what's stored in TA-18. The Libyans could make a dozen gun-type bombs out of that stuff. We can't let Wilson anywhere near there until we know every damn thing there is to know about his relationship with this Aziz/Saafi character."

"Simmer down, Rowe," snapped JJ, "and try to remember who's in charge of this investigation. The experiment can't take place without Wilson, and we've got a car watching his house, and a tap on his phone. There's no way he can get to the material in the kiva before we've talked to him. We don't need to create a possible political flap."

Link simmered down, ungraciously. He still thought it was a mistake, but JJ WAS in charge, and on the face of it, his position sounded reasonable. Nonetheless, Link resolved to stay in Los Alamos and wait for Wilson's return. He intended to be right there for every minute of the interview, whenever the sonofabitch came back. And where the hell was he, anyway?

Link was telling the Santa Fe CP that he would be staying in Los Alamos when they got a call on another line from the New Mexico State Police about the car driven by the Moroccan, Abdel Kader. It was registered to the Hertz Corporation. Link told the CP to call Hertz in Santa Fe and Albuquerque and check it out.

They called him back ten minutes later. The girl at the Albuquerque airport Hertz counter confirmed that the car had been rented to Kader on August 12th. Unless he had checked it in today, he still had it.

"Put an all-points bulletin on that rental car," Link told the agent in Santa Fe. "Stop it on sight, detain the driver and bring him in for questioning."

JJ, who had been eavesdropping from across the room, broke in. "Hey, wait a minute. We will NOT repeat NOT make an arrest without probable cause. You can stop the car, check his documents, and ask for his cooperation, but if he won't cooperate, and there aren't any other legal grounds for detaining him, all you can do is let him go and tail him."

Link gritted his teeth. "Change of instructions," he told the CP. "Find him, check him out and if he won't come in voluntarily, stick to him like stink on shit. And ask him about the woman he had breakfast with at the Ramada on August 17th, too!"

A new idea occurred to him. He re-dialed the Santa Fe CP. "Hello, it's me again. Have Headquarters ask the State Department to send a telegram to the US Consulate in Morocco – all of them, if there's more than one. See if they've issued any visas to someone named Abdel Kader in the last six months. We need to know as soon as possible."

"I'm losing my grip," he muttered to himself, as he hung up. "I should have thought of that hours ago. I wonder what else I've overlooked?"

He stared into space for a minute, trying to think of contingencies that he hadn't covered. One came to him almost immediately. He turned to JJ.

"Look, we've got Delta Force up in the Big Meadow, sitting on their asses. How about bringing a company-size unit down into TA-18. Have them set up machine gun positions around Kiva 3, just in case?"

JJ snorted. "We've got twenty Special Agents in TA-18. There are only three of these rag heads. We don't need the goddam Army."

Link could feel his frustration level heading toward escape velocity. He tried Plan B. "Okay. What about running a bluff out there, just in case the Libyans really have recruited Wilson and are planning something for tomorrow?"

"Like what?" asked Adams.

"Beef up the guard force at TA-18. Triple the guard force, and make 'em real visible. I'll provide the manpower. We can arm everyone with shoulder weapons, turn on the lights, and generally make a show of force. If the Arabs are out there in the weeds someplace, maybe we can scare them off."

To his surprise, Adams bought it. "Well, why not?" he said. "In fact, it sounds like a good idea. Maybe I can get some sentry dogs from Kirtland Air Force Base, too." He got on the phone.

"Well," Link thought, "We've plugged that hole in the dike, at least partially," but he still wasn't a damn' bit happy, either with the situation or what he was doing about it.

They had hit an absolute dead end in the search for both Willis Wilson and the Libyans. It was getting late in the day. His troops in Santa Fe had pretty much covered the places that were open on Sunday. By the time they got started again tomorrow, the experiment would be under way.

Presumably, Wilson had to come back for the experiment, and when he did, they'd talk to him, but if he stonewalled them, they couldn't do anything about it with the evidence they had in hand at this point, and Dr. Long might very well allow the experiment to go on.

And speaking of evidence, what did they really have? What were the hard facts?

Well, Aziz had been in Santa Fe all summer, using an alias and a false nationality. Wilson knew him. Aziz's so-called sister was a Sabana look-alike, was registered at La Posada while Wilson was there, and they had checked out at the same time, same date—so, maybe together.

More facts: three weeks after the check out from La Posada, a man who looked a lot like Wilson had spent the night in the Lamplighter with a woman, likewise a dead ringer for Sabana, who had registered as Andrea Johnson (but probably wasn't). – No, forget the last thought. Stick with facts.

OK, facts. The Johnson woman was from Dallas. Sabana had lived in Houston. So, could they know each other? Houston Field Office was trying to find out the answer to that right now.

Still more facts. The two so-called Moroccans in the Ramada were the same size as Da'ud and Ibrahim, but didn't look much like their composite pictures. But—one of them had breakfast on the 17th with a woman who spoke their language and did look like Sabana, and that happened just about the time Wilson – or the guy who looked like Wilson – checked out of the Lamplighter, a few hundred yards away, alone. And, speaking of that, if it WAS Willis, and if the woman he'd spent the night with WAS Andrea Johnson, where had she been while he was checking out?

Any more facts? He pondered. Not really. The Dallas woman's identity and present location, the reason for Aziz's departure, etc., etc. were all in the twilight zone of supposition, conclusion and how-the-hell-should-I-know.

Final conclusion? It smelled. He didn't have enough evidence to get a search warrant, let alone a conviction, but to Link, the whole damn story smelled to high heaven, and what it smelled like to him was camel shit.

He had that nasty cop's feeling in the gut, the scary subjective certainty that something bad was about to happen. He'd had the feeling before, and nine times out of ten, disaster had followed close behind. This time, the extent of the possible disaster was so enormous that he didn't dare ignore the feeling.

It was time to bite the bullet.

He picked up the phone and looked across the room at JJ. "I'm going to send a coded cable to the Chief of the Criminal Division, and ask for approval to arrest Wilson 'on suspicion', the minute he hits Los Alamos. I want to put him in custody and keep him there until it's too late for his experiment."

JJ looked at him as if he had lost his mind. "If I wouldn't let you pull in the Moroccan, why do you think I'll go for this?"

"I'm not asking you to go for it, JJ. I'm telling you what I'm going to do. Don't worry. Your ass is covered. I'll make it clear that you don't agree."

JJ's face got as red as a tomato. "Let me tell you something, Rowe. Chief, CD put me in charge of this task force instead of you, Rowe, precisely because he didn't trust you not to pull some stupid cowboy trick like this."

Link kept dialing. "If he tells me no, JJ, okay, but at least he's going to understand what's at stake. And furthermore, if Wilson shows up before Chief CD tells me no, I'm going to collar him, probable cause or no probable cause, and it'll take Chief, CD to make me let him go."

Santa Fe answered.

"This is Mr. Rowe. I want you to send the following message to Headquarters, highest priority, for the eyes of the Chief of the Criminal Division only."

He dictated three paragraphs outlining the facts and his conclusions, being very careful to label them as such and keep them separate. He concluded the message with a final paragraph.

"We do not have probable cause at this time to make a legal arrest of Dr. Wilson. However, TA-18 Director refuses to cancel experiment, and C/ATS John Maloney refuses to appeal to LASL Director to overrule him. Believe grave risks of this case justify requested action. My request is opposed by C/ATS, who will present his views of situation here by separate message. End."

With JJ sputtering in the background like a lit fuse, he ordered it sent night action and directed that he be notified immediately of the response. Then he held out the phone to JJ, who snatched it from him and began dictating his own message.

What he had just done might well cost him his job and his pension, Link reflected, but he didn't see how he could do anything else. The Libyans were here. He was sure of it. They were within fifty miles of where he was sitting right now, probably a damn' sight closer, and getting ready to make their move. He felt it in his bones. He had to preempt them.

If he was going to be fired, he'd rather it be for violating Willis Wilson's civil rights than for letting the Libyans steal Skua while he sat around with his thumb up his ass.

Chapter Twenty-nine

August 24
Los Alamos

JJ finished dictating his own message to Chief, CD, during which he mentioned Link's name frequently and unfavorably. Afterward, he wouldn't speak to Link. Ed Adams, horrified by Link's insubordination, wouldn't speak to him either. Link wished that was all he had to worry about.

Time dragged by. At a little after eight, the phone rang. Link beat JJ to it by a hair. It was the Santa Fe CP, passing along Headquarters confirmation that the State Department had sent a telegram to the American Consulates in Rabat and Casablanca about the issuance of a visa to Abdel Kader.

State advised FBI that the hour of receipt in Rabat was 3:00 a.m. The Consulate opened at nine in the morning. A response could thus be expected at some time after three in the morning Los Alamos time.

"Those cookie-pushing assholes!" Link exploded down the phone line at the hapless duty operator. "Can't they get themselves up before breakfast, even for a case of nuclear theft?"

He really hadn't needed that tidbit, not with Wilson and the Libyans still somewhere off the face of the earth. He, JJ and Adams went back to staring silently at the phone, willing it to ring.

It stared back, but it didn't ring. The sweep second hand on his watch went around. And around. And around.

Santa Fe

In the cabin, they finished a late, virtually silent, dinner. Da'ud was preoccupied by the activity around TA-18 that Ibrahim had seen during the afternoon. The American couldn't explain it, but his protestations of ignorant innocence were convincing.

Da'ud's original intention had been to have Wilson return to Los Alamos tonight, so he would be out of the way during the final preparations. In view of the unexplained activity at TA-18, it now seemed safer to keep him at the cabin until morning.

If the Americans had become suspicious, he didn't want to give them a chance to talk to Wilson any earlier than he had to. The physicist couldn't resist a hostile interrogation for five minutes.

Willis didn't put up any argument. He knew he would be too frightened to get any sleep at home in any case. At least, now he would be with Samira for a little longer.

Da'ud gave him amended orders.

"You will be taken to your car no later than six a.m. Drive to Los Alamos, change clothes, eat and go to work at the regular time.

The LIBYAN BOMB

Call us from your office, as soon as you can after eight-fifteen. Use the same number I gave you earlier. Give us one ring to go ahead, two rings for danger. Understood?"

The Arab took a length of nylon cord and motioned for Willis to lie down on the bed. "We must leave you here alone for a short time. Samira has to go with us for a while, but she will be back soon and untie you."

Willis submitted to having both wrists tied to the headboard and one ankle to the footboard. With some contortion he could roll from side to side, and the knots were not so tight that they cut off circulation.

"Lie quietly," Da'ud told him. "It will not be long." He fixed Willis with a long, hard stare.

"I will not see you again until the operation is under way, Dr. Wilson. What you do tomorrow will govern the rest of your life. Do not even dream of betraying us. You have only to act the innocent, obey orders and you and Samira will be fine." He left the room.

In the living room, the two men made the final equipment checks. They put new, fully charged batteries in the radios. They loaded the guns. Sabana put one of the walkie-talkies into her shoulder bag as well as the PPK, a round in the chamber, the safety on. It terrified her to have to carry it, but she was to pick up Aziz on the Paseo de Peralta on her way to the airport in the morning, and pass it to him. The sooner she got rid of it, the better. She hated guns.

Da'ud and Ibrahim walked out on the back stoop and fired a round apiece into the trunk of the nearest tree. The snap of the slide actions made more noise than the "plop" of the silenced shots. They reloaded the magazines and put the pistols in shoulder holsters.

Da'ud put his radio and binoculars into the backpack, closed the flap, placed the pack on Ibrahim's back and carefully adjusted it for fit.

Ibrahim put the M-79 ammunition into a khaki shotgun case, bought in town, which he slung over one shoulder. Da'ud had rigged the sling, which would leave both hands free. He tried it on, one last time, for fit.

Both men wore black overalls and jogging shoes. Da'ud took three western-style hats off the dresser top and passed them out. "While we are in the car, we will wear these. They will make us look like locals to other drivers."

They emptied their pockets. Da'ud put all their identification documents into the fireplace, except his forged alias Texas drivers license. He poured fire-starter on them and set them on fire.

Da'ud handed his car keys to Sabana. "I should have turned this car in, but there was no time. When you come back here, put it behind the cabin, so it cannot be seen from the road. You will use your own car from then on. Aziz' swore his boss made him work tonight, so I must trust you with Wilson." He fixed her with a stare that chilled her. "Remember our bargain."

At 10:06, Deputy Sheriff Jess Lopez yawned. The lights of a car were coming up Route 502 from the direction of Santa Fe. The

car crossed the bridge over the Rio Grande. As it passed his position, twenty yards west of the bridge, Jess noted its make.

It was a white 1986 Pontiac Sunbird with New Mexico tags, Bernalillo County indicator. The occupants, three in number, were wearing western hats.

Lopez noted the information on a legal pad and compared it with the car makes and license numbers he had written at the top of his clipboard. They weren't the same.

He looked in his mirror again. No more cars were coming. The Pontiac started up the hill towards Los Alamos. Lopez fished out a Marlboro and lit up. God, he wished eleven o'clock would come, so he could go home and get some sleep. He was scheduled for the morning shift tomorrow.

☆ ☆ ☆

By eleven, everyone in the LASL CP was glassy-eyed with fatigue. "Screw this," Adams said. "If Wilson came home right now, I couldn't think straight enough to talk to him. How about it, John?"

"Until Headquarters shoots down Rowe's request to arrest Wilson," said JJ, "I'm not going to let him out of my sight."

Link was dead tired himself. He decided it wasn't worth the damage he was doing to himself to keep JJ up, and it really didn't make any difference whether they took Wilson tonight or tomorrow morning. Just so the experiment didn't take place, and he got some time to sweat Wilson and/or find the damned Libyans.

"Okay, JJ," he said, making a T with his hands, "Time out 'til morning."

As they trooped groggily out of the conference room and down the hall to the dormitory that had been improvised in one of the adjacent suites of offices, the white Pontiac passed in front of the Administration Building, heading in the direction of Pajarito Road.

Da'ud and Ibrahim were out of the car an instant after it stopped. They pulled the aluminum ladder from the trunk and disappeared into the power line right of way. Sabana drove off down the hill. A couple of minutes later she passed the entry road to TA-18.

She looked over her shoulder at the entrance gate. The whole area was brightly lit. She could see men moving around inside the gate. Some of them had rifles slung over their shoulders. To her eyes, it looked like an armed camp.

Her hand moved toward the walkie-talkie on the seat beside her, then stopped short. To conserve battery power, Da'ud wouldn't turn on his radio until morning. It was too late to go back and look for them. She had no idea where they had gone. There was no way to communicate with him until she was up in the helicopter. All she could do was get back to Willis and see what he thought. She sped on down Route 4, turned left at the White Rock junction and started down the steep hill toward the river.

Jess Lopez watched her car go by. He recognized it from its earlier passage. There was only one person on board now. He logged the car on his legal pad and yawned again.

227

The LIBYAN BOMB

Lying on his stomach in the darkness at the edge of the canyon, some seventy-five yards up-canyon from Kiva 3, Da'ud peered down into the illuminated perimeter of TA-18.

Something was very wrong. He squinted toward the administration building of TA-18. Even from this distance, he could see people moving around.

As he watched, a truck pulled away from the gate area and moved up the blacktop road that led toward Kiva 1. A finger of light shot from the spotlight on its roof and probed the trunks of the cottonwoods that bordered the stream bed in the canyon floor. Da'ud swore viciously under his breath.

Ibrahim nudged him, and motioned with his chin at the far wall of the canyon. A uniformed man was walking slowly along the perimeter fence of Kiva 3. He had a guard dog on a chain and an M-16 rifle slung on his shoulder.

He rounded the rear of the fenced area and moved along the north wall of the canyon, passing less than fifty yards away from them. Da'ud was relieved to feel the wind blowing directly into his face. There was no danger of the dog catching their scent.

As the man and dog passed their position, Da'ud could make out the fatigues dark blue beret of the U.S. Air Force Police. Whatever it was that had alerted the Americans, the knowledge of it was not limited to LASL Security. Was Wilson responsible? It seemed doubtful to Da'ud. The physicist had been under the Libyans' control since Friday evening.

As the man passed out of sight into the darkness, Da'ud checked the luminous dial of his watch. He would have to time the rounds of the guard and consider that factor in carrying out the operation—if there could now be an operation.

He shook his head angrily at the defeatist thought. He wouldn't give in to despair before he had even begun!

They could do nothing until daylight in any event, and unless there was a search along the fence line where they lay, they could remain there in safety, and observe what other precautions the Americans might have taken. He wasn't beaten yet! Not yet.

Chapter Thirty

August 24
Santa Fe

Sabana glanced casually at the instrument cluster of the car, then stared at it, startled and frightened. When the three of them started for Los Alamos, the gauge had shown between a quarter and a half-tank, more than ample to make the trip to Los Alamos and back, and still deliver Willis to his car and make it to the airport in the morning. Now, however, the needle was falling very rapidly toward the empty mark. They should have filled it on the way. She had to get some more gas soon!

She became more and more anxious as she passed one closed filling station after another. When she had driven the route before, there had always been stations open, some well into the night. But today was Sunday. The stations were closed. She hadn't foreseen that problem, and neither had Da'ud, the idiot!

She couldn't get stranded out on the highway, with a radio and a pistol in her purse, and Willis tied to the bed in the cabin! The fear that made its home in her belly had climbed up into her throat.

When she reached the eastern outskirts of Santa Fe, still without finding an open station, she was almost hysterical. Struggling not to lose control of herself, she decided to go ahead and try for the cabin, rather than waste time and precious fuel in what might be a vain search for gas.

The cabin was only three miles away from her present position, so if she ran out of gas before she got there, she could walk the rest of the way. She could use the car rented by Ibrahim for her trip to the telephone and the airport tomorrow.

The gas held out. She sagged with relief against the steering wheel as she turned off the road. She drove the car behind the cabin as Da'ud had told her, locked it and let herself into the cabin. She ran to the bedroom door, opened it and snapped on the light. "Willis?"

He jerked into wakefulness, his pale eyes blinking in the bright light. She untied the knots. "Is everything all right?"

"Something is wrong. TA-18 is all lit up and there are men with rifles everywhere."

His surprise was clearly genuine. "Are you sure? I don't understand it. Where are the others?"

"They are in place, waiting for daylight."

"You mean we're alone? Come on then, let's get out of here. We can go to the FBI."

"No, Willis, we don't need to, now. I want to run away, too, but it is so much safer for both of us if we don't. If we go to the FBI now, there will be a gun fight. Da'ud and Ibrahim may be killed, but in Tripoli there will be people who will blame us, and perhaps come after us. We don't have to risk that. We can just wait for tomorrow."

He frowned, not convinced.

"Don't you see? Tomorrow, when you call, I am the one who is to listen for your signal. I will answer. You can tell me what is going on, but no matter what you say, I will radio Da'ud and Ibrahim that your experiment is cancelled; that their plan is impossible."

She desperately wanted to convince him. An interview with the FBI would quickly destroy any chance she might have to keep his love. "I can't call him now. He won't turn on the radio until morning. Once I tell him my story, he will have no choice but to believe me. He has probably already seen for himself the men and guns that I saw. He will have to give up the attempt to steal Skua, and he will not blame us for the failure. This is the only way we can be sure they will let us live together in peace."

She convinced him. She had convinced herself, too. It was the perfect solution.

At 3:40 a.m., Link was shaken awake to take a call from the duty officer in the Santa Fe CP.

The American Consulate in Rabat had issued a six-month tourist visa to Mr. Abdel Kader of Meknes, on the 16th of May.

Mr. Kader's visa application appeared to be in order. Nonetheless, in view of the FBI's interest, the Consulate had checked with Mr. Kader's home by phone, and had been told by Mrs. Kader that her husband was on a trip to Europe and the United States. She did not know his precise whereabouts.

Link absorbed the information in sleepy silence, wondering if he should withdraw the order he had given to stop Kader for questioning. He decided to leave it in effect. He still wanted to know with whom Kader had eaten breakfast in the Ramada on the 17th. It damn sure hadn't been Mrs. Kader.

The insistent buzz of the alarm finally dug Willis out of the refuge of sleep. He groped for it and turned it off, feeling Sabana stir beside him.

They got out of bed and dressed in silence. Willis pulled together the few articles he had brought with him for the weekend. While he finished dressing, Sabena looked for the keys to Ibrahim's rental car.

She couldn't find them. She turned the cabin inside out, becoming more frantic with every passing minute. Where were they? Ibrahim hadn't taken them with him. She had watched him empty his pockets. She couldn't use her own car—it was out of gas—and Da'ud had told her not to use his.

She ran outside and looked in Ibrahim's rental car. There were the keys, dangling from the ignition! Weak with relief, she pulled on the door handle. It didn't open.

She jerked at it savagely. It was locked. So were all the other doors. Ibrahim had locked the keys in the car!

Willis came around the side of the cabin. "What's the matter? What are you doing out here?"

She tried to mask her anger and frustration. "Oh, stupid Ibrahim locked the keys in the car we were going to us. Never mind. We'll take Da'ud's car instead."

Thirty minutes later, they pulled up beside his Volkswagen in the empty lot of the Santa Fe Opera. He pulled her into his arms for what he feared might be the last time. The idea made a gigantic knot in his stomach.

She kissed him with cold, dry lips. "I will wait for your call, darling," she whispered. "We are doing the right thing to do it this way. We won't be apart for long, I hope. Be brave."

He returned her kiss, his cheeks wet. "Goodbye, sweetheart. Take care of yourself." He started the VW and drove away, blinking furiously to keep the tears from blinding him.

Forty-five minutes later he stood inside the front door of his house in Los Alamos, trembling in terror.

He hadn't thought a thing about the sheriff's car parked at the corner of Camino Cereza, until he glanced in his mirror after passing it and saw the officer talking urgently into a microphone, his eyes glued on Willis' VW.

They had been waiting for him to come home! The activity that Ibrahim had seen at TA-18 yesterday was no coincidence. Something had alerted LASL to danger, and Willis was obviously suspected of being involved.

He undressed, showered, shaved and dressed again, expecting at any minute to hear a knock on the front door. His mind revolved furiously.

Perhaps he ought to call Ed Adams right now. He could say that he had learned over the weekend that he had been made the dupe in a conspiracy to steal one of the critical assemblies, and that the Libyans were on the canyon rim near Kiva 3.

The Arabs would be overpowered and captured or, better yet, killed. Samira could get away. He would have saved his job and reputation, and in time he could leave LASL, rejoin her and start a new life somewhere else.

He was actually dialing the LASL operator when he put the telephone slowly down again. What Samira had told him last night was right. The people in Libya were madmen, at least by western standards. His kidnapping was proof of that. He and Samira would really be safe only if Da'ud himself ordered the operation called off.

What he had to do was wait and call her from his office, just as soon as he could give her some details of what was happening. Then, when he was sure that she was in the clear, he would call Ed Adams and tell him some story that would protect Willis's own reputation, and at the same time keep Samira out of it.

Link was shaken awake a little after six-thirty. "Wilson's coming home," the duty Agent told him. "He's over the bridge."

"Okay, here we go." JJ was climbing stiffly off his own cot. Link went to the bathroom, taking his shaving kit with him. When he got back, Ed Adams, who had gone home for the night, was there. He nodded to Link without speaking.

There had been no response on Link's request for arrest authority.

Link called the Santa Fe CP and asked them about the status of his request. Headquarters had acknowledged receipt of his message. There wasn't any point in repeating it. They knew what he intended to do. The ball was in their court.

He decided to give Headquarters more time in which to act by waiting to see Wilson when he got to TA-18. After all, the man's house was under surveillance and the phone was tapped. He couldn't contact the Libyans without Link knowing it.

They drove silently over to the LASL cafeteria and had breakfast. Just as they walked back into the CP, the Santa Fe line rang. It was the Chief of the Criminal Division in person, patched to them on the secure voice link from Headquarters.

"Good morning, Link. I'm sorry I've made you and John wait for the answer to your calls, but under the circumstances, I thought it best to check with the Director and Attorney General first."

"The answer is no, Link. Despite the seriousness of the situation, there can be no arrest without probable cause, at least not of a native-born US citizen."

"The Libyans, however, are a different story, even if they are naturalized citizens. You can arrest them on sight, with or without probable cause, but Dr. Wilson's civil rights are not to be violated, period. I'll overlook your coming to me over Mr. Maloney's head in this case, Link, but from now on, you've got to go by the book."

Link played his last card. "Sir, will you please personally call the Director of LASL and ask him to overrule Dr. Long and postpone this morning's experiment? We're just about out of time, and we still don't have any idea where the Libyans are or what they're doing. JJ doesn't want to do it, but I think we've got to."

"I will do that, Link. I think that is entirely justified in the circumstances. I don't understand why Mr. Maloney didn't want to do it. Let me talk to him, please."

Three minutes later, after a lot of "yessirring" and "nosirring," JJ hung up and turned on Link, red-faced and baying like a wasp-stung beagle. "You sonofabitch, you think you're pretty smart, don't you, getting Headquarters to overrule me? Well, I'm still in charge of this operation, and when we talk to Dr. Wilson, I'll conduct the interview, not you."

He stared at Link with angry eyes. "You've completely lost your perspective about this man," he pontificated. "He may be a suspect, but he's an American citizen, he's got rights and I'm going to see to it that they're protected."

Link didn't care how JJ put his ego back together again, any more than he cared how they stopped the experiment, just so it got done.

They drove in two cars to TA-18 to wait for Wilson.

Chapter Thirty-one

August 25
TA-18, Los Alamos

The slanting rays of the morning sun moved slowly down the canyon wall opposite Da'ud. He and Ibrahim were huddled in the pile of boulders and detritus where they had spent the night.

In deep shadow on the north side of the canyon, the new site was almost as good a staging point for their final move on the kiva as the original one, but it was high enough off the canyon floor that the sentry dogs could not catch their scent.

The dog handlers—there had proved to be two of them, walking in the opposite directions—had passed their vantage point time and again during the night. Their schedules were precise enough to plan around. They alone would not interfere with the operation.

As the clock moved toward eight o'clock, however, the full strength of the enemy became all too clear. Da'ud could see down-canyon now through his binoculars, all the way to the control building of TA-18. There were at least two dozen men in sight there, all carrying shoulder weapons. The Americans were clearly alerted.

Further, they would soon have Willis Wilson in their hands. Da'ud had no illusions about the scientist's ability to withstand interrogation. The experiment would certainly be called off. The kiva would never be opened.

The best that he could hope for now was that Wilson, in an effort to protect Sabana, would not break completely under questioning, and that Da'ud and Ibrahim could escape overland under cover of darkness according to their alternate plan.

He recognized that as a slim hope. A more probable alternative was that Wilson would tell all he knew, and that he and Ibrahim would die in a gun battle long before sundown. If that happened, they could only try to take as many of their attackers with them as they could. Neither of them would be taken alive.

In either case, however, the mission was to be a failure. That was a bitter blow. Had it succeeded, Da'ud's name would have lived forever. Still, insh'Allah. What was written, was written.

He settled deeper in the shadow of a scrub cedar to wait for Sabana's radio call, or the sound of approaching men, whichever came first.

The car from the Sheriff's office stayed behind Willis all the way from his house to TA-18. As frightening as that was, it was nothing to the fearful sight that greeted him at the area gate.

The four regular LASL gate guards were all carrying shotguns —a thing Willis had never seen before—and there were a dozen more men in civilian clothes close by, armed with rifles. Two of them even had sub-machine guns.

Willis showed his pass to the guard. "What in the world is going on?" he asked, as they checked the car with Geiger counters. It was hard to keep his voice steady.

"Can't say, Dr. Wilson," was the terse answer. "Orders from Security."

The sight of all the weapons frightened Willis terribly. He had to be certain that none of these gunmen had a chance to shoot Samira. He might lose his job if it were learned that he had colluded in Da'ud and Ibrahim's escape, but he was prepared to accept that risk, if it would just keep Samira safe. He had to stall, give her enough time to contact the two men and frighten them off. Then the danger would be over.

In the hall of the building, he saw Tim Long talking to Ed Adams and a white-haired man in shirtsleeves with a pistol on his belt. Nearby, scowling, stood another stranger, powerfully built, with coal-black hair and dark blue eyes. Further down the hall were another half-dozen armed men.

"Tim, what is happening here?" asked Willis, trying to seize the initiative. He ignored Ed Adams.

Tim turned toward him with a grave face. "I'm glad you're here, Willis," he said. "These gentlemen think we have a security problem." He gestured at the white-haired man. "This is Mr. Maloney of the FBI."

Willis nodded in acknowledgement of the introduction. "How do you do?"

"Mr. Maloney would like to talk to you for a few minutes, Willis," Tim said. "Why don't you use my office?"

"Okay, sure. Uh, has Bert Lundstrom come in yet?"

"Yes, a couple of minutes ago."

"If this is going to take some time, you'd better alert him."

"It shouldn't take very long, Dr. Wilson," said Maloney, addressing Willis for the first time. He waved Willis ahead of him into Tim's office. Ed Adams and the black-haired man followed. Tim remained in the hall.

"What can I do for you, Mr. Maloney?" Willis tried to sound like a concerned citizen.

"The Libyan government is conspiring to steal nuclear material from this facility, Dr. Wilson," Maloney replied, looking straight in Willis' eyes. "We believe you may be able to tell us something about that."

Willis felt as if the man had just kneed him in the groin. They knew! He was sure his reaction was written all over his face.

"Steal nuclear material?" he echoed dumbly. "I don't know anything about that."

"We've been trying to reach you all weekend, Dr. Wilson. Would you mind telling us where you've been?"

Willis had anticipated that question. "Well, I met this woman while I was on leave recently, and, uh, I spent the weekend with her in Santa Fe."

"Could I know her name, please?"

He hoped to God that he remembered it correctly. He had only heard Samira say it that one time at the hotel. "Yes, of course. Her name is Andrea Johnson. She's from Texas."

He looked at Maloney with what he hoped was a convincing mixture of embarrassment and diffidence. "Uh, this is sort of embarrassing, but this woman is married. I mean, she's getting a divorce, but I'd hate to have her husband learn about us. He might do her bodily harm."

Maloney nodded reassuringly. "If you can tell me where I can reach her locally, there won't be any danger of that."

"She left this morning to drive back to Texas." Willis had thought of that, too, but as soon as he said it, he panicked. Suppose they asked him where he had spent the night with her? He obviously couldn't mention the cabin. If he gave the name of a hotel, they would check it out and immediately learn that he was lying. They had been watching his house, so that was out. What had he got himself into, lying to his own government like this?

Maloney frowned. "Well," he said, "I guess we'll just have to wait and see her in Texas when she gets home, but you can rest assured that we'll be very discreet. Now, here's another question. Do you know the bartender at the Staab House Bar in Santa Fe?"

Christ! From the frying pan into the fire. Willis nodded affirmatively, not trusting his voice.

"Did he ever introduce you to his sister?"

Jesus, they knew so much? What could he say to that? He hesitated, feeling the silence lengthen as he groped for an answer.

The black-haired man broke into the silence, his voice threatening. "Dr. Wilson, you had better level with us, or you are going to find yourself in really deep trouble. Tell us about Samira Khalid."

The size of the man, his menacing tone, and the mention of Samira's name almost overwhelmed Willis. He was right on the edge of telling them everything, when out of the corner of his eye, he saw Ed Adams standing in the background, a smirk on his face.

The sight infuriated Willis, and brought back into his mind a line he had used during his confrontation with Adams, years ago. "Do I understand that you are accusing me of the commission of a crime?" he demanded.

He tried to make his voice as cold as that of his accuser. "If that is the case, I refuse to answer any more questions until I have my attorney present with me." He got out of the chair and started toward the door, fully expecting the powerful man to grab his arm and throw him back in the chair again.

"Wait a minute, Dr. Wilson." It was the white-haired one who came after him, and his tone was placatory. "Mr. Rowe used an unfortunate turn of phrase just now. You are not a suspect at this time."

Willis saw Maloney shoot a furious look at the black-haired man. He seized on the tension between them. "I am not going to be treated like a gangster by you people," he repeated. "I will not talk to you any further without advice of counsel."

He opened the door and went out into the hall, his legs so shaky that he could hardly walk. Tim Long was waiting. "Through already?" he asked hopefully.

Willis couldn't trust his tongue. He just nodded and walked on down the hall to his own office. Locking the door behind him, he went to his desk and picked up the telephone. He had to use both hands to hold it steady. Pray God that Samira was at the phones in the shopping center early!

After leaving Willis at the Opera parking lot, Samira drove back to the cabin. She tried to eat something, but the food stuck in her throat. What was happening at TA-18? She prayed that the experiment would really be called off. Surely, if the Americans suspected something dire enough to warrant all those armed men, they wouldn't let the experiment continue!

She was determined to tell Da'ud that was the case, in any event, but she would feel much safer in her own mind if it were true. She paced the cabin, and the dial crawled around the electric clock on the kitchen wall. Finally, it read a quarter to eight. Willis was to call at 8:15. She would be early, but she couldn't stand the waiting any longer. She could drive around the Paseo de Peralta to kill time, and make sure of the spot where she was to meet Aziz on the way to the airport.

The drive around the Paseo did in fact kill the extra time, but it did nothing to calm her anxiety. At 8:13, she was standing outside the row of three pay phones on the outside wall of a convenience store, fidgeting and checking her watch. A little over a minute after she arrived, the center phone rang. She pounced on it. "Hello?"

"Samira?" Oh, thank God" Panic was clearly audible in his voice.

"What's happened love?" He sounded so frightened!

"They know, Samira," he panted. "The FBI is up here. They know Libya is after nuclear material. Contact Da'ud and Ibrahim. They mustn't come near the kiva. There are armed men everywhere. I'll stall these people as long as I can, but hurry, darling, hurry! Make Da'ud call it off, and leave Santa Fe."

Fear nibbled at the edges of Samira's self-control. Willis babbled on. "They know about you, too. They know we were at the hotel. I told them you were the Johnson woman. Run, darling, run!"

She had heard enough. "Stall them as long as you can," she told him, "and be brave. I love you." She slammed the phone back on the hook and ran for the car.

Chapter Thirty-two

TA-18, Los Alamos

Willis sagged in his chair. He had done it. She was gone, out of his life for who knew how long. God keep her safe!

Now, what was he going to do? His own situation was much worse than he and Samira had dreamed it would be. He had only put off the FBI. They would be back again, any second now. They would learn the truth. He might not only lose his job, but even be sent to jail. The idea was horrifying. Still, he had saved Samira. There would be no bloodshed. That nightmare, at least, was over.

A knock sounded on his office door. The FBI! Very reluctantly, he crossed to the door and opened it.

Bert Lundstrom, his co-experimenter with Skua, was standing in the door. He looked quizzically at Willis. "Are you all right? You don't look well, Willis."

Small wonder, thought Willis. "I'm all right, Bert," he said. "What can I do for you?"

Now Lundstrom looked surprised. "What do you think? We've got an experiment scheduled."

Willis could scarcely believe his ears. They were going to let him continue? He looked down the hall. The group of armed men was still standing there, but there was no sign of the two who had interviewed him, nor of Tim Long.

Lundstrom was looking at him with a mixture of curiosity and impatience. Well, thought Willis, if they were willing to go ahead, why not? The danger was past now, and anyway, the longer he waited to see the FBI again, the more time Samira had in which to get away.

"Okay," he said to Lundstrom. "Sorry to keep you waiting." He opened his safe, got out the experiment paperwork, and followed Lundstrom on still-shaky legs to the control room.

They signed for access to the blue and gold keyboards, checked out their respective keys and showed them to the control room duty officer, who turned off the door and interior alarms on Kiva 3. They got back in their LASL van and drove in silence up the canyon to the kiva. Willis could still scarcely believe that Tim had allowed the experiment to proceed.

☆ ☆ ☆

Behind them, the control room began to fill with the men who would monitor the preparatory activities in the kiva on the closed-circuit television system.

The LIBYAN BOMB

Each of the three kivas had its own console in the control room, containing a television monitor, sensor instrumentation which showed the radiation level inside the kiva, and finally, the remote control system.

The control team turned on and checked the equipment on the Kiva 3 console, then sat back in their chairs and sipped coffee while they waited for Willis and Lundstrom to finish their quarter-mile drive and open the kiva.

On the TV monitor before them appeared the interior of Kiva 3, in which were stored the three experimental reactors: Flat-top, Godiva, and Skua. At the far end of the kiva, a large sign was visible on the wall.

If horns blow and lights flash

Get out of the Kiva

FAST

Over the years, a lot of people had laughed at the arrangement of the message, but no one had ever ignored it.

"You're finished, Rowe! You are fucking history! I told you that I was going to interview Dr. Wilson and that you were to keep your mouth shut. You disobeyed a direct order, butted into the middle

248

of the interview, and scared him into taking the Fifth. You've been a loose cannon on the deck ever since we got here, but that is absolutely the last straw. Start reading the want ads, Rowe. Your career has ended."

JJ's face was beet-red, and he was screaming at the top of his lungs. Both Ed Adams and Dr. Long, their eyes wide, were standing at the far end of Long's office, as far from JJ and Link as they could get and still be in the same room.

The diatribe had been going on, non-stop, ever since Wilson stormed out after invoking the Fifth Amendment.

Link was trying his hardest to keep his own temper in check, while he waited for a lull in the storm. The bad part was he didn't really have any excuse for what he had done. He shouldn't have jumped into the interview the way he had. He hadn't done it deliberately—he just hadn't been able to keep quiet.

Wilson's face during the interview had been a signed confession. And when Link had hit him with the name of Samira Khalid, the physicist had damn' near shit in his pants. He knew her, he knew where she was, and he knew what the Libyans were doing, too. Link had to get JJ off his case, and back on Willis Wilson's.

JJ took a breath, and Link jumped into the breach. "You can do whatever you like about me when we get back to Headquarters, JJ," he said, trying to sound reasonable. "Right now, we'd better concentrate on Willis Wilson. Tell Dr. Long something for me, JJ. Do you think Wilson is innocent?"

For a couple of seconds, it looked as if JJ were going to strangle on the question, but finally, the old cop in him won out over the asshole. With an accusing finger still pointed at Link, he turned to the Facility Director.

"That question, anyway, is good," he said. "Wilson's reactions to my questions were all those of a guilty man, Dr. Long. He's in this thing up to his eyeballs. You really have to postpone the experiment now."

That particular ball was still in Long's court. There had been no results from Chief/CD's promise to speak to the head of LASL, probably because—according to Long—the LASL Director was on his way to Europe.

Long frowned. "I really can't imagine why Willis would take the Fifth Amendment," he mused. "Of course," he added, "he had every right to do so." His voice had lost most of the conviction it held during his earlier defenses of Wilson.

Link was trying desperately to think of some way to capitalize on Long's doubts when the idea hit him. It was a very simple idea, and, as usual in the past day or so, an idea he should have had a lot earlier.

"Maybe we can save ourselves a lot of heartburn here," he said to the physicist. "Once the experiment has been set up, the kiva is re-locked, isn't that right?"

Long nodded guardedly.

"So, if our theory about a Libyan plot is correct, the time of maximum danger to Skua is during the next thirty minutes or so, isn't that right?"

Long's nodded. "As a practical matter, that's right. It would take high explosives to blast one's way into kiva, once its re-locked, and when the experiment is going on, the radiation level in there would kill anyone inside."

"Okay," said Link. "How about this? Just let me send a team of men up there now to keep watch while the kiva is open. They won't bother your people. Hell, Wilson and the other guy won't even know my men are there. They'll all stay outside. They'll come back here with Wilson when the kiva is re-locked."

Long looked tempted. Link could sense that his belief in Willis Wilson had diminished. Link pleaded. "Please Dr. Long. I promise no interference at all with the experiment."

Dr. Long shrugged his consent. Link dived for the office door. The gaggle of Special Agents was still in the hall. "All of you, drive up to Kiva 3," Link yelled at them. "Cover the place, but stay outside. If you see any strangers up there, arrest them. If you see guns, shoot first. GO!"

The agents ran off down the hall. Link went back into the office. It was time to kiss and make up. "Thank you very much for your cooperation, Dr. Long," he said. "If I'd had enough smarts to think of that earlier, we could have saved a lot of hard feelings around here."

Long was gracious. "I still can't believe that Willis is involved with some Arab Mata Hari," he answered, "but if I'm wrong about that, I'm going to be very glad you thought of it, too."

Ed Adams looked a bit shame-faced. Well he might, thought Link. After all, he was responsible for the security of those devices. It made Link feel better to know that he wasn't the only slow thinker in the crowd.

251

JJ didn't say anything, the turkey.

Well, screw JJ. He could do whatever he wanted about Link's career, but Link felt as if a thousand pounds had just been lifted from his shoulders. He didn't have Delta Force out there, but he had something. It should be enough. He hoped to God it was. If the Libyans intended to make a move on Kiva 3, they had to do it soon.

Chapter Thirty-three

Kiva 3, TA-18

"What are they doing?" Ibrahim whispered, as Wilson and the other man unlocked the kiva and went inside. "Can they be going ahead after all?"

"Apparently so," Da'ud hissed back. "As unbelievable as it seems." He had been certain that the experiment would be cancelled. Now he wondered if he was looking at a trap. He checked the volume and squelch controls on his radio for perhaps the tenth time since turning it on fifteen minutes earlier. Where was Sabana? Why hadn't the bitch called?

Sabana pulled up in front of the little super market on the Paseo de Peralta where she was to pick up Aziz. There was no sign of him.

She checked her watch. He was five minutes late. Of all the days for him to sleep in! She needed to get in the air and tell Da'ud of the danger, now!

She shut down the car, angrily snatched open the car door and ran to the pay phone on the wall of the store, digging in her hand bag for her coin purse as she ran. Her hand touched the handle of the PPK. Thank God they didn't need the damned thing now!

She fumbled with the snap of the coin purse, got it opened and found a dime and a quarter. He fingers shaking, she dropped the two coins in the slots. She heard the phone ring, and ring again, and again. He wasn't there. He must be on the way!

"Hello?" It was a strange woman's voice. Samira started with surprise. Damn! Had she dialed a wrong number?

"Saafi?" she ventured timidly.

"Saafi?," echoed the woman. "Oh, he's gone."

Thank God. He must be on the way. She shot a glance down the sidewalk. It was empty.

"Oh," she said. "What time did he leave?" Who was she talking to? A cleaning woman?

"Yesterday" answered the woman. "Moved out."

Samira couldn't believe it. "What?" she gasped.

"Yep," responded the voice, now sounding chatty. "Say, are you his sister?"

"Ah, ah, why yes, I am," mumbled Samira, dumfounded.

"Well, he left a message for you with me, in case you called."

"Oh?" She could scarcely get the word out of her mouth. "What was it?"

"He said, 'I'm gone on my honeymoon. You ought to do it, too.' Did you just get married, too, sweetie?"

Samira's shock turned to anger, then to fear. "Why, no, no I haven't. It's a joke."

"Oh? Well, he was a real joker all right. Great sense of humor."

"Yes. Yes, thank you." Samira hung up and ran back to the car. Aziz had fled! And what was that about a honeymoon? Had he talked some woman into marrying him? The idea almost brought a smile to her lips, in spite of her roiling emotions, then the thought of Da'ud's reaction wiped the humor from her mind. She got in the car, started it and backed out, trying to sort out the implications.

She pulled out on to the Paseo and headed toward the airport. Aziz's advice to her was clear enough, in any event. He was urging her and Willis to follow his example. She weighed it for an instant, then discarded it. No need, now. As soon as she got airborne and contacted Da'ud, the danger would be over.

She glanced at her watch. She was going to be late! Damn Aziz! He could have warned her in advance! She immediately recognized the thought as idiotic. He wouldn't have dared warn her in advance, any more than she would have warned him, had she and Willis decided to flee or go to the FBI. Well, at least Aziz hadn't done that, and left them all to be arrested.

When she reached the Cessna hangar, the large helicopter was parked out in front, with the pilot standing beside it. Sabana didn't want to take time to park the car, and in any case, Da'ud had not wanted her to use it, for some reason. She gestured for the pilot to start the engine, and ran into the office of the hangar.

"Would you be good enough to park this for me," she asked the man behind the desk, giving him a smile. "I'm running late."

"Sure," he said, holding his hand out for the keys. "I'll put it in the hangar, to keep it out of the sun."

✧ ✧ ✧

The helicopter lifted gently into the wind, then banked around and climbed away from the Santa Fe Airport to the north. They leveled off at fifteen hundred feet above the city. This was a Bell Jet Ranger, both larger and faster than the helicopter they had been up in yesterday.

Sabana sat in the front right hand seat. Her shoulder bag was on the rear seat floor behind her. The pilot took off his earphones after takeoff, and tried to engage her in conversation. She answered him automatically, her mind thirty miles ahead of them. She could see the morning sun's reflection on the water towers and building roofs at Los Alamos.

She looked at her watch again. "I am supposed to contact my client," she told the pilot. "He is a late riser and I didn't want to phone him before we took off. Will it be all right if I call him now, on my radio?"

"Sure, go ahead." He didn't seem too surprised that she had a radio.

She unbuckled the seat belt, turned, and knelt on her seat to open the shoulder bag and fish out the portable transmitter. Her hands were still shaking. She had exceeded the speed limit by hundred percent or more all the way from the grocery store to the airport.

She turned around and sat down again. Without bothering to re-buckle the seat belt, she turned on the radio. She checked her watch again, biting her lip with impatience, as she waited for it to warm up.

When the speaker clicked in response to her thumb's pressure on the transmitter button, she pointed the antenna toward Los Alamos, flashed the pilot a smile, and keyed the mike. She had already assured herself that he spoke nothing but English.

"Da'ud, Da'ud, this is Sabana. Do you hear me?"

There was no reply. Her heart sank. God, surely they hadn't already entered the kiva? She looked again at her watch. Ten minutes after nine. She pressed the mike button and called again.

✫ ✫ ✫

Da'ud's hand shot to the radio and turned down the volume, but his eyes remained glued on the van which had just pulled up in front of the kiva. Four men got out and took up positions around the entrance to the building.

He could just barely see them from his vantage point, which was up-canyon from the kiva entrance, but he noted that they had no shoulder weapons, just short-barreled revolvers in belt holsters.

Sabana called again. He answered. "I hear you, Sabana." I hear you."

"I can barely hear you. Turn up your volume." The relief in her voice was plain.

He edged up the volume control a hair. "What is happening," he demanded. "Wilson has opened the kiva, but there are armed men outside. Did he give you the safety signal?"

"No, he gave the danger signal, so I picked up the phone and talked to him. He said he had been questioned by the FBI about a Libyan plot to steal Skua. They asked him about both Samira Khalid and Andrea Johnson, too. He warned that you should not try to approach the kiva, that it is a trap."

Even though he had half-expected to hear them, the words were bitter for Da'ud. The experiment was not to take place after all. The FBI had sent Wilson to the kiva as a Judas goat, to lure him and Ibrahim in for the kill.

All the months of planning and work; the miraculous second chance after the failure in California; the textbook recruitment of Wilson; all had been for naught. The mission was a failure.

He looked at his watch. The King Air in Taos would only wait for them for another two hours, and they didn't dare move from here now, in broad daylight. They would have to use the alternate plan, tonight.

He keyed the radio again. "Sabana, go back to the cabin. Pack us up. Clean out everything, and drive to Taos for the day. Come back and pick us up tonight at eleven o'clock, the same place you dropped us off. Understood?"

He listened woodenly to her acknowledgement, then turned to Ibrahim, who had been listening. "It was written, my friend," he said.

"Insh'Allah," muttered the big man.

"Da'ud nodded. He didn't believe in the will of Allah to the extent that the big man did, but if it made Ibrahim feel better, fine. He couldn't think of anything that could make HIM feel better.

☆ ☆ ☆

Since eight o'clock, Special Agent Charles West had been routinely checking the private flying services at the Santa Fe Airport, showing everyone the composite pictures of the Libyans in an effort to find some trace of their arrival or departure from the city. So far, he'd had no luck.

At nine-twenty, he parked behind the Cessna dealer's hangar and prepared to try again. As he passed the open hangar door on his way to the office, he glanced inside, then stopped, turned, and stared. In the corner of the hangar was a blue, 1984 model Ford Escort.

He fished out the notebook from his shirt pocket and compared the Ford's license number with the one he had written there. They matched. He ran the rest of the way to the hangar office and burst in on the startled manager. West leaned over the counter and showed his credentials.

"I'm an FBI Special Agent. Whose car is that, parked in the hangar?"

"A customer. A lady."

"Where is she? What's her name?"

"She's up in one of the Sundance helicopters. I don't know what her name is–wait a minute, I do too." He dug out a note from a drawer and looked at it. "It's Khalid, Samira Khalid. She's Moroccan."

"What's she look like?" West asked.

The manager grinned lasciviously. "Like the world's greatest lay."

West pulled out the composite picture of Sabana. "Like this?"

The manager squinted at the picture. "Yeah, as a matter of fact. A lot like that."

"Hot damn! Let me use your phone." West came around to the inside of the counter, picked up the phone and dialed the Santa Fe command post number.

"Hey, what's this all about anyway?" The manager sounded nettled.

"I can't give you the details," West answered, "but believe me, it's important." He pulled the photo of Willis from his coat pocket. "Have you seen this man with her—or anywhere, for that matter?"

"No."

"Does the name Abdel Kader mean anything?"

The manager shook his head. West handed him the other composites. "Ever seen any of these guys?"

Another negative shake of the manager's head.

"Has the woman been here before today?"

"Yeah, yesterday. She was up in the little chopper for two hours. The pilot told me she's in real estate. Looking for property for a rich oil Arab."

The Santa Fe CP answered. "This is West, out at the airport," West told the operator. "I've got urgent information for Mr. Rowe. We have a make on the woman, only now she claims she's a Moroccan. She's driving the Kader rental car, too."

He fidgeted while the CP operator took notes. "She's up in a helicopter right now, supposedly looking for land to buy. She did the same thing yesterday.—No, only the pilot is with her. The guy here doesn't recognize any of the other composites, or the picture of Wilson, or Kader's name. —Hang on a sec'."

He turned back to the manager. "When's she due back here?"

"I dunno. Couple of hours, the pilot thought."

"Ten-thirty or eleven o'clock," West said, glancing at his watch. "——Okay, I'll ask." He put his hand over the mouthpiece and looked at the manager again. "Can you reach the chopper by radio?"

"Yeah. The pilot said he'd monitor Unicom so we could talk if anything came up."

West spoke into the phone again. "Yes, he can reach them. Okay. —Okay, will do. You going to get me some backup out here? Okay. It's the Cessna dealer's hangar. You can't miss the Cessna sign on the building."

He hung up and spoke to the manager again. "Look, this is an important national security case. It's vital that we get that woman back here as fast as we can. Can you call the pilot and ask him to come back?"

"Sure, but he's going to want to know why."

"Tell him the FBI needs to talk to his passenger, but not to let her know that. Have him tell her the engine doesn't sound good, or the controls feel funny or something, and that he wants to come back and check it out. Have him land as close to the office door as he can."

"What if he has the speaker on? She'll hear what I'm saying."

West thought about that for a moment. "Hmmm. Well, use as much flying slang and airplane jargon as you can. She's a foreigner, after all. Hopefully, she won't understand."

The manager nodded agreement and picked up the pedestal mike on the desk top. He keyed its transmit button. "Sundance, oh-seven-four Foxtrot, this is Santa Fe Cessna on Unicom. Do you read me?"

☆ ☆ ☆

The radio call interrupted the pilot's attempt to get Sabana to go out to dinner with him. He looked puzzled, and took the microphone from its bracket. "Roger, Santa Fe Cessna, this is oh-seven-four Foxtrot. Go ahead."

"Uh, oh-seven-four Foxtrot," the distorted voice said through the loud speaker in the headliner of the helicopter, "I have a request from federal fuzz here. They need a debrief from the right-seater, ASAP. Have you got that?"

The pilot's look of puzzlement deepened. "Uh, roger, understand federal fuzz. Is that the FAA?" "Negative," crackled the speaker, "That's the Foxtrot Bravo India, but don't tip your mitt."

Sabana didn't understand the phonetic alphabet, but the strangeness of the transmission, the world "federal", and the look it produced on the pilot's face set an alarm siren screaming in her mind. She snapped her seat belt open, whirled around on the seat, and dug into the shoulder bag.

Her sudden movement made the pilot look at her. "The FBI?" he said at the same time into the mike. "What the hell is that about?"

Sabana pulled the PPK out of the bag and pushed its muzzle to within an inch of the pilot's startled face. "Listen to me," she hissed. "If you say one word out of place, or make one false move, I'll kill you. Tell them you understand."

He stared at her in utter stupefaction, but raised the mike unsteadily to his mouth. "Uh, roger, oh-seven-four Foxtrot. WILCO."

"What is your ETA?" asked the voice over the speaker.

"What does that mean?" Sabana snapped.

"They want to know when we'll land. They want us to come back immediately."

Tell them it will take us an hour."

The pilot keyed the mike. "Uh, Cessna, our ETA is one hour."

The speaker clicked an acknowledgement, and fell silent. The pilot was still staring at Sabana with a face like an ox.

"Turn the helicopter toward Los Alamos and fly there as fast as you can," Sabana ordered. She groped in the shoulder bag with her left hand for the radio. "Now!"

The helicopter banked sharply to the left, and the sound of the motor increased in pitch.

Sabana was so frightened she could scarcely think, but one thing was crystal clear: she was destroyed. They were all destroyed. She couldn't meet the FBI with the radio and gun in her purse. She would be arrested on the spot, the Sundance Helicopter people would identify her as Samira Khalid, the General Atomics engineer would identify her as Maria, a Salvadorian, her neighbors in Houston would identify her as Sabana al-Murtada, the wife of Da'ud, and she would spend the rest of her life in prison.

Everything had fallen to pieces. The only chance she had for escape now was to rescue Da'ud and Ibrahim, force the helicopter to fly them to Taos, where the airplane was waiting. They might be able to make it to Mexico, and Willis would be safe.

She keyed the transmitter of her radio. "Da'ud, this is Sabana. Do you hear me?"

✡ ✡ ✡

Da'ud's head jerked up off the boulder where he was resting. What was this? He snatched the radio. "Yes, I hear you. What is it?"

Sabana's voice was rich with fear. "I have been discovered. The pilot got a radio call from the airport. The FBI is there. They want to speak to me. With the radio and gun, I can't talk my way out of it." Her voice almost broke. "I am coming to get you."

Her words lit a fire in Da'ud's mind. Now they would have to fight with the men in front of the kiva for their very survival. Very well then, he would fight. Only not just for survival, but for victory as well.

He keyed the mike. "All right, Sabana. Stay calm. As you approach Los Alamos, fly to the left side of the town of White Rock and up the canyon which will be in front of you. Not the one with the highway leading to TA-18, but the next one to the left. Do you understand?"

"I understand," she quavered. "I see White Rock in front of us now."

"Good," he said soothingly. "Make the pilot fly right up the bottom of the canyon, so his approach can't be seen from TA-18. When you reach the end of the canyon, have him pull up and to the right over the top of the mesa. TA-18 will then be right in front of you. Have him land in front of Kiva 3. It will be the one farthest to your left as you come over the mesa. There is plenty of flat land in front of the kiva to land on. We will meet you there."

He snapped off the radio and looked at Ibrahim, who was watching him expectantly.

"How will we get to the front of the building without being seen by the guards?" the big man asked.

"We will kill them," Da'ud answered, reaching for the knapsack. "Since we are blown, we will take the uranium out with us. Do you agree?"

"Yes, by Allah!" The light of battle shown in Ibrahim's eyes.

"Very well. Bring the ladder, and come on. We must be quick, but also very quiet. If they spot us before we get into place behind the kiva, we will have no chance at all."

Da'ud threw a last look through the branches of the pinon bush which shielded their position. He could see only two of the four guards. The others were either on the other side of the building, or inside. He had lost track of them while talking to Sabana on the radio. He beckoned to Ibrahim and began slipping down the rocky draw toward the perimeter fence.

Now that there was no going back, he found that he felt not only calm, but happy. This was far better than slinking off into the night like a jackal.

The LIBYAN BOMB

The odds against them were enormous, but as least if they died, they would have done so fighting the damned Americans, not running away from them. This was far better than returning to Tripoli a failure. Had silence not been essential, he would have sung a battle song.

Chapter Thirty-four

Kiva 3, TA-18

"Sundance oh-seven-four Foxtrot, this is Santa Fe Cessna." The voice of the Cessna manager crackled over the speaker in the helicopter's cabin. The pilot looked at Sabana for permission to answer.

She nodded. He picked up the mike. "Oh-seven-four-Foxtrot, roger."

"Seven-four-foxtrot, say present position." The pilot looked at her inquiringly.

She glanced out of the cockpit. Ahead, perhaps ten miles away, was the gorge of the Rio Grande and on the mesa above it, the town of White Rock. The airspeed indicator of the helicopter quivered at one hundred thirty-five knots.

"Tell them that we are forty miles north of Santa Fe," Sabana ordered.

"Roger," said the pilot into the mike, "oh-seven-four-Foxtrot now four-zero miles north of Santa Fe."

"Roger," replied the voice over the speaker. "Understand four-zero north."

"Go lower," Sabana told the pilot.

✡ ✡ ✡

Link, JJ and Ed Adams joined Timothy Long and his technicians at the Kiva 3 console in the control room. Tim pulled in extra chairs from adjacent console areas and watched on the TV monitor while Willis Wilson and Lundstrom installed Skua in its reactor.

The device wasn't much to look at, reflected Link, considering all the excitement it was causing: a gray metal sphere, about the size of a basketball. It obviously weighed a whole lot more than a basketball, however, in view of the equipment that Wilson and Lundstrom had to use to install the device, after removing it from its vault and wheeling it over to its reactor.

The reactor itself was on an elevated metal platform, about six feet off the floor, with metal steps leading up to it. The scientists had used an hydraulic lift to raise it to the level of the reactor, and were now rolling Skua into a sort of cradle in the middle of the platform, on either side of which were metal panels, which looked to be about a foot wide by four feet or so high.

Tim Long had explained to Link that one side of the panels was coated with carbon, a neutron-absorbent material, the other side with beryllium, an excellent neutron reflector.

Once Skua was in place, its safety chain removed, and the scientists had locked the kiva and returned to the control room, they would be electrically manipulating the panels from there. As long as the carbon-coated sides faced Skua, it would remain sub-critical. The instant the beryllium-coated sides faced it, however, it would go critical, emitting a burst of deadly gamma radiation, some facet of which (Tim didn't elaborate) was the subject of the experiment.

The console crew, plus Long, Ed Adams, JJ and Link, ate doughnuts and drank coffee. The control area was quiet, aside from the insistent ringing of a telephone down the hall. After a moment it fell silent. Then the phone on the console rang. Tim Long picked it up, listened for an instant, and passed it to Link.

"Hello," he said, "Rowe here . . .Yeah, I'm sorry. I didn't think to leave you the number here – didn't know it, in fact . . . Huh? What??" He listened for a moment, said, "Okay, thanks," and hung up. He turned to Tim Long.

"That was my guy on the phone tap, up at the telephone company. Wilson made a long distance call from his office this morning, and charged it to his home phone. The number he called is a public phone in a shopping center in Santa Fe. This had to be right after he talked to us and took the Fifth. The call lasted for less than a minute." He looked at the TV monitor. "How much longer before they get finished up there and come back here?" he asked Tim Long.

Long glanced at the screen. "Just a few more minutes, I'd say. They have the assembly in the reactor, and are removing the safety chain. All that's left is hooking up the monitoring instrumentation now." He looked very unhappy. "What are you going to do?" he asked Link.

"We're going to have another talk with Dr. Wilson just as soon as he gets here. If he takes the Fifth again, I'm going to ask you again to postpone the experiment."

The telephone rang again. This time it was Link who picked it up. "Rowe speaking . . . Yes . . . What? . . . . Where? . . . . . Good! Good work! How soon will they be down? . . . . Have you got enough people out there to handle it? . . . All right. Keep me posted, up to the minute."

He hung up and turned to JJ with a grin. "We've found Sabana. Positive ID on the composite and furthermore, she's driving the car that Abdel Kader rented from Hertz. Right now she's in a helicopter north of Santa Fe, posing as a real estate agent. They've pulled a gimmick with the chopper pilot to get them back on the ground."

Da'ud and Ibrahim reached the bottom of the draw and moved up to the perimeter fence. From his position, crouched next to one of the fence posts, Da'ud could now see only the left side of the body of the guard nearest to him. The rest of the man was screened from his sight by the side of the kiva, as were the three others with him.

"I will go first," he hissed to Ibrahim. "Cover me with the grenade launcher. If they spot me, wait a moment to let them bunch up together before you fire. We don't want any survivor making radio calls."

Ibrahim grunted his understanding.

"If I make it over the fence unobserved," Da'ud continued, "throw me the grenade launcher and I'll cover you while you climb over. Then follow me to the back of the kiva. When I give you the signal, we'll take them from both sides of the kiva at once with the silenced pistols."

Ibrahim nodded and dropped a round in the chamber of the M-79. The barrel closed on the 40mm. rifle grenade with a click that wasn't audible over two yards away. Da'ud peeked at the kiva again. The guard was almost invisible, his back still toward them. Da'ud took a deep breath and picked up the ladder. "Here we go."

He placed the ladder against the fence post, scrambled up it, and pushing off against the top strand of wire, jumped over the fence. He hit the ground with a thud, and looked immediately at the kiva. He could see only a tiny part of the guard's arm.

He turned and gestured to Ibrahim, who threw the M-79 over the wire. It fell heavily into Da'ud's waiting hands. He pulled it to his shoulder as he whirled back to face the kiva again. There was no sign at all of the guard now.

Ibrahim followed the weapon, scaling the ladder at a run. He landed beside Da'ud, then sprinted off across the grass of the canyon floor toward the kiva, with Da'ud 20 meters behind him, running hard, but keeping his eyes glued on the front corner of the building.

When they had both reached the shelter of the rear of the kiva, Da'ud hissed. Ibraim stopped running, and a second later, Da'ud caught up with him. He passed Ibrahim the grenade launcher. The big man slung it over his back, then continued on to the far corner of the massive concrete blockhouse. Da'ud himself ran silently to the near corner.

He slid one eye around the edge of the building. He could see no one. He pulled the silenced .22 from his belt, raised it, glanced at Ibrahim, nodded, and then charged forward, along the side wall of the kiva. He ran as fast as he could without making any noise. Surprise was all-important.

As he rounded the front corner, all four of the guards, spread evenly across the front of the building, had their backs to him. Da'ud stopped, pointed the pistol at the back of the closest man's head, and squeezed the trigger twice. The gun made a noise like a hiccup, and the man fell silently forward.

As Da'ud shifted his arm to the next man, out of the corner of his eye he noticed the farthest guard falling. Ibrahim had opened fire, too.

Da'ud's target was turning toward Da'ud in surprise, making head shot tricky. Da'ud dropped the barrel to the center of the man's chest and pulled the trigger three times. Phut! Phut! Phut!

The man crumpled to the ground, and at the same instant, the remaining man fell also. None of the four had even managed to pull his weapon.

Ibrahim ran up. "Easy," he said, grinning.

"Pass me the pack," Da'ud told him, "and then cover the road with the grenade launcher."

Ibrahim unbuckled the pack from around his waist, and shrugged it off his shoulders. Da'ud took it in his left hand and with his pistol still in his right, raced through the open door of the kiva.

Right inside the door, he collided with Willis Wilson. At the sight of him, the American let out a wail of pure anguish. "Get out, get out," he screamed. "There are guards everywhere."

Da'ud caught him by the arm and spun him around. "The guards are all dead, and you will be too, if you don't do exactly as I tell you. Lead me to Skua." He shoved Wilson ahead of him into the kiva.

✵ ✵ ✵

Link's euphoria at having located Sabana lasted only a few moments, before second thoughts made him frown. "What the hell is that broad doing up in a helicopter?" he demanded of no one in particular. "I don't like the sound of that at all."

He pulled the radio from his belt and keyed the mike. "West, this is Rowe. Can you hear me?"

There was no answer. He called again. "West? Rogers" Anyone up at the kiva. Can any of you hear me?"

Still no response. It was probably interference from the terrain or the 4-foot thick magnetite sand concrete of the kiva itself. Nonetheless, it bothered him. He turned to JJ. "I'm going to the kiva to reinforce the troops up there. I'll stay in touch by radio." He got up and headed for the door before JJ or Tim Long could start an argument with him about it.

There was a gaggle of four or five agents with shoulder weapons in the parking lot. "Keep your eyes open for a helicopter," he shouted to them as he jogged toward the LASL van. "If you see one trying to land in the area, open fire. Aim right under the rotor mast."

He jumped in the LASL van. Thank God he'd been smart enough to ask Tim Long to leave the keys in the ignition. He started the vehicle, backed out, and exited the parking lot toward the narrow blacktop road that ran from the control building up the canyon, where the three kivas were located.

He passed through the open gate into the inner perimeter, and turned left along the tiny watercourse which ran down the canyon floor, bordered by ancient cottonwoods.

Half a mile later, he had Kiva One on his left. Ahead he could see the face of the canyon wall where the canyon divided into two forks. The stream bed crossed under the road here through a culvert, on its way down from the left-hand fork, which housed Kiva Two. In a couple of seconds, he would be clear of the trees and be able to see up the right-hand fork to Kiva Three.

He pulled the radio from his belt and tried his agents again. "West? Rogers? Can you read me?" There was still no answer. He couldn't understand that. At this range, he should be coming in loud and clear. They certainly had their radios on under the present circumstances.

He drove out from behind the screening trees, and the kiva came into view. At the same instant, he saw the bodies of his four men sprawled on the grass by the front entrance, and, crouched at the corner of the building, another man, with a curious-looking shoulder weapon in his hands.

The man was big. Link knew him, despite the distance. It was Ibrahim! It had to be. Where was Da'ud then? Inside the kiva?

Jesus! They must have been out here in the canyon for God knows how long, waiting. His bluff hadn't frightened them off, and the bastards had killed four of his men. A surge of sheer hatred flooded through him.

He saw the big man raise the weapon to his shoulder. As he did so, Link recognized it from his Vietnam experience. An M-79 grenade launcher. Oh, my God! He stood on the brake pedal and simultaneously felt frantically for the door handle. He finally found it and yanked, slamming his shoulder into the door.

The car was still moving, but screw that! He threw himself out of it onto the shoulder of the road, trying to hit the ground rolling, to lessen the impact.

It hurt like hell when he landed. It not only hurt, it knocked the wind out of him, but breath or no breath, he had to keep moving or die. He, scrambling on all fours toward the meager protection of the little stream bed, now ten yards away from the road.

He never heard the shot, but he couldn't miss the concussion of the blast behind him. A quarter-second later, he heard the sound of the explosion, followed instantly by the secondary blast of the van's gas tank blowing up.

The concussion shoved him face-first into the gully, followed by a tremendous wave of heat. Gobs of burning gasoline landed all around him, instantly setting the brush along the stream on fire. Oh, Jesus, he thought. Don't let one land on me!

But one did. A big one, that burned shirt and flesh over his entire back. He heard himself scream like a woman, and he rolled frantically over on his back, trying to smother the flames that he felt reaching down inside his body after his life.

He thrashed and slithered like a wounded crocodile into the trickle of cool water in the bed of the stream. The flames died, and for a brief, blessed moment he felt nothing. Then the pain returned, terribly, remorselessly.

He rolled back on his belly again, and lay flat on the sand, panting in agony. Thirty feet away, the skeleton of the van was a raging inferno. "High explosive round," he instinctively diagnosed. "Hope to Christ he hasn't got any more of them." He knew as he thought it that it was a vain hope.

He tried to organize his mind by doing a quick mental check of his condition. The first pain he had felt was probably glass from the van's windows, blown out by the concussion. He could keep moving with that for a long time. The pain of the burn was a different story. Before very long, that would incapacitate him.

Therefore, while he still could move, he had to get himself away from this area. He reviewed the canyon's geography in his mind. What he had to do was crawl up the stream bed toward Kiva Two far enough so that the protective mass of the canyon wall would screen him from the Libyan's sight.

Once there, he could cross the canyon floor and work his way along the base of the lava cliff toward Pajarito Canyon and Kiva Three.

If Ibrahim thought that Link had died here in the ditch, Link would have the advantage of surprise. At the worst, he and the Arab would see each other at the same time. No, he realized with a sick feeling in the pit of his stomach, that wasn't the worst case. The worst case was that the Libyan would see him moving up the stream, drop another 40 mm. round into the gulley and blow Link into a bloody pulp.

He felt at the back of his belt for his Browning, being very careful not to let his arm show above the stream bank. The movement hurt like hell. Thank God the gun was there, secure in the inside holster.

Next he brought his arm back forward and felt for the radio. If he could summon Force Delta down from the Big Meadow, they would wipe out the Arabs in seconds.

Shit! The radio was gone. It must have been scraped off back by the road, when he hit the ground. He couldn't turn around to look for it in the narrow stream bed. Anyway, he didn't have to. The men in the parking lot must have heard the explosion, and would have immediately called for reinforcements. Link fervently hoped so. Wounded, and armed only with a handgun, he didn't like his chance of winning this fight all by himself.

Still, he had to get in position to try, if that became the only option, so it was time to move. The creek bed was only eighteen inches or so below the level of the canyon floor, and it got progressively shallower as it approached the wall of Kiva Two. So that Ibrahim wouldn't see him, he would have to crawl flat on the sand, his face almost in the water, wriggling like a snake.

At the first movement of his body, agony from the burn on his back nailed him to the sand, motionless, for twenty seconds. God. He'd forgotten how much you could hurt. He took a deep, ragged, breath, and started forward again.

Chapter Thirty-five

Kiva 3, TA-18

"What the hell?" The technician's voice brought up every head around the control console. On the Kiva Three TV monitor, Bert Lundstrom was climbing down from the Skua rector, and shouting at the two men who were moving toward him from the direction of the kiva door.

One of the men was Willis Wilson. None of them had ever seen the other man before, but JJ Maloney knew, with an awful emptiness in his gut, who it had to be. The man didn't look a lot like the composite drawing the FBI had made up, but it had to be Da'ud.

Maloney's gut turned into a square knot. How had the Libyans got into the kiva? What had happened to the four agents Link had sent up there? And where was Link? He should have reached the kiva by now. Why hadn't he called the control room?

Before Maloney's horrified eyes, Da'ud pointed a gun with a bulbous barrel at Lundstrom. No sound came to them over the speaker, but the physicist collapsed onto the floor like a rag doll.

The violence released Maloney from temporary paralysis. "Shit!" he shouted, and ran to the door. Ed Adams got up to follow him. "No!" Maloney shouted at Adams over his shoulder. "Stay here. Get on the radio and call Delta down from the Big Meadow! Alert the police and sheriff's department, too."

He crashed through the outer door, startling the group of agents outside. "Come with me!" he shouted. "Where is the duty vehicle?"

The sound of an explosion up-canyon stopped them all in their tracks. A rolling ball of fire-tinged black smoke lifted suddenly into view over the tops of the cottonwoods inside the perimeter fence.

Maloney thought he might be sick. His career had just vanished into the sky along with that puff of smoke, which signaled only God-knew-what disaster. Maloney could never survive this, even if the Arabs didn't get away with Skua. Link had wanted to have the LASL director cancel the experiment. He, John Joseph Maloney, had refused. Link had suggested bringing Delta Force down to protect the kiva. Again, Maloney had refused.

There were witnesses to both those conversations. Maloney's lifetime of service in the Bureau was turning to shit right in front of his eyes. There was only one possible way he could salvage something from the debacle, and that was to make damn' sure that the Libyans didn't make off with the nuclear device.

He snatched the radio from is belt. "Attention all personnel," he shouted into it. "An assault on Kiva Three is in progress. Notify all civil and military authorities in the area." Running for the van, he called again on his radio, trying to reach Link and the four men Link had sent to the kiva ahead of him, but no one answered. Feeling as if he had to vomit, Maloney piled into the rear of the vehicle after the others.

☆ ☆ ☆

Willis gasped in horror. "What do you mean, Samira's coming?" It couldn't be true! Not even an animal like Da'ud would bring his own sister into what was certain to end as a gun battle.

"In a helicopter," Da'ud grunted, shoving Willis up the ladder of the reactor platform ahead of him.

"Helicopter?" Willis repeated. "But you told me that she wouldn't be anywhere near here!"

The boom of an explosion outside reached them. It was muffled by the thick walls of the kiva, but it terrified Willis. "She'll be killed!" he wailed.

"The whore takes her chances like the rest of us," snapped Da'ud. He shoved his pistol into his belt and put the backpack in his left hand on the floor. "Help me pull the thing out of the reactor," he ordered.

Willis stared at the Arab from across the reactor. Fury at the gross insult of the woman he loved flooded through him. "What did you say?" he stammered in rage. "What did you call her?"

Ignoring him, Da'ud reached into the cradle holding the nuclear device and tried to lift it. He grunted with the effort, but he wasn't able to get enough of a purchase on its slippery sides to overcome its great weight.

Wild with grief and rage, Willis reached between the metal panels of the reactor, and shoved the Libyan backward, as hard as he could. Off balance, Da'ud stumbled, tripped over his own feet and sat down heavily on the floor of the platform. Willis looked down at him, his fists clenched. "Take it back, you sonofabitch," he shrilled.

Cold hatred looked back at him from Da'ud's eyes. "Whore is what I called her, you fool," he shouted at Willis. "That's what she is. Not my wife. Not my sister, but my agent. A common whore recruited to make you betray your country." He got to his knees.

Willis' mind rebelled at the words, refused the meaning. "No," he heard himself scream. "No! It's not true. It's a lie!" He looked around wildly and clutched at the air as if for support. Not that any support on earth would have been strong enough to hold him up against the awful realization that was slowly gripping his mind and soul.

Da'ud had regained his feet and was approaching the reactor again. He looked at Willis' face, and suddenly laughed. Laughed!

Da'ud's laughter stripped Willis of his last illusions. What Da'ud had just told him had to be true. Samira's reluctance to call the FBI last night had not been due to lessen the danger of revenge on them by the Libyan government. She hadn't been in any danger at all. She was with them, a co-conspirator. She had been on the other side the whole time!

Her declared love for him, the love that had brought his life back from darkness to light, had been only play-acting, a charade, a lie. She had hooked and played Willis just as she had hooked and played the trout at Red River.

And very soon, Willis would be as dead as that trout. If she was on their side, then there had never been any intention to let Willis go.

Da'ud was going to kill him.

With that realization, a great calm came over Willis. Samira had made a fool of him, and not just a fool, but a traitor as well. She had gulled him into betraying his flag, his colleagues at LASL, his countrymen everywhere, and his own precious little daughter. And now, she had led him to his death.

There remained nothing at all for Willis. Nothing, except to atone, in the only way remaining to him, for the terrible thing he had done.

He leaped forward, grasped the edges of the vertical carbon-coated reactor panels with shaking hands, and, grunting with the effort, began pulling them around, toward each other.

The Arab watched him for an instant without reacting, incomprehension written on his face. And then, suddenly, as the panels passed the half-way point in their travel, Willis saw understanding, and mortal terror, leap into the Libyan's eyes.

He saw Da'ud snatch the pistol from his belt and point it at Willis's chest. Willis felt a terrible impact, as if he had been hit with a baseball bat, and then another. He felt himself staggering backward under the blows. There was no pain, but he sensed that something vital within him had come to a stop.

He couldn't stand any more. His eyes were dimming, too, but he could still see Da'ud, standing on the other side of the reactor with the gun in his hand. The reactor! The thin edge of its panels was both pointing in, toward Skua. It was in neutral. Even with the safety chain out of it, there was not enough reflection of its neutron flux to make it go critical. Even in his last effort to make amends, Willis had failed.

He saw Da'ud point the pistol at him again. Another awful impact. God, he . . . . . .

Link couldn't possibly have covered more than a hundred yards, but it felt to him as if he had been crawling forever, through Hell. Every movement of arms and legs caused incredible agony to his flayed back. He could only force himself forward a few feet at a time before the pain became unbearable, and he had to pause to let it ease. The further he moved up the little watercourse, the longer those pauses became.

He heard a helicopter coming, and for an instant, the familiar "whopa-whopa-whopa" of the rotor tips slicing through the exhaust filled him with hope. In his pain, his mind took him back to Vietnam, where that had been the sound of reinforcements, of air cover, of medevac choppers and survival.

He rolled his eyes upward and saw the helicopter turning into the wind above him, preparing to land. Its civilian colors brought him abruptly back to the brutal truth: in the war he was in now, it was the other side who had the air support. He gritted his teeth and dragged himself forward for another agonizing yard.

He knew he wasn't moving fast enough; that the Libyans were going to get away before he could get to the kiva and stop them, but there wasn't anything he could do about it.

Now a new sound came to his ears: the noise of a car engine, turning over fast, coming up the road behind him. Thank God! Friendlies! His relief turned instantly to dread. Ibrahim was waiting for them with the grenade launcher. Link had to warn them! He squirmed around, at the cost of indescribable pain.

A LASL van was just crossing the little bridge over the stream. It was coming fast, almost fifty miles an hour, and it was full of men. He could recognize some of them as the agents he had talked to in the control building parking lot. On the far side of the van, with his upper body hanging out of an open window, was JJ.

JJ's service revolver was in his right hand, and his white hair was streaming in the wind. As Link stared, JJ shouted something to the driver and pointed ahead with the barrel of his pistol. The van slowed, swerved around the still-burning skeleton of Link's vehicle, then speeded up again.

Link shouted with all his might in an effort to warn them of the deadly danger ahead, but all that came out was a croak. The pain of the effort left him trembling.

Without any warning, the van disintegrated in a blinding flash. Oh, God, no! Ibrahim had fired another high explosive round from his M-79. Link stared in fascinated horror.

The van screeched to a grinding stop. Its entire front half was a shambles of charred metal. Miraculously, it stayed upright, and the fuel tank didn't explode. For perhaps fifteen seconds, there was no movement to be seen at all. Then there was stirring in the rear, and Link saw JJ's mane of white hair appear unsteadily above the seat back.

He was moving very slowly, and certainly suffering from shock, if not physically wounded. That was scarcely surprising. It was a miracle that he was alive. Link saw him fumbling with the van's door, trying to get it open. He finally succeeded, and tumbled out of the van onto the road.

He was out of Link's sight now. Link called out again, trying to warn the older man to get off the road and under cover, but his voice didn't carry two yards.

Suddenly, JJ was in view again, in front of the devastated van. He was upright, but moving haltingly and shaking his head, as if trying to clear his vision. His whole left side was covered with blood, but he still held his .38 in his right hand, and he was moving forward, toward the kiva.

Then, abruptly, he just wasn't there anymore. Where he had been was a blossoming fountain of brilliant white, shot through with pink and orange lights. Link heard the crack of the explosion, and then an awful, high, soaring scream.

White phosphorous! It burned at a temperature near two thousand degrees. Link had seen it used before, had heard that awful screaming before, and had never wanted to hear it again in his life. He closed his eyes, wishing with all his heart that he could close his ears as well.

The scream stopped as if it had been snipped off with a pair of scissors. Thank Christ! The only sound now was the sound of the helicopter, its engine turning over at idle. It must have landed.

Now there was no more time for Link to out-flank the Libyans. He had to take them head-on. If Ibrahim had any more W.P rounds . . . . Link tried to keep himself from finishing the thought.

The LIBYAN BOMB

He had to take a look, to locate the targets. There was a large bush of some sort growing on the bank of the stream about eight feet away. He could use that for cover. Foot by nerve-rasping foot, he crawled toward it.

✵ ✵ ✵

His hands shaking, Da'ud threw down the silenced gun, grasped the sides of the Skua, and with an enormous effort, lifted it clear of the sided of the cradle.

The metal was slippery to the touch, and hot. Wilson had told him to expect that. The heat resulted from alpha particle decay within the radioactive device.

Wilson! Who would have dreamed that the foolish, scrawny American would have enough balls to try to kill them both with the device? He had nearly succeeded, too.

Da'ud couldn't hold the weight of the sphere any longer. He set it down on the floor of the reactor platform as gently as he could, then rolled it the rest of the way to the top of the steps. When he reached them, he recovered the backpack, which was lying a few feet away, and placed it on the top step, beneath Skua. Holding the pack open with one hand, he pulled the Skua forward.

It rolled off the platform floor and into the open pack, striking the metal step under it with a hollow clang. Da'ud turned around and felt with his arms for the back straps. Finding them, he shoved his arms through them and scrambled backward until the pack was on his back.

He heaved himself erect, grunting with effort and pain as the full 143-pound weight of the device struck his back. Staggering under his burden, he descended the steps to the kiva floor and hurried toward the door.

He came outside into brilliant sunlight. The helicopter was there. Allahu akbar! He hadn't even heard its approach.

He could see Sabana in the front seat, next to the pilot, with her pistol pointed at him. Ibrahim was already in its rear seat, the M-79 beside him. He motioned for Da'ud to hurry. Da'ud moved as fast as his burden permitted around the rear of the machine, through the dust churned up by its idling rotor blades. He reached the door and turned his back to it. "Help me with the pack," he ordered.

The big man put the M-79 on the seat beside him, grasped a thick nylon shoulder strap in each hand and pulled the pack off Da'ud's back. Da'ud turned and dived into the rear passenger compartment behind it. "Go!" he shouted.

"Is Willis all right?" Sabana screamed at him, scanning the door of the kiva.

"He's dead," Da'ud snapped. "I killed him. He tried to fry us both with the device."

She twisted around in the seat to stare at him, the color draining from her face. "Go!" he shouted again, slapping the pilot on the shoulder over the back of the front seat.

"Dead?" she repeated. "But you.." Her mouth continued to move, but the words were lost in the sudden roar of the jet turbine. The rotors turned faster, and the helicopter began to lift off the ground. Da'ud felt for the backpack. It was almost under his feet.

The LIBYAN BOMB

He shoved the pack across the floor of the passenger compartment. Chunks of the cadmium packing with which they had lined the pack fell out of its open top. Da'ud brushed them aside, and jammed the pack, with its precious cargo, under the rear seat.

Link was finished. He had made it to the bush, but he could go no further. Through its branches, he watched the Libyans climb into the helicopter, first Ibrahim and then, coming out of the Kiva, another one, whom Link knew had to be Da'ud al Musa. On his back was a back pack, and he was hobbling under the weight of its contents. It had to be Skua. They had stolen the nuclear device and were getting away with it!

The bastards had beaten him; beaten him decisively, every inch of the way. They had killed Leo, littered the floor of the canyon with the bodies of JJ and seven other Bureau special agents, and now they were getting away with a nuclear device from which they could make half-a-dozen atomic bombs.

It was the worst moment in Link's life. He had had a number of good chances to stop them, and he'd blown them, every one. Now he was down to one last chance, and it was a pathetically feeble one, a bare possibility. Still, it was the only one he was going to get, and he had to make it count.

The helicopter lifted off the ground. It turned, and came in Link's direction, gaining altitude rapidly. He pulled the Browning, grunting at the pain the movement cost him, thumbed off the safety, and braced himself for what the next move would do to him.

As the helicopter passed overhead, Link rolled over on his back.

He knew about pain. All told, he had spent almost a year of his life in hospitals. He had been badly hurt in a car accident in college, had suffered multiple fractures landing in a tree during his smoke jumping days, and had been wounded twice in Vietnam, but none of that prepared him for what he felt when his charred back touched the sand and gravel of the canyon floor.

He screamed like a woman in hard labor, screamed with all his might, and screaming, emptied the thirteen rounds in the Browning into the helicopter above him.

He tried to blot out his body, tried to compensate for the plane's direction and speed, tried to keep his eyes working despite his agony for just a second or two longer, to shoot slowly, to probe the fuselage below the rotor mast with his bullets.

As the final spent cartridge case ejected, the pain crushed him like a huge falling rock. The noise of the helicopter faded in his ears. His mind saw one final image of the sky, and then darkness swallowed him up.

Chapter Thirty-six

White Rock, New Mexico

Da'ud heard the rhythm of bullets striking the skin of the helicopter. So, apparently, did the pilot, who wrenched the machine into a tight turn. They cleared the pinon bushes on top of the mesa with what seemed like only inches to spare, and dropped back down again into Potrillo Canyon.

Da'ud unbuckled his seat belt and leaned over the pilot's shoulder. "Are we all right?" he shouted over the sound of the engine.

The pilot was just opening his mouth to answer when the helicopter bucked like a bee stung-horse. Whatever the pilot had intended to say, it now came out, "Shit!" He began scanning the instrument panel. "We must have taken a round in the hydraulic system," he shouted over his shoulder. "The pressure is dropping like a bomb."

The pilot manipulated the controls, and the bucking stopped, but Da'ud could see one of the needles on the instrument panel falling remorselessly toward zero. "How far can we go?" he demanded of the pilot.

"Mister, we can't go anywhere but down, and damn' soon at that," the pilot answered. A red light began to glow on the instrument panel, and Da'ud could hear the insistent beeping of a warning horn.

"Turn left," he told the pilot, "toward the bridge on Route 4." If they could make the bridge, they could commander a passing car and make a run for it. The odds were almost insurmountable, but their destiny would still be in their own hands, not intertwined with the fate of some senseless piece of machinery.

He looked forward through the windscreen. They were just emerging from Potrillo Canyon, about to fly over the town of White Rock. Immediately beyond the town, the highlands ended in a cliff hundreds of feet high, which dropped vertically down to the Rio Grande River. "Can we make the river gorge?" he asked the pilot.

"Don't know," was the reply. "Real soon we're going to have to auto-rotate, and she'll go down real fast then. If we make the river gorge, we'll be okay. It's a long way to the water."

Da'ud glanced at Sabana. She was belted into the front right-hand seat, and her left hand was still holding the Walther against the pilot's right ear, but she was immobile, as if she had been turned to stone, looking straight ahead. Da'ud grunted in contempt. Love-sick bitch! When they reached the bridge, he would leave her body with the helicopter.

They were very close to the sage brush when the land beneath them suddenly vanished, and they were high in the air again, over the valley of the Rio Grande. The pilot swung the helicopter left, in obedience to Da'ud's orders. Da'ud could see the river, a shining ribbon below them, and the tiny silver structure of the bridge, far ahead.

Sabana's mind had frozen the moment she heard that Willis was dead, and the sound of the bullets striking the helicopter had frozen her body as well. Now, with the relative normalcy of their descent toward the river, she regained the capacity to think.

Ahead of them, on the bridge which was their destination, she could see black and white cars. Police. Waiting.

They were all as good as dead. Da'ud would never surrender. Not him. He would fight to the last bullet, and she would be killed along with him, shot to pieces in a gunfight in which he had no say. And Willis! Willis, the only decent man she had ever known in her life, was dead at Da'ud's hands, Da'ud's promise to her just a bitter mockery!

What had she done to deserve this? She was a simple, uneducated woman, who had had to make her way in life with the only assets she had: her face and body. She had no interest whatsoever in politics, and she didn't give a shit for Moammar Gaddhafi. All she had ever wanted was a quiet life with a good man who loved her. And she had almost had it; or at least the hope of it.

And who had done that to her? Da'ud al-Musa. Ever since she had been forcibly recruited and sent to live with him, her life had been inexorably forced into a pattern which could only end in tragedy for her. He had destroyed every possibility she might have had for a normal, happy life, and now he was forcing her to die with him, into the bargain.

She craned her head to look in the rear compartment. Ibrahim looked as unemotional as the ox that he was, but Da'ud, leaning forward to give orders to the pilot, was transformed. His eyes shone with excitement.

She couldn't believe her eyes. He had murdered Willis, they were all about to die, and Da'ud was happy! Hate gushed up from her guts like water from a geyser. Her eyes fell on the PPK, still resting on the pilot's shoulder. She looked from the gun to Da'ud's face. She didn't know enough Islamic theology to know what it would do for his chances for Paradise, but Paradise or no, one thing was certain. The bastard wasn't going to die in any holy war. Allah was going to get him straight from the hands of a frightened, angry whore.

"Da'ud," she screamed at him at the top of her lungs. "Da'ud, you goat-fucker, die!"

She saw his eyes widen in alarm and disbelief. She pointed the PPK at his chest and pulled and the trigger.

Nothing happened. Unbelieving, she looked at weapon. The safety was on. Shit! She thumbed it down and re-aimed the gun.

Out of the corner of her eye she could see Ibrahim pulling out his own pistol. She pulled the trigger. The gun kicked in her hand and barked. She saw Da'ud shudder at the impact.

Ibrahim had the gun in his hand now and was raising it, but never mind him. Da'ud was the important thing. She pulled the trigger again, and again. Da'ud seemed to sag and shrink with each shot. For the first time ever, she saw fear — real, bone-deep, unmistakable fear — on his face. It was a beautiful sight, and the last thing she ever saw.

✳ ✳ ✳

A blistering hot ejected shell case hit the pilot's face, and the woman's gun went off in his ear. For a heart-stopping second, he thought that she had shot HIM, but then she fired twice more in rapid succession. Jesus Christ, they were having a gun fight in the chopper!

Before he could react to the thought, the windscreen on the right side suddenly turned pink and shattered. The woman jerked, sagged and fell on his right arm.

Unprepared for the contact, his hand was wrenched loose from the cyclic handle. The chopper yawned violently. He tried to disengage his arm from her body. The dead woman's face looked up at him, distorted by the rage of her final seconds on earth. There was a small, neat hole in the center of her forehead, but most of her long shining black hair was gone, together with the back of her skull.

A surge of bile rose in the pilot's throat. He fought it down. He couldn't get sick! They'd crash for sure. The bird was about to get away from him as it was.

Her seat belt and harness were holding her in the seat, but the full weight of her upper body had sagged onto his arm. He heaved his elbow up into her lifeless face with all his might. She flopped slowly over to the right, sagging against the door. The pilot grabbed the stick again, and fought to bring the falling aircraft back under control.

They had lost a lot of altitude. The river was much nearer. Only inches deep after the summer drought, the water was transparent, with an occasional spot of green marking holes in the gravel stream bed.

The pilot heard movement behind him, but didn't have time to look for the cause. "Will we make the bridge?" The voice was right in the pilot's ear. It was the man who had been shot, the one the woman called Da'ud. He had spoken to the pilot before, but his voice was different now; labored, rasping. He sounded as if he had been hit badly.

"Will we make it?" he gasped.

"Maybe," grunted the pilot. He didn't have time for chit-chat with this bastard. If they DID make it, it wouldn't be by much, but the bridge was getting closer. There were two police cars parked on it. He saw one of the policemen point in their direction, then run to the nearest car and lean inside—making a radio call, no doubt. The other officers drew their pistols and took cover behind the bridge abutments.

The pilot didn't like the looks of that. As soon as the chopper touched down, a gun fight was going to start. The pilot was directly between the cops and the two in the rear seat. He'd get hit by both sides. He made up his mind that the second the bird made contact, he would throw himself out of the cockpit door and run for the thicket of willows on the bank of the river.

He might still get shot, either by the police, supposing him to be one of the criminals making a break for it, or one of the hijackers might shoot him too, but it seemed like his best chance. Hell, it was his only chance.

They weren't going to make the bridge. They had lost too much altitude when the woman knocked his hand off the cyclic. "We can't make it," he told the men in the back. "I'm going to put her down there." He pointed with his chin at a broad bench of gravel on the west side of the stream, about three hundred yards from their present position and a hundred or so yards short of the bridge.

There was no response from the back seat. The gravel bar was coming up at them fast. Time to flare out and break their descent. He pulled the nose up sharply to bleed off airspeed, but the helicopter kept sinking. Damn, he thought. He should have flared sooner. They were three thousand feet higher here than at Albuquerque, where he practiced his emergency landings. The air was a lot thinner.

The tail boom touched the river, and the resistance of the water brought the helicopter to an almost immediate full stop. It fell heavily into the water, thirty yards short of the gravel bench the pilot had been aiming for.

As soon as he recovered from the impact of the hard landing, he yanked open his harness release with his right hand, pulled the door open with his left, and rolled out the door into the river.

The water came up to his armpits. He had fallen into a pothole. He slogged desperately toward the bank in front of him, dreading the impact of a bullet in his back, praying that the hijackers were too shaken by the unexpected impact to shoot.

After about ten feet, the gravel bottom turned upward. When his knees came out of the water, he broke into an awkward run, splashed from the edge of the stream onto the gravel bank, and dived head-first into the cover of the salt willows.

Behind him, the helicopter tipped slowly left into the same hole the pilot had fallen in. It sank into the water almost four feet before the left landing skid touched bottom. The river rushed in through the open cockpit door, swirled across the floor and around and into the backpack jammed underneath the rear seat.

In just a few seconds, Skua was completely immersed in water. Its eternally-escaping neutrons, moderated by the water, were reflected back into the interior of the device.

In less then three-tenths of a second, Skua went critical. By the time that first second had ended, nuclear fissions were taking place in its heart of enriched uranium at the rate of ten to the tenth power per second.

The water around the backpack seethed and smoked with the heat generated and an eerie blue glow appeared and grew in intensity as the hydrogen atoms in the water were ionized.

Under such conditions, the device would normally have blown itself apart in a steam explosion, but the tight backpack provided it with mechanical support, and the cold water of the Rio Grande provided a measure of cooling, and so it remained in one piece, and at critical mass.

The immense flood of gamma radiation engulfed Da'ud and Ibrahim in a soundless river of death. The gamma rays, capable of piercing five feet of lead, poured through the aluminum seat bottoms as if they weren't there, and destroyed millions of their body cells every second.

Da'ud, critically wounded by Sabana's shots, had been mercifully numb, his body failing but his mind still alert and aware of the increasing desperation of their situation. Suddenly, he felt as if he had been doused in gasoline and set on fire. Skua's unseen outpouring of radiation was devouring his skin cells like the breath of a furnace.

At the same instant, his nervous system, deluged by the gamma rays, reacted as if he had touched a high-tension line. He arched almost double in a violent convulsion. A scream of agony broke from his sandpapered throat.

Ibrahim was simultaneously racked by terrible convulsions, one after another. With the last of his great strength, he managed to unbuckle his seat belt, wrench open the rear compartment door and hurl himself into the stream. If he thought the water would put out the invisible fire that was burning him alive, he was deceived, but for all that, he was lucky. The next awful convulsion brought his skull down hard against a boulder on the stream bottom, and unconscious drowning ended his suffering.

Da'ud was not so fortunate. His uncontrollable seizures rocked the helicopter, and his screams made the policemen on the bridge turn pale. Almost two full minutes passed before his nervous system disintegrated beyond the ability to torture him further.

Long after both the Libyans were dead, Skua continued to pour its murderous tide of neutrons into the cool, sweet air over the murmuring river.

Chapter Thirty-seven

August 29
National Burn Center,
San Antonio, Texas

From the windows of Link's room in the National Burn Center, located on the north side of the city of San Antonio, there was a fine view toward Lackland Air Force Base.

Link hadn't seen it. He hadn't seen anything, or felt anything, or known anything, but the awful endless red pain of the back that had been flayed off him by the burning gasoline from the exploding van.

No, that wasn't true. He had also felt the icy fingers wrapped around his gut.

Link knew what the fingers meant. They meant death. He had felt them before, the second time he got hit in 'Nam, but after the second day in the hospital at Da Nang they had gone away. This time they hadn't let go.

The doctor in charge of his case had been non-committal when Link told him about the fingers, but the too-hearty voices of Link's nurses when they praised his good progress scared him. He'd heard medics and nurses bullshit dying men before.

The doctor and nurses wouldn't even bullshit him about anything else, though. Since he'd come here, the only word he'd had from outside his private, sterile hell was a telegram from the Director, read to him over the phone by SAC of the San Antonio field office. The telegram commended Link for his work at Los Alamos, without providing details.

That had made no sense at all to Link, even taking into account the (largely useless) pain-killers he was pumped full of. From all he could recall of it, his performance at Los Alamos had been a litany of disasters. Every time he thought about it, the fingers squeezed his gut a little more tightly.

The only relief was that thinking about the debacle at Kiva Three made the icy grip seem less important. What the hell did it matter if he died? He'd stop hurting, at least, and he didn't have all that much to live for: no family, no career, no reputation. And no girlfriend.

He'd thought a lot about Barbara since he'd been here. He'd even imagined hearing her voice once or twice. Thinking of her, however, hadn't made him feel any better. On the contrary. He'd had a chance to marry a wonderful woman, and he'd blown that, too. It was the story of his fucking life. He wondered if she'd heard what happened.

Next to the pain, and the darkness of his soul, the worst part about being in the burn ward was the smell of the place. Actually, he supposed it was mostly the smell of his own charred back.

Anyway, it smelled terrible. Which is why he noticed the new smell right away. It smelled wonderful, and it was a smell he recognized.

He opened his eyes and sniffed. The smell remained, but he couldn't see anything except the sheet disappearing over the edge of the bed. He didn't move his head to look farther. It hurt too much.

Then a hand came in sight, a slender, shapely, feminine hand. It was incased in a surgical glove, but that couldn't disguise it.

"Hi, Link. Can you hear me?" God, what a soft, sweet, voice she had!

"Hi, Barbara," he said. "I hear you fine. Hunker down by the bed so I can see you." Speaking of voices, his own sounded that of a little old man.

Her face came in sight, or at least her soft blue eyes, in between the mask and the surgical cap she was wearing. The sight was almost immediately blurred. For God's sake, was he crying?

"Thank you for coming," he croaked.

"I got here the same day you did, Link," she said. "They wouldn't let me in until now."

The sonsofbitches, he thought. He HAD heard her voice. They could have at least told him she was here. Which raised an interesting question. WHY was she here? He voiced the question.

"Oh", she hesitated over the answer, "I'm on leave."

Her eyes moved to his back as she said it. He saw them flinch, and hurry back to his face. He couldn't blame her for that. Not if the back looked like it felt.

"Barbara, no one will tell me a damn' thing. What happened?"

"They couldn't tell you, Link." She lowered her voice. "They don't know. The President ordered a complete news blackout, for fear of panic."

Oh, shit! The bastards had got away! The icy fingers caressed his guts

"You stopped them, Link."

Huh? What had she said? He hadn't stopped anyone. "Say that again!"

"You stopped them as they were flying away with the Skua thing. Your shots hit the hydraulic lines on their helicopter and made it crash in the Rio Grande. Skua became a critical mass and killed them all." Her voice became somber. "It killed four other people, too, before they finally got it out of the water. That's why the news black-out was imposed. The White House didn't want the whole state of New Mexico to think they were going to die."

Well, Link reflected, now the telegram from Director made sense. He didn't feel any better about himself, because hitting the hydraulic line had been pure luck, but his career was saved, and in fact, probably enhanced. The Bureau, ever sensitive to its Congressional relations, would not hesitate to take credit for luck as well as for competence.

"They'll lift the blackout tomorrow," Barbara said, but the story will be that the device was being transported from Los Alamos to Sandia Laboratory for an experiment, and was forced down in the river by mechanical problems."

That made sense, too. The Administration wouldn't be anxious to have the voters know how close Libya had come to getting away with material for an atomic weapon.

He saw the latex-gloved hand come closer, and felt it stroke his cheek.

"The doctors say they're worried about you, Link. It's not the burn that bothers them, but your apathy. They say you aren't trying to get well."

So, the icy fingers were real. Which meant that now was the time to tell her what he'd been thinking as he lay here.

"Barbara, I want to say something, while I still can. I'm sorry for the way I treated you. You're the most wonderful woman I've ever known. I've been miserable since you walked out on me. I – I love you, Barbara."

Her blue eyes filled with tears. Her hand tightened convulsively against his cheek. "Don't you dare talk like that," she said in an anguished voice. "Don't you dare say, 'while there's still time'. There's a whole lifetime for us, Link. All you have to do is get well. You've got to try, Link. For me. For us."

She leaned forward and tried to kiss his forehead through the surgical mask. It didn't work.

He saw frown lines between her brows for an instant, and then suddenly, inexplicably, with tears streaming from her eyes, she giggled. "That wasn't very satisfactory, was it?" she asked.

He couldn't be sure if she was laughing or crying, but whichever it was, the sound was wonderful. "Okay," he told her. "I'll try harder."

She whispered in his ear. "As soon as you're out, and I don't have to wear this mask anymore, we can make up for lost time."

Link liked the sound of that, but apparently not everyone was happy. A disapproving female cough sounded in the background. His nurse, no doubt. Spoilsport.

One of the blue eyes above the mask winked at him. "I have to go now," she said, "but I'll be back to see you every day until we walk out of here together." He liked the sound of that, too. A lot.

She gave his brow another masked kiss, and her face disappeared from view. Her steps crossed the floor of the room, she said something indistinct to the nurse, and the door clicked shut behind her.

He wished she hadn't had to leave so soon, but she'd be back. Tomorrow, and the day after that, and if he was smart and lucky, every day forever.

He suddenly realized that the cold fingers had eased their grip on his gut, just a little.

OTHER BOOKS BY THIS AUTHOR

THE CHAMPA FLOWERS

9574152R0018

Made in the USA
Charleston, SC
24 September 2011